ire

EVERY STEP YOU TAKE

M. A. HUNTER

B

First published in Great Britain in 2024 by Boldwood Books Ltd.

Cover Design by 12 Orchards Ltd

Cover Photography: Shutterstock

Every effort has been made to obtain the necessary permissions with reference to copyright material, both illustrative and quoted. We apologise for any omissions in this respect and will be pleased to make the appropriate acknowledgements in any future edition.

A CIP catalogue record for this book is available from the British Library.

Paperback ISBN 978-1-80549-572-7

Large Print ISBN 978-1-80549-571-0

Hardback ISBN 978-1-80549-570-3

Ebook ISBN 978-1-80549-573-4

Kindle ISBN 978-1-80549-574-1

Audio CD ISBN 978-1-80549-565-9

MP3 CD ISBN 978-1-80549-566-6

Digital audio download ISBN 978-1-80549-569-7

Boldwood Books Ltd
23 Bowerdean Street
London SW6 3TN
www.boldwoodbooks.com

For my beautiful children,
I love you both more every day.

1

NOW

21 April 2024, Blackheath, London

My skin pocks with tiny bumps as something brushes past my ankle. I yank my leg back under the thin sheet and force my eyes apart, staring into the dimness of the room I don't recognise. My pulse quickens as I try to make out the odd shadows cast by unfamiliar furniture. There is a strong smell of cleaning products in the air.

This isn't my room.

The television hangs from the wall beyond the end of the bed, instead of balancing on the single chest of drawers unit to my right. Where my tiny kitchen area should be is a large wardrobe, and the door to the bathroom is on the wrong side of the room.

Where the hell am I?

My phone isn't on the nightstand where I usually charge it, and when I check my wrist, my watch is missing too. I pinch at the tan lines where my watch should be, trying to wake myself from whatever nightmare this is. I try to recall the last thing I can remember, but there is a black hole that I can't get past.

Think!

I drag the edge of the bedsheet up to my nose as if the fabric will act as any kind of force field should I be attacked in this moment. I check the shadows for any sign of movement, and strain my ears for any sound, but there's nothing above the constant, gentle whirring. I blink away my exhaustion, willing my mind to process what I'm seeing. And then, after what feels like an age, I remember I checked into the hotel room late last night at my agent Jamie's suggestion. The cool breeze of the rotating fan at the foot of the bed once again passes over my covered feet, and my racing pulse begins to slow.

I can't remember what I was dreaming about – I never do – but the sheen of cold sweat at my hairline suggests it wasn't a dream worth remembering. With everything that's happened in the last five months, it doesn't surprise me that my subconscious is working overtime to process. There have been so many moments that have felt nightmarish that it's a wonder I'm able to decipher reality from dreams. I pinch myself again just to make sure, and am relieved when I open my eyes and am still in the hotel room.

Sitting up in the almost-too-comfortable bed, I gingerly straighten my tired legs, careful not to overstretch my calf muscles, and then I repeat the process with my arms. There's a slight crook in my neck from where the cloud-like pillow embraced my head, and I now wonder whether staying in a strange bed ahead of the biggest race of my life was such a good idea. I never feel rested after sleeping in a strange bed. If anything, this bed is more comfortable than those I've become accustomed to since moving to London in November, and whilst I would like to get used to the finer things in life, it's going to take time to adjust.

Jamie said it made sense to be closer to the start line than having to commute across London from my tiny flat, in amongst the fun runners and thousands of supporters estimated to be cheering along the route of this year's London Marathon. There were 48,000 runners who completed the course last year, and although the elite runners are segregated from the rest of the pack, battling across the city is an added stress I just don't need. With so many roads closed and diversions in place, navigating through London is going to be a nightmare for everyone. At least I can see the start line from the window here, even if it did wipe out the last of my savings. And it's not like I've had an easy route to be here.

I close my eyes and take a deep breath, then slowly exhale through my mouth.

That is all behind me now. I remind myself that *he* is in prison, and cannot get close to me again. I have one objective today: cross the finish line in the quickest time possible, and qualify for the summer Olympics. I try to picture myself as my feet fly over the white painted line, and all the glory that will bring. One of the sports psychologists I spoke to said many athletes benefit from visualising their goals and almost manifesting the outcome. I've tried, but I can never escape that cynical voice in the back of my head that always wants to put me down and tell me I'm not as good as the other Team GB runners. Mam used to say my inner cynic allowed me to be more pragmatic about life, but I don't agree. Every day feels like a battle of wills: mine versus cynical me. And more often than not, I don't win.

I take another deep breath to try to ease the nerves, and push back the bedsheet. Standing, I shuffle across the carpet, and play with the light switches by the door until I find the right compromise: not the main lights in the ceiling, but bright enough to see. I have no idea what time it is as the floor-to-ceiling blackout curtains are doing a great job of blocking out the real world. How easy it would be just to stay in this moment, away from judge-mental critics, and safe from *him*.

My running vest and competitor number stare back at me, hung over the back of the heavy wooden chair beneath the desk. This is why I can't keep hiding. Six months ago, I would have given anything to be here right now. Lying in that hospital bed, the pain so eye watering and the doctor reciting the potential complica-tions of spinal surgery, it felt like I would never recover, let alone be able to run competitively. My career as a professional athlete was in tatters, and coming so soon after I lost Mam... I came so close to just giving up. Although I'd said goodbye and repeatedly told her how much I loved her, when the doctor's call came, it still felt like I hadn't told her enough. She was my guardian, my guide, my best friend. I don't think I've even acknowledged my grief yet, but now isn't the time to start. Considering everything that followed the funeral, maybe I should have listened to that cynical voice in the back of my head.

I shake the negativity away. No, I have fought to be here today, and the months of uncertainty and terror have only served to make me a stronger person, even if I don't always feel it. I have to remember that there are hundreds of other athletes out there who would swap places with me in a heartbeat; many of whom will likely be running today as well. I've come too far to give up, and no matter what happens today – whether I realise my lifelong dream, or fall at the final hurdle – I'll know I'll have given it my all. I was only milliseconds away from a bronze medal three years ago, and I have to prove to myself that I can go one step further.

My phone vibrates in my hand as I collect it and my smart watch from their respective chargers on the large desk that domi-nates the room. A message from my coach Finn, advising me he's already at the start line, and has a specific warm-up he wants me to complete ahead of the race. Today is the forty-fourth consecutive marathon in London, and although I'm not here to try to win it, I know I need to complete it within two hours and twenty-eight minutes if I am to qualify for the Team GB Olympic squad. The fact that I have recovered from a slipped disc to be here today only serves to show how hard I've worked. The last British athlete to win the race was Paula Radcliffe almost twenty years ago, and though I'm not in her league, I deserve my crack at it. When I close my eyes and try to visualise myself crossing the finish line, all I can see is the large clock telling me I wasn't fast enough.

My finger hovers over the Instagram app. I shouldn't look. I know *he* is in prison so won't have access to the app or have any means of messaging me today. I should just lock my phone and shower as I'd planned to do, but I continue to stare at the screen, unblinking. If I don't check it, I'll never know whether he's messaged or not, and I don't think I will be able to move forward without knowing for certain.

I stab at the screen with my thumb and open my messages. My eyes widen and I gasp as I see there is a new message request.

No, not again. This can't be happening!

I don't need to look at the message. I know I should just close the app, and get in the shower. I can let Detective Zara Freeman know about it, and move on. She told me *he* was in prison and if that's the case, there's no way he could have messaged me overnight. No. Way.

I put the phone down, and march myself into the small bathroom, reaching behind the shower curtain, and running the water until it's hot. But rather than climbing into the bathtub, I march back out to my phone and scoop it up. Curiosity has got the better of me, as it always does, and I open the message, expecting the worst. But instead of the usual abuse I've become accustomed to, I see two words:

Good luck

I click on the sender's avatar, and although they're not someone I've interacted with before, their profile appears genuine. They have posted hundreds of times, have dozens of followers, and have been following my account for a few weeks. Is the message just a genuine attempt to wish me well? I take a screenshot of both the message and profile as Zara has instructed, just in case.

The bathroom is a fog of steam as I step back in and allow the shower's hot stream to wash away my lingering doubt. I keep my head under, massaging the shampoo into my scalp, and try to focus on what I need to do today. I know the course, and having watched recordings of last year's race, I know what to expect. Adrenaline will push me at the start, but I know the first 5K is downhill so I need to avoid the temptation to run faster, so I can maintain a steady and manageable pace. I will have Finn in my ear for when I need his encouragement, and I have handpicked the soundtrack I intend to run to.

I switch off the shower, and tie the large towel around my chest, then wrap another around my dripping hair, and return to the main room. I start when I hear what sounds like scratching at the door, and I hurry to the peephole. All I can see is what looks like an empty corridor.

You're imagining it!

I listen again, but don't hear any noise, but just as I'm moving away, I hear the strange scratching again. I scan the room for something I might use as a weapon, and pick up my umbrella, holding it out like a truncheon, as I unlock and open the door, peering through the gap. I open the door wider, and poke my head into the corridor, turning one way and then the other, but there is nobody there. I'm sure I didn't imagine the sound, but there's nobody who could have made it. Closing the door, I decide to dress and get myself to the track, knowing that seeing Finn will help put my mind at ease. I need to load up on carbs and protein before the race, but my stomach is turning and I have no appetite. I'll just have to grab some fruit on the way to the park.

After drying most of the water from my hair, I pull my track-suit over my shorts and vest. According to the forecast, it's supposed to be a mild start to the day, with the threat of rain before lunchtime, but I'm hoping it stays dry until I finish. Grabbing my sports bag, I open the door again, and jolt at what I see.

2

NOW

21 April 2024, Blackheath, London

Blue orchids?

They were Mam's favourite. I can remember her telling me they symbolised the rare and beautiful. She used to call me her blue orchid. But why on earth is there a box of them outside my hotel room? Were they there when I opened the door a few minutes ago, and I somehow missed them?

I'm sure I would have noticed them on the lime-green carpet, but then I was distracted by the scratching noise and was searching for someone in the corridor. I lean out now, and peer in both directions, keen to find out who left the flowers, and check that they're for me. I'm certain there was no knock at the door from the person trying to dispense them, and surely a staff member wouldn't just leave flowers outside a guest's door if they'd been asked to deliver them?

'Hello?' I call out, surprised by how strained my voice sounds.

There's no answer, and I'm not surprised as it doesn't look as though anyone has been along this corridor recently. I sniff the air, trying to sense a trace of perfume or cologne, but there's nothing. Whoever left the flowers either was scent-free or left them some time ago.

I reach out and lift the cardboard box, only now realising there is a ceramic plant pot inside containing water. Careful not to spill any of it, I carry the box over to the large oak desk, and carefully rummage through the leaves in search of a card. When I first saw the flowers on the floor, I instinctively thought they must be from Mam wishing me luck, which, of course, is ludicrous and impossible. But who else would have chosen this particular plant to send to me? It can't be coincidence that someone would gift me Mam's favourite flower on the morning when I would really benefit from a boost of dopamine.

There's no card amongst the leaves, and as I continue to rummage, one of the delicate blue buds snaps off and floats down to the desk. Mam always used to say that anyone can grow and maintain an orchid, so long as they're careful, and treat them like they would a child. That was the year she sent me two as a birthday present. They died within a week, and in the days running up to her visiting me I'd had to go online to source replacements. She never said, but I suspected she knew what I'd done.

But if she didn't send the flowers to me, then who did? I can't think of anyone who would know about Mam's love of blue orchids, aside from Aunt Rachel, Mam's sister. The last time we spoke was when I visited at Christmas, and although I did tell her I was hoping to compete today, I can't imagine she would have remembered. Nor could she know I'd be staying in this hotel. In fact, the only person who knows I'm here is Jamie, so presumably he must have sent them. Maybe I mentioned Mam's love of the blue orchid in passing. I'll be sure to phone and thank him for the gesture.

The flowers smell incredible. The sweet and salty scent evokes so many memories of growing up surrounded by these beautiful and dainty plants; so powerful and yet delicate too. I'm going to treat these with the respect they deserve, and in homage to Mam, I'm not going to let them die this time.

I carefully grip the side of the ceramic pot and extract it from the box. It's a beautifully decorated glossed white pot, with green spots, and as I rest it on the desk, a piece of paper the size of a business card flutters to the carpet. It must have been squashed inside the box. I reach down to the floor to retrieve it and as I do so, I see it's an envelope. A chill runs the length of my spine as I remember the last time I held a similarly sized envelope in my hands.

I chase away the doubt.

He's in prison. They can't be from him.

I slip my finger beneath the lip and then extract the card from inside. My jaw drops as I read the printed words.

I'M RIGHT BEHIND YOU.
SEE YOU AT THE RACE.
xxx

Not again.

It's like I'm immediately transported back to that night at the television studio when I received a similar message in my dressing room. If he's in prison, how can he have sent me these flowers? And how could he know the significance of the blue orchid, and that I would be in this room, in this hotel, on this day?

Like last time, there's no name, and nothing to suggest a company was used to deliver the plant here. Which means they must have been delivered by hand. I shudder at the thought of him being on the other side of my door, and I instinctively dart into the bathroom in case he's there right now, peering through the wrong side of the peephole.

Condensation continues to cling from the corners of the large mirror above the sink, but my reflection is painfully pale as the blood has drained from my face, neck and shoulders.

'It might not be from him,' I say loudly to the terrified girl staring back at me. 'Detective Freeman said he's in prison. And there's no way he could know you're here.'

The words provide scant relief, and I fight the urge to cry as my eyes water and the reflection blurs before me.

I unlock my phone, and locate Jamie's number.

He answers on the third ring.

'Good morning, Molly. Are you all set for the race?'

I open my mouth to reply, but I don't want him to hear how upset I am, so I swallow the emotion down. 'Um, sure. Ready as I'll ever be.'

'That's what I wanted to hear! Not that I want to add any additional pressure, but I have Nike and Adidas ready to battle it out for your signature if you qualify today. Everything that's been building in the last five months has led to this. And, if we play it right, you won't ever have to do a real job after this summer's games; even after you officially retire from competition. This race could set you up for life.'

My stomach turns at the excitement in his voice. I could remind him that I didn't take up running to make money, but I know all the endorsements he's lining up are for my benefit (as well as his own).

'I just received some flowers,' I say, struggling to get the words past the lump in my throat. 'Did you send them?'

'Flowers? Nope, not from me.' He pauses. 'Of course, I meant to send you something, but I figured you'd have enough on your mind without having to worry about all that. But I promise I *will* take you out for a slap-up dinner tonight if you qualify. We'll celebrate and it'll all be on me; well, on the agency, but you know what I mean.'

The blue orchids aren't from Jamie.

'Jamie, did you tell anyone I was staying here in the hotel tonight?'

'Tell anyone? Like who?' He sounds confused.

'I don't know. Did you mention it in passing to anyone else at the agency? Or the press?'

'No, why would I? I'd assumed you wouldn't want to be disturbed.' He pauses again, and when he returns there's a sound of recognition in his voice. 'Wait, are you disappointed that the press aren't at the hotel to follow your story? You don't need to worry about any of that. I've got interviews lined up with the BBC at the start line, and given everything we've been leaking to them about your stalker, you're definitely a runner they'll be tracking throughout the race.'

He still doesn't understand that I don't want my whole life exploited for the sake of headlines. It was Jamie's idea to set up the Instagram profile in the first place, and maybe if he hadn't convinced me, *he* wouldn't have found me.

'No, it's not that,' I correct. 'Somebody has left me a pot of blue orchids, but as far as I'm aware, you're the only person who knew I was here.'

'Isn't there a card with the flowers? That should tell you who they're from.'

I roll my eyes. 'There's no name on the card. But...' I stop myself. If I tell Jamie who I think they're from, I can't help but feel he'll try to use it to increase publicity further. 'Never mind,' I say instead. 'Are you going to be at the race today? I could do with all the support I can get.'

'Um, yeah, I should be. I'm not dressed yet, and actually I'm not at home either,' he adds with a whisper. 'Once I'm done here, I'll nip home and change, and I'll be waiting at Buckingham Palace to cheer you over the line.'

I hang up the call, and stare back at my reflection, but the girl in the mirror is trembling. Flipping through my calls list, I locate Detective Freeman's number and press dial. The call rings out, so I try again, but she still doesn't pick up.

Is she refusing to answer because she's annoyed by all my calls?

She did tell me to call at any time, and although my last few calls have probably been based more on my own paranoia than any actual danger, I should tell her what he's done today. I try a third time, but when the answerphone engages, I decide to leave her a message.

'*He's* back. I'm in The Clarendon Hotel in Blackheath and he's just left flowers outside my room. Blue orchids, no less! How does he know where I am? And how does he know they were my mam's favourite flower? Please call me back. I need you, Zara.'

I hang up, and study the phone as I wait for her to call me back. Focused breathing does little to control the shaking of my hands.

What if he's outside my room right now, waiting, watching?

I scoop up the phone again and redial.

'Hi, Zara, it's Molly again. Listen, I need to get to the race. It starts at 9.25 for the elite women. I need you to meet me there as soon as you can.'

I hang up, and take five deep breaths, willing the terrified girl in the mirror to pull herself together. Shoving the card into my sports bag, I arm myself with the umbrella, and slowly open my bedroom door, ready to thrust. The corridor appears empty again, so I pull the door closed behind me, ensuring it locks, and hurry towards the stairs. I don't care that I'm on the fifth floor, I want to keep my wits about me. I take the stairs two at a time, and when I emerge into the lobby, the adrenaline is pumping through me.

There are people milling about, some apparently checking out, others heading for the dining hall. I head there, and quickly explain to the man at the front desk that I just want to grab some fruit on my way. I don't know whether it's my Team GB tracksuit or if he recognises my face from all the media attention I've garnered, but he doesn't ask for my room number, and later, when I emerge with two bananas, a granola bar, and a bottle of water, he wishes me good luck.

It's a relief that there are no journalists gathered outside the hotel, but as Jamie said, there's no reason they would know I'm here. As far as I'm aware, none of the other elite runners booked to stay here overnight. But despite the lack of people outside, I can't escape the feeling that I'm being watched.

3

NOW

21 April 2024, Greenwich Park, London

My head spins left and right as I plough through the dozens of people milling about in the park as I approach the entrance to the marathon. I have to show my letter of race confirmation to the security guard in the high-visibility jacket. She scans the QR code at the bottom, stares at me with all the enthusiasm of an accountant, and then allows me through to another area where my sports bag is rifled through by another guard in a bright, glowing jacket. At least she smiles when she hands it back.

'Enjoy the race,' she says, adding, 'we're all rooting for you.'

She's already looking at her next target before I can acknowledge or respond. And she's just one of a hundred faces I don't recognise, all here for a reason and with a single purpose etched on their faces. I am surrounded by people and yet I've never felt so alone. Any one of these people could be my stalker, but none of them appear to be showing any interest in me. But is that just to hide their true intentions?

I continue along the concrete path through the park, the air filled with the buzz of excited chatter, but none of it distinguishable. I should be excited. This is my first time competing in this particular marathon. I've completed Boston, Chicago and New York, and after today I'll only have Tokyo and Berlin to go to complete the World Marathon Majors. But I can't let that distract me; I need to focus on just getting through today.

My body fills with relief when I finally spot Finn standing a short distance from the portable toilets, where he said he would be waiting. He smiles that goofy grin when he sees me approaching, and I can't stop myself throwing my arms around his neck and pressing my body against his. It's so good to finally find a face I know. He gently taps my shoulders, and I release him from the embrace.

He fixes me with a concerned stare, his brow furrowing, and his ice-blue eyes narrowing slightly, as if he's trying to read my mind. His usual short, fair locks are buried beneath a woollen beanie hat, and his coach's tracksuit top is zipped to his neck.

'Everything okay?' he asks, his Derry origins carrying through on his voice.

I want to tell him that everything is far from okay; that I'm convinced my stalker is here right now and intends me harm; that I'm worried I'm not ready to compete today either physically or mentally; that I'm terrified of not achieving the qualifying time and failing to reach my dream of competing at this summer's games in Paris.

'I'm fine,' I say instead, hoping that once the race starts, my mind will smother all of these doubts and focus on the task at hand.

'Good, then we should get you warmed up and ready. Have you eaten breakfast?'

I nod. I managed to stuff down the granola bar and one of the bananas on the short walk from the hotel.

'Good, then let's find somewhere quiet, and you can strip down and start stretching. Any twinges or aches since you woke up that I should know about?'

I have a flashback to the moment we shared on the track in February when I made a pass at him and he told me nothing could happen while he's employed by Team GB. He muttered something about official rules, but if they do exist, I've never seen a copy. I can't be the first athlete to be attracted to their coach, especially when working in such close proximity. I never would have made the pass had I not been told he was keen on me too. Thankfully, he didn't transfer me to a different coach, as I like Finn, and I like the working relationship we've established. He knows when to push me, and when to stop me pushing myself too hard.

'Molly? I said are there any twinges or aches I need to know about?'

I follow him to the clearing, shaking my head. 'Nope.'

I strip out of my tracksuit and squash it into my sports bag, and proceed to raise my right leg behind me, pressing my heel into my bottom and holding it there for twenty seconds, before repeating the action with my left leg. I then raise my right knee to my chest and hold it for twenty seconds before moving on to the other. Over the next ten minutes I complete hip rotations, knee circles, forward skips, shoulder rolls, and leg swings. The cool of the air is a distant memory, and it's good to be able to focus on an activity I'm so familiar with.

'Earth to Molly,' I catch Finn saying. 'Where's your head at today?'

I shake away my internal mutterings. 'Sorry, what did you say?'

'I need you to do forward and side lunges next. Did you hear any of what I've said?'

I begin to nod, hoping he doesn't call my bluff, but he fixes me with a hard, low-brow stare, and I cave.

'I'm sorry, can you repeat the last bit?'

He shakes his head dismissively. 'I said, the official qualifying time of two hours and twenty-eight minutes may be reviewed should the race be impacted by rain. There is a heavy downpour due around ten, but it remains to be seen whether it will arrive or not. I think it's safer to aim for the five-and-a-half-minute miles we've practised for, rather than hoping for a late reprieve. I know your training has been disrupted by minor strains and turbulence, but if you keep your mind on the race, there's no reason you can't hit the time.'

He fails to acknowledge that I've never actually managed to run twenty-six miles any quicker than two hours and twenty-nine minutes.

'Stick with Thea, Kat and the other elite pack for as long as you can and then maintain your own pace.'

I almost snort at the mention of Kat's name, as I know for a fact she'll do anything not to have me tagging along. Given Thea's already qualified for Paris, I'm hoping she'll stick with me for at least the first half of the race.

'Seriously? What is wrong with you today?'

I look up and realise Finn has been talking to me, and again I have failed to take in any of what he has said.

'Sorry, am I boring you discussing race strategy?' he says pointedly.

My shoulders sag, and I look down at my feet so he won't see my watering eyes. 'My stalker is back.'

'Wait, what? He's back? I thought he was in prison in Germany?'

I close my eyes to keep the tears at bay. 'So did I. But this morning I found a pot of blue orchids outside my hotel room with a message that I know is from him.'

I can't see his reaction to this news.

'I don't know what to say... Do you want to withdraw from the race?'

My head snaps up and I glare at him. 'I can't afford not to compete!'

His face softens. 'I'm sure – given the circumstances – I could speak with Gloria Hutchinson, and explain why you couldn't—'

'Oh, sure, because I'm her favourite athlete right now, aren't I?'

My face burns as I think about my last encounter with the battle-axe Head of the Olympic Committee.

'Have you reported the flowers and message to the police?'

'I've left messages for DC Zara Freeman, but she isn't answering her phone and hasn't called me back. I asked her to meet me here, but there's no sign of her. If I give you her number, can you keep calling her for me? She needs to know that he's back on the scene.'

He nods and I send him her contact details.

'Is there anything else I can do?' Finn asks sincerely.

'I... I'm worried he's here somewhere, but there are so many people that it's like looking for a needle in a haystack.'

Finn reaches into his pocket and tosses something towards me that I just about manage to catch. I look down at the elasticated headband.

'It's got a Bluetooth speaker and microphone built in,' he tells me, taking it from my hands and slipping it over my head and pressing it against my ears. 'It means I'm only a phone call away, which you can dial from your watch. If you think you see him or become alarmed, you can call me, and I'll do whatever it takes to keep you safe.'

His hands are still holding my cheeks, and again, for the briefest of moments I think he's going to kiss me, but then he catches himself and pulls away.

'You'd better do your front and side lunges. Not long to go.'

I search the faces of the athletes, coaches and race stewards passing nearby, looking for the face of the man who I saw lurking outside the door to my flat back in February. He could be anywhere, and I can't shake the lingering doubt in the back of my mind that he has a partner who's been helping him terrorise me for the last five months. What if Zara was wrong and there are two of them at work?

I finish my warm-up, and am about to hunt for the second banana when I realise Finn has taken my sports bag with him, so there's nothing for me to do but make my way towards the elite runners' enclosure.

'Molly? Molly?'

I start when I hear a man with an accent calling my name. My pulse races as I turn to face him, wishing Finn had escorted me to the start line. And for the briefest of moments, I see the face of Otto Bistras staring back at me. But in the blink of an eye he's gone and I realise it's a BBC journalist and they're calling to me.

'Molly Fitzhume?'

I recognise the journalist as Denmark's former London Marathon runner-up Henrik Anderson.

I'm flustered as I make my way over. At least there's safety in numbers.

'And now here is one of Britain's brightest stars, Molly Fitzhume,' Henrik says into the camera, the spongy microphone pressed so close to his lips he's practically chewing it. 'She narrowly missed out on a bronze medal in Tokyo three years ago, but hopes to go one better in Paris this summer.' He turns to face me, and pushes the microphone so close, I have to take an involuntary step back. 'How are you feeling ahead of the race today?'

'Um, I'm excited, obviously,' I say, trying to recall how Jamie had made me rehearse responses to questions from the press.

'Any nerves?'

'Of course, nerves are a necessary evil for all athletes, but that builds adrenaline and helps us push through the wall.'

'Many of our viewers will know the setbacks you've undergone since slipping a disc in your back last year, but is everything feeling good? Are you ready to compete?'

I look at the crowd of spectators beginning to gather beyond the railings draped in banners of sponsorship, searching for Otto, but come up empty.

'Molly? Are you ready for the race today?'

My attention snaps back to Henrik. 'As ready as I'll ever be, I suppose,' I reply, forcing a smile I'm not feeling.

'Everyone knows how close you came to the podium in Tokyo, and that the games in Paris are likely to be your last chance to compete at the Olympics. Does that add any unnecessary pressure ahead of what is likely to be a hugely competitive London Marathon?'

Pressure? He has no idea.

The crowd of spectators is cheering now as Sifan Hassan, last year's Dutch winner, takes her place at the start line. She's then joined by Ethiopia's Yalemzerf Yehualaw, 2022's winner, and the crowd's cheering becomes overwhelming.

I can't concentrate, and apologise to Henrik as I pull away, desperate to cover my ears and plead for silence. I can barely hear myself think.

Is he here now? Is he watching?

I scan the faces of everyone around, their eyes all seemingly staring back at me.

Where's Finn? Where's Thea? I need a friendly face.

There are now nineteen other elite runners standing in numbered vests and shorts surrounding me, and as I glance down at my watch, I can't believe it's already 9.25. The loud air horn breaks through the crowd's cheering and the elite women runners charge forward.

4

BEFORE

Friday, 17 November 2023, Streatham, London

Molly shivers as she pulls up the sleeve of her tracksuit top and checks her watch. She is certain Jamie said to meet here at ten, but there's no sign of his car; not that there's anywhere to park. Google Maps had her walk past the address several times before she worked out she had to slither through the darkest, narrowest alleyway to get to the road. And as she emerged and looked up at the tall, grey corner building, she prayed she'd got the address wrong. Sheltering inside the doorway of a long since abandoned kebab shop, she wishes she'd got the umbrella out of her suitcase while she was still on the train. There isn't enough room in the doorway to open it now, and she doesn't want all her carefully packed clothes getting stained by the polluted rain.

The road bends around the building in a U-shape, and must come out somewhere, as there's no way cyclists could fit through the alleyway. The front sheet of a soggy newspaper blows past,

catching the bottom of a sign. More NHS strikes due, according to
the headline. Molly can't remember the last time she saw a posi-
tive headline on a newspaper; all scaremongering; it's no wonder
the public are fed up.

A man in a turban walks past, chattering loudly into the phone
pressed to his ear, while battling with a large golfing umbrella
threatening to blow inside out. She smiles and nods in his direc-
tion, but if he sees her, he doesn't acknowledge it.

She unlocks her phone and checks to see if Jamie has sent a
message, but he hasn't, so she reluctantly pockets it again, rubbing
her arms against the sleeves of her tracksuit, hoping the static
generated will warm her.

She had no idea London could be so cold in late autumn, and
she's certain the thick, dark clouds overhead and torrential down-
pour aren't helping. And this certainly isn't the London she
pictured in her head when Jamie suggested she move here to aid
her recovery. He said recuperating and training close to the British
team would ensure nobody forgot she was still hoping to make the
Olympic squad. She pictured a townhouse or an apartment
building overlooking the Thames, the way London movies had
portrayed.

Growing up in Dumbarton, she's not used to things being so
built up. And she lost count of the number of taxis she passed on
the walk from the train station. Roads full of cars, people
marching with heads down, glued to their phones. She's never felt
so far from home.

'Molly?' a voice says, snapping her attention back to the dingy
street.

Jamie closes the door of the black cab and pays the driver
through the window, before scurrying across the road, extending
his umbrella.

'You found it okay then?'

Her heart drops a little; so this really is the place he's proposing she rent for the next five months.

'Aye, I found it,' she says, forcing a smile she isn't feeling, but knowing that he's gone out of his way to help her find somewhere.

'Listen,' he says, with a playful wink, 'I know it's not much to look at, but it's got great access to the Underground, and is only a short ride from the hospital and the Crystal Palace National Sports Centre. Given the limited budget you suggested, it's the best I could find.'

'And I appreciate you finding it for me,' she says.

'As your agent, it's important for me to make sure you're happy. Got to earn my commission, right?'

She nods.

'Great! Shall we head inside then?'

'Don't we have to wait for the letting agent?'

Jamie opens his hand and shows her a ring with two keys in his palm. 'No need. I picked up the keys on the way over.'

Jamie leans past her and lifts the case out, under the cover of the umbrella, and wheels it away, leaving her to jog to catch up. Once around the corner, he uses one key to open the communal entrance and closes the umbrella as he holds the door open for her to duck in. The lobby smells of damp trainers and sweaty men, and throws up memories of the athletics club back home. There is a wall of small, numbered letter boxes immediately to her left, and there are worn patches of carpet immediately beneath them. It reminds her of the Hall of Residence she stayed in during her first year at university, only worse. Her mam would have said beggars can't be choosers, but even she would be telling Molly to forget the idea and just head home.

'The flat is number five,' Jamie says, leading the way along the dark, narrow corridor.

A light flickers overhead, giving the whole place a sinister vibe.

There must be better accommodation, she tells herself, but she can't turn this place down without at least seeing inside the room.

Jamie unlocks the door and wheels the case through, stopping abruptly as he reaches the windowed wall.

'This is it,' he says, and Molly has no idea how he's managing to make his voice sound so positive.

The room is about the size of the living room in her mam's old house, but the space here is dominated by a double bed, a desk and a chair on one side, and a small sink, draining board and countertop on the other. There are two cupboards beneath the counter, but no other apparent storage in the room. A sliding door beside the bed leads to a room barely big enough for the shower cubicle and toilet.

'Is this it?' Molly says, unable to believe that her agent would have looked at the place online and believed it was adequate for her needs.

'It's got charm,' he says, but his face doesn't agree.

'I've stayed in hotel rooms bigger than this!'

'I'm sorry, but it's the best I could find. How much time are you really going to spend here anyway? When you're not at the track, you'll be undergoing physio. Think of this as a means to an end. Okay, it's small, but if you only sleep here, does it really matter?'

She crosses to the bed and turns her nose up at the light brown stain dominating the nearest corner of the mattress. She also notes the damp patch in the ceiling above the window.

'What if I increase the budget?' Molly says. 'How much more for somewhere that doesn't look like something out of a horror movie?'

He pulls a face. 'That's the thing... this place is actually a bit over the budget you gave.'

Her mouth drops. 'This dive is more than eight hundred a month? You're kidding, right?'

He shakes his head.

'How much over?'

'It's twelve hundred a month, but that includes utilities costs.'

'I budgeted for eight. I can't afford twelve hundred a month.'

He heaves the case onto the bed before manoeuvring her into the chair by the desk. 'Honestly, this was the cheapest place I could find so close to the track and hospital. I know it's shit, and I probably should have warned you before you got here, but I was worried you wouldn't get on the train. There are cheaper places, but so far away that you'll end up spending most of your time commuting.'

'But I don't have the money, and between physio and training I don't have time to get a job to pay rent too.'

'Listen, don't worry about the money. I have a plan for that too.'

She frowns at him, already suspecting what he's about to suggest.

He reaches into his pocket and extracts a small cardboard box that he hands to her. 'I can find you lucrative endorsement work. All you have to do is post to your Instagram followers, telling them how much you love whatever the product is. Advertisers are desperate to get their products endorsed online, and you definitely have enough followers to demand a decent return.'

She stares at the box in her hand. 'Sports bra?'

He shrugs. 'I know, I know, but they've been on at me for months to discuss this with you. One picture of you in that bra will pay half the rent on this place for a month. It's easy money.'

She wants to tell him that there's no way she'll sell her soul, but the London Marathon is her last chance to prove she deserves a spot in the Olympic squad. And Jamie's right, by training in London, she can show the committee she's serious about the sport and doing everything within her power to be ready.

Jamie waits outside while she slips into the sports bra, and snaps an image. He doesn't agree that she's smiling enough and uses her phone to take several more. He uploads one of the images to her Instagram account, flagging it as an advert and tagging the manufacturers. Molly feels physically sick as she watches the number of views and comments steadily rise. She tells herself it will be worth it when she's boarding the flight to Paris next summer.

5

NOW

21 April 2024, Greenwich, London – Mile 1

Instinct cuts in, and although I wasn't standing in the second row beside Thea and Kat where I should have been, I move forwards, almost as if a puppeteer is controlling my legs and arms with string. I am already several yards behind my competition with barely a minute on the clock. The cloud overhead is so thick I cannot see the sky. A mixture of greys hang above us, and if I was a betting person, I'd say rain will fall a lot sooner than forecasted. The breeze I felt on my journey from the hotel has also accelerated and is buffeting towards us. These are not clement conditions for distance running, especially with everything that's at stake.

The race favourites Sifan Hassan and Yalemzerf Yehualaw have disappeared behind the wave of baseball caps and heads of hair ahead of me. I've no doubt they're setting the pace for this early part of the course. More troubling is that I can't see Thea or Kat either, and they're the two I need to set my pace by. Too fast now, and I'll suffer later in the race. But too slow, and I'll never stand a chance of catching up. The gathered crowd behind the barriers is cheering, and holding up homemade cardboard signs, but they all pass in a blur. If *he's* amongst them, I don't spot him.

London looks so different on race day, with roads closed off to allow runners to compete on the course. We're passing residences and businesses like they're not even there. Traffic lights have been switched off so as not to cause us any distraction. A motorbike with a cameraman perilously positioned on the back is at the very front, with another twosome to the rear and side. I briefly glance up to see the one nearest has his camera pointed straight at me. I can't tell if they're broadcasting this particular footage, but in my head I imagine myself being referred to as the 'surprise straggler'.

I can also imagine that Jamie will be fuming to see me bringing up the rear so early in the race – if he's even watching.

There are twenty elite female runners this year – the cream of the crop – but even amongst that group, there is a hierarchy of speed, skill and experience. Finn and I have worked on the tactic that the pack will branch off the further the race develops, with the favourites to win forming a group of three or four before we reach Cutty Sark, ten or so grouped together in the middle, until the latter stages, and then the remainder at the back who will generally become further segregated from the rest. That's why the women's course record is 02:17:01, set by Mary Keitany in 2017, and yet my qualifying goal is a flat 02:28. There will be runners today that finish closer to the 02:20 mark, a margin of nine minutes' difference between the favourites and the stragglers.

Get your head in the game!

We pass a vacant petrol station on my left. The gathered crowd has dispersed somewhat now, and the cheering has died down. Not that I can hear anything above the roar of blood in my ears.

My watch buzzes with a message, and as I glance down at my wrist, I see it's from Finn, asking if everything is okay.

Does he really expect me to type out a reply?

No, of course he doesn't. He's my coach, and he's probably alarmed to see how off the pace I am already and is checking on my well-being. If he was here now, I know he'd tell me to accelerate and at least catch up enough so I can see Thea and Kat.

I focus on my breathing, and pump my arms, feeling the hard concrete through the cushioned soles of my trainers, kindly donated by the sports company as part of the incentive-pushing that Jamie has been coordinating on my behalf. Although I wasn't keen on all the endorsement activity he has arranged in the last few months, I also acknowledge that beggars can't be choosers. It's not like I'm financially proficient to afford my own trainers, not with the cost of rent on my flat.

I turn the next bend, onto a street lined with short trees, brick walls, and semi-detached houses. My eyes widen when I see how far ahead the first pack already is. We've only been running for three minutes, and within that half-mile distance my plan for today is already out of the window. Despite everything Finn warned me about in terms of running too quickly early on, I really have no choice right now. I pump my arms and legs quicker, passing the pack of four stragglers quickly, and slowly close the gap on the fifteen ahead. I spot Thea's maroon baseball cap bobbing somewhere in the middle of the pack, and target it.

The motorbike and cameraman appear to be following my increased progress, and it's hard to ignore them as they stay just far enough ahead that I won't stumble into them.

Leave me alone!

I want to yell at them, but I need to keep my breathing focused and in rhythm with my arms and legs – just like we've been working on at the track. There's a fresh smattering of applause to my right as we pass local residents who've come out to cheer us on, but I keep my eyes on Thea's baseball cap.

The wind is now whipping in from the right, and there are drops of rain in the air. A wet road makes grip more difficult and will inevitably slow the whole pack. But I can't think about any of that right now.

Concentrate!

I've caught up with the two runners at the back of the main pack, and although I'm not yet feeling the strain of my increased pace, I know I will later. Hopefully, Finn's concern will be eased now. The pack is already starting to splinter with Kat and Thea at the front of the second half. I ease my way around the others and position myself beside Thea.

'Hey,' I call out, breathlessly.

'Wondered where you were,' she pants back. 'You okay?'

I want to tell her that no, I'm not, that discovering those blue orchids outside my door this morning has totally thrown me on what is the most important day of my life.

'Fine,' I puff instead.

Kat side glances, and increases her pace, pulling away from the two of us, and hurrying towards the tail of the first pack. I guess some things never change. I wish I knew exactly what her problem with me is. I get that we're in direct competition, but there's no need to be so outwardly rude. Maybe I should just accept that the two of us will never be friends.

I still remember the first time I realised how much I love distance running. I was eleven and had just started secondary school in Dumbarton. We were told we would be running for four miles over fields and hills, and that the course would be marked out by orange flags and teachers at key points along the route. We were running with those in the year above who knew the route already, so it was easy enough not to get lost. The games teacher told us at the start that the key was to maintain a consistent pace throughout the course, and that stuck with me. There were those who tore off at the start, but were flagging before the end of the first mile, and ended up walking most of the course. I remember the feeling of my feet slapping against the ground in rhythm with my heart being the most natural thing in the world. While those I passed were panting and struggling, it felt like I was born to run. I loved the isolation, getting lost in my own thoughts with that steady rhythm of my heart driving me along like a metronome.

I was the sixth student to cross the finish line that day, and first in my year group, but when I went home I was disappointed, as I knew deep down I'd been holding back. I knew I could run faster and still maintain a consistent pace, so the following week that's precisely what I did, and I finished third overall. And yet still I was disappointed, because although I'd increased my pace, I knew I'd had reserve energy in the final mile. And so the following week, once the final mile started, I accelerated, and sprinted the last stretch, finishing first overall to the delight and amazement of the games teacher. At eleven years of age, I was running faster and more consistently than runners almost two years older than me.

Within a month I was being entered into competitive events across the county, and that drove me to become quicker and more competitive. I didn't like not placing first, or finishing a race knowing I could have pushed myself harder. By the time I was sixteen, I was competing in competitions across Britain in my age group. I didn't choose running, it chose me.

Ahead I can see a parade of shops, most with their shutters down, though it isn't clear if that's because of the race, or just because it's so early on a Sunday morning. There are more people gathered on the streets, but they're no longer behind metal barriers. There aren't even that many race stewards to keep them in check. There's nothing to stop any one of them bursting out into the road and disrupting the race... or worse.

I try to shake the ensuing images that flood my mind: Otto Bistras running out and tackling me to the ground; Otto Bistras jumping forward and plunging a knife between my ribs; a van driven by Otto Bistras careening into all the runners just to take me out.

If he is there, I can't see him, but I can't escape the feeling that I *am* being watched by someone. I'm not thinking about the viewing public camped around their televisions in the warmth and dry, but someone specific here today who is keeping their focus solely trained on me.

If Zara was wrong and Bistras *does* have a working partner then they could be here now, watching and waiting to strike. And the worst part is: I have no idea who that is or what they look like.

I shiver as a feeling of ice shudders through my body, but I can't tell if it's the blustery wind or the thought of my stalkers watching me.

Where are you?

The faces in the crowd continue to pass by in a blur, and my head is all over the place as I try to commit each to memory in case one reappears later on. I realise, almost too late, that Thea is gaining on Kat's pack, and I'm once again falling behind.

I need to stay focused on my running. Thea is a more experienced marathon runner than me, and if I can keep pace with her for as long as possible, then I should get close to the required time. I accelerate again, falling into line with her.

'What are you listening to?' Thea asks, and it's only now I realise that I haven't started my pre-planned playlist.

No wonder the voice in my head is so loud. I fiddle with my watch, but the bouncing of my arms makes it difficult to start. I should have had it going before the start of the race, but I was distracted, and I don't have time to extract my phone from the sleeve on my upper arm and tune it in. I'm still fiddling with the dial of my watch, trying to get it started, when suddenly my right leg lands on a raised bit of road I'm not expecting, my body twists as it tries to compensate, and then my left leg also lands on the raised road. I realise too late that I'm running over a speed bump that I hadn't noticed.

I wince at the bolt of heat that sears through my left calf muscle upon impact. But I don't slow my pace, quickly straightening, and pushing on through the pain. It was only a few weeks ago that this same calf muscle required rest and recuperation, and I dread to think that the injury has returned as we complete the first mile. With twenty-five more to go until the finish, I can't afford any more setbacks. I should let Finn know that I can feel a constant twinge in the leg now, but he'd probably tell me to withdraw, rather than risking it. I grind my teeth, and try to push it to the back of my mind. I just hope I can make it to the end without the strain becoming a full-blown tear.

6

BEFORE

Monday, 27 November 2023, Streatham, London

Molly can't get over just how many additional followers she's gained since the sports bra photo on her Instagram story. And all she can picture is dirty old men who've started following in the hope that she'll expose more flesh. She's been firm with Jamie that future endorsements need to be more wholesome as she knows she has an aunt and cousins following who wouldn't approve of her totally selling out.

'I just want to make enough money to cover food and rent,' she said pointedly the last time they spoke, and he said he'd see what he could do. The sports bra company offered to double their payment if she would post a video including their product, but she's drawn a line, and hopes she remains strong enough not to crack under financial pressure.

The latest endorsement is for a multivitamin, and although she was asked to record a video in sports clothing, she feels she has kept her dignity. And that particular video led to a host of weird messages from – she presumes – men telling her how beautiful she is and how they'd show her a good time. She rolls her eyes just thinking about the additional attention. She's comfortable enough in her own skin not to require male attention of any kind. Her only focus is on making it to and competing in next year's Olympics. It's what her mam would have wanted, and it's what everything in the last three years has been building towards. Slipping a disc while emptying furniture from her mam's old house wasn't planned, and but for that, she probably would have already qualified for the squad.

She bites down on her lip, a silent chastisement to remind herself that she can't change the past and should focus her attention on the future. But there is something that's starting to trouble her, and it stems from a message she received online last week. A Dr Jürgen Oppenheimer, claiming to be a renowned physiotherapist, messaged offering to give her injury a cost-free assessment. There was nothing remotely sexual in the wording of the message, and when she looked him up online she discovered that he'd worked with the German Olympic squad a decade earlier. The image in his profile picture matched the one she saw on the German Athletics website, and so she responded politely to thank him for his interest, stressing she was being well looked after by the British Athletics physios.

15 Nov, 11:39
Are you sure they have your best interests at heart?

15 Nov, 12:01
Why wouldn't they? It's in their best interests that I'm able to perform.

15 Nov, 12:03

I'm sure you're probably right, but I know so many former athletes who were bullied into pushing their injuries too soon. I just don't want you to suffer in the same way.

She didn't respond, but it led her to undertaking more research on him, although she couldn't find anything of note in the last eight years. He messaged again several hours later to say he would be more than happy to fly to London to assess the injury if she wanted, but she didn't answer, hoping he'd take the hint.

But days later and the question is still playing on her mind. She's been receiving sports massages on the muscles surrounding the injury, as well as ice baths and punishing gym sessions. She's yet to take to the track since moving south two weeks before, working on optimising her leg muscles with weights while the scar tissue around the slipped disc continues to heal. Sleep has been almost impossible, such is the pain when she lies on her back, but she knows achieving an Olympic dream doesn't come easy.

But what if the tenderness in her lower back is more than just her body trying to recover? That's why she's made the appointment to speak with her athletics coach, Finn, at the track.

He looks flustered when she arrives, but in fairness, she didn't tell him the real reason for the meeting. She takes a seat when directed.

His office actually looks bigger than her flat, with a massage table against one wall, a punch bag hanging from a bracket in the ceiling, and a watercooler near the window. The slatted blinds are open, revealing the athletics track below, but there's nobody running as rain bounces off the surface.

He is frowning at his phone, cursing under his breath, and she feels compelled to ask if he's okay.

'Personal stuff,' he replies, his Derry accent laced with tension.

'I don't want to pry,' she says, trying to get her own thoughts in order.

'My girlfriend broke up with me last night, and now she's trying to steal my dog,' he says. 'Can you believe that? I mean, he was my dog before we met; she moved in with me, and takes care of him when I'm overseas with work, but he is still *my* dog.'

Molly regrets booking the meeting and wishes she could just go home.

'Sorry, what was it you wanted to see me about?'

She desperately tries to think of any other reason she can offer that won't make her sound like a spoiled brat, but her mind is empty. 'I, um, was just wondering how you think things are going?'

He puts his phone face down on the desk, but confusion shrouds his eyes. 'It's only been a couple of weeks. I think it'll be a wee while longer before we know when you'll be ready to make it back onto the track. How do you think it's going?'

She thinks about the sleepless nights, and the agony even just standing up when she's been sitting for too long. 'I'm worried that we might be pushing too soon,' she says quietly.

Finn stands and crosses to the watercooler and fills a cup before returning to the desk. She wishes she could read his mind, but she doesn't have to wait long until he shares it.

'You're the one who wants to compete at the marathon in April. If you now think that's an unrealistic target, then we should probably stop.'

This is what she didn't want him to say.

'I one hundred per cent want to compete in the marathon; that's not what I'm saying.'

'So what are you saying, Molly?'

'I guess I'm just worried that... I don't want to do more damage and set my career back further. Paris 2024 is probably my last chance of competing at the Olympics, but I'm young enough to continue with nationals.'

'What is it you want from me, Molly? You approached me and said this is what you wanted to do. You said you'd do anything to make the squad. Remember? We agreed the physio and training plan before you moved down here, but if it's too much for you, then I also don't want you doing anything to make matters worse. Is your back not getting any better?'

Molly thinks back to the moment when the disc slipped while she was trying to manhandle the large sofa through the door without help. She'd barely been able to crawl to the phone to call for an ambulance, such was the excruciating pain.

'It is better than it was, of course, but I'm just worried about making it worse.'

'You're working with the physio daily, though, right? And she's checking the tissue each time?'

Molly nods.

'Well, if she had concerns, I'm sure she'd make them known. What's this really about?'

Her brows knot. 'What do you mean?'

'Well, I've known you for a while now, and I know how much competing in Paris means to you. Maybe you're worried that you won't make the squad? Team GB has never had so many elite female distance runners as it does right now. It's only natural to feel threatened.'

'This isn't that. If I'm on my game, I'm capable of beating any of them.'

'Good, then what can I do for you?'

Annoyed at his presumption about her own doubts, she tells him she needs to get back to work, and leaves.

She messages Dr Jürgen Oppenheimer that evening to thank him again for his offer, but reassures him that she's in good hands.

21 Nov, 19:53
If you change your mind, just let me know, and I'll stop by. How is the new flat?

She hasn't posted anything about moving to London, but wonders whether he still has contacts in the sport who might have mentioned her training at the Athletics Centre.

21 Nov, 20:01
I'm settling in thanks, but it's only temporary.

21 Nov, 20:02
Maybe I can see it some time? It's been years since I've visited Crystal Palace.

She quickly closes the app, and tells herself there could be a million different ways he could know where she's now living. She reminds herself that she checked him out before replying and that he is a familiar name in the industry. Yes, she's just being paranoid, she tells herself. His profile image matches that of Dr Jürgen Oppenheimer, so there's no reason to question who's been messaging her. But as she later wills sleep to take over, she can't stop thinking about why he would be showing such an interest in her.

7

NOW

21 April 2024, Charlton, London – Mile 2

Every time my left foot lands on the road, it's like a hot dagger is scratching at the back of my calf. It's putting me off my stride because now I'm over-compensating, trying to ease the impact when I place the foot, rather than keeping a natural rhythm and gait. I know from experience this isn't a long-term strategy. Forcing myself to do something unnatural with my left leg puts more pressure on my right, indirectly manipulating it into counterbalancing, which in turn will put additional strain on all the muscles and tendons in my right leg.

The pain right now is manageable, and I'm hoping that if I can just ease the pressure on the calf muscle for the next mile or so, the twinge will settle and I'll find my rhythm again. Ideally, I would stop, elevate it and apply an ice pack and rest it for a few hours, before applying a strapping and trying again. But I don't have the time or the tools to do any of that, so I just need to push on through.

In my periphery, I can see Thea eyeing me suspiciously; she can probably sense that something is wrong, but I don't want to put her off her own race. Whilst she has already qualified for the Team GB distance running team from previous competitions, this is the last full-length marathon before the Paris Olympics, and there is no better practice session. We usually train at the athletics track, but running around in circles – no matter how many laps are completed – doesn't compare to running a full course. There's something special about a day like today. The added pressure of competing against fellow professionals, the crowd watching on and cheering, the different landmarks that are passed along the way; nothing compares.

'Are you okay?' she asks me next.

When I meet her glance, I can see the concern etched across her face.

'Fine.' I grimace.

'I saw you land awkwardly on that speed bump,' she puffs.

'It's just a twinge,' I snap back, not wanting to acknowledge the potential seriousness of the injury.

I see her eyebrows raise, but she doesn't respond, and now I feel awful, as she doesn't deserve to bear the brunt of my frustration. I really don't know how I would have coped without Thea these last few months. She's the only real friend I've made since arriving in London, and she's the only one who knows how much stress *his* antics have caused.

My eyes dart back to the smattering of spectators lining the streets as we pass by the parade of shops. I hate that the voice in the back of my head has brought him back to the front of my mind.

Is he here now? Is he still watching?

The sense of dread makes me shudder, and I almost lose my footing again, but recover in time. My right thigh is starting to ache, and I know that it's too big a risk to keep running in this manner. There are medically trained stewards scattered along the course to offer support for any injuries, but stopping to explain the problem and receive treatment is going to take too long. It's taking all my effort just to keep in time with Thea; I can't afford to fall further back. If I stop for treatment, I might as well just quit the race and wave goodbye to my dream.

We turn the next corner, putting the shops and most of the spectators behind us. There is the odd one here and there along this stretch of road, but I'm able to scrutinise and dismiss each one.

Where is he?

I check my watch for any messages from Zara or Finn, but there's nothing. It's seven and a half minutes since we started running, so we must be about halfway through the second mile of the course. Just another twenty-four and a half to go then. There are more speedbumps along this stretch, and I finally stop placing my foot, and test the twinge. It holds and it's the first bit of good news I've had today. I don't want to push it, but the sooner I can rediscover my rhythm, the better.

A loud cheering to my left catches my attention and I see a group of four men, their formal shirts untucked, unfastened bowties draped around their necks, falling into one another, with brown bottles in their hands. If I had to guess, I'd say they're still drunk from wherever they spent last night. One of them gropes his groin and shouts obscenities, and the others fall about laughing. I try to ignore them, hoping the race stewards step in and move them on, but I inadvertently make eye contact with the ringleader and he shouts out my name, asking me for a picture. I lower my eyes and continue to run past them. But they're now running along the pavement, and despite their drunken state they're doing a good job of keeping up.

'Come on, darling, I could give you exactly what you need,' he shouts out, but I don't look up.

My cheeks burn at the unwarranted attention.

'Oi, Molly, give us a smile,' another one shouts.

Just keep running. Don't give them any reason to continue.

Mam always used to tell me, 'The best way to deal with bullies is just to ignore them,' and so that's what I'm trying to do, although it clearly didn't work where Otto Bistras is concerned.

Could this group have something to do with him?

The thought seems so absurd that I almost burst out laughing, but isn't this exactly the sort of thing he would organise to put me ill at ease?

'What's the matter, Molly? Am I not your type? You a fucking lesbian or something?'

Thea stiffens at this comment, probably embarrassed to be running beside the focus of their attention, and I wouldn't blame her if she upped her pace to avoid being associated with their actions.

Two uniformed police officers are suddenly running in their direction along the pavement, and with that, the pack turns and runs in the opposite direction, but only after one of them – and I don't see which – lobs one of the bottles towards me. It smashes on the kerb so close that some of the froth splashes up my shin.

I try to ignore it, and as much as I want to charge after them and demand to know what gives them the right to be so abusive, I keep running. I've no doubt the world would feel ten times safer if that kind of animal was forced to wear a muzzle.

We're now passing a sports complex, and the overhanging trees cast shadows over the road. It's the safest I've felt all day. I notice some of the race stewards are now holding up placards warning of speed bumps ahead; I wish I'd noticed them sooner.

Running in fear of being watched isn't the solution. I am frustrated that Zara still hasn't phoned me back, and so I fiddle with my watch again – keeping one eye firmly on the road ahead – and press redial when I find her number. I hear the line ringing through the Bluetooth headband, desperately hoping this time she'll answer, but the answerphone kicks in, and my shoulders sag. I leave her another message.

'Are you phoning someone?' Thea puffs incredulously.

I can't keep these fears to myself any longer. Mam always said, 'A problem shared is a problem halved,' and although I've no right to drag Thea into my nightmare, two pairs of eyes watching the spectators will double my chances of finding him.

'My stalker is back,' I say, before I can convince myself not to come clean.

'What? That's awful.'

I shake my head, already regretting saying anything, but also relieved that her first response is to believe me.

'He left a gift and a card outside my hotel room this morning.'

She frowns empathetically.

'The card was just like the one he left at the television studios before. Do you remember?'

She nods. 'That's awful, mate. I'm sorry.'

I fight against the sting at the edges of my eyes. 'He said he would see me at the race, and now I'm convinced he's here and planning to do something, but I don't know what or when.'

'Have you reported him?'

'I've left messages for that police detective, but she's not answering my calls.'

'What about reporting it to the race stewards?'

'And say what? Some guy I don't know – who may or may not

be here – is planning to do something at an unspecified time, God knows where or when?'

Again, I don't mean to snap at her, but I feel like I'm falling down a well, and there's nobody who can save me.

'But you know his name and what he looks like, right?'

'Yes, but... I think he has a partner.'

'A partner?'

'There's someone helping him. I don't know who, and I can't prove it, but in my bones I'm certain he's not acting alone. Even after Zara told me he'd been caught, strange stuff has still been happening.'

'Like what?'

I sigh. 'I don't know... just *odd* stuff. Things inexplicably moved; the feeling that I'm being watched *all* the time. It's driving me crazy.'

I've reported all the strange goings-on to Zara, and I think maybe that's the reason why she's refusing to take my calls. I realise that such claims make me sound paranoid, but that doesn't mean I'm not right. Either that or he's made me so stressed out that I'm actually losing my mind.

No matter how much I try to rationalise it, I can't see how the flowers could have been from anyone else. I've now mentioned them to Jamie, Finn and Thea, and none of them have claimed the credit. And the lines in the card are almost a carbon copy of what came before, and I know for a fact that he was the one who left it last time, so it *has* to be him again. I hate that I don't know what his endgame is. What happens when making me feel uneasy isn't enough of a thrill? What if he escalates? And what if he's angry at me because I reported him and he was arrested? What if revenge is now on his mind?

'Is there anything I can do?' Thea asks, drawing my attention back to the race.

I offer her a grateful smile. 'Just stay with me? I feel safer having a friend nearby.'

She raises her fist and I press my own against it, and a tear escapes. I quickly brush it away with the back of my hand.

I start at a ringing in my ears: someone is phoning me. I look down at my watch, expecting to see Finn's name, or better still Zara's, but all I see is the word 'WITHHELD'.

It must be Zara calling me from a work phone, so I stab my finger against the watch screen to answer the call.

'Zara, is that you?' I stammer.

There's no response, and I have to double-check my watch to ensure the call hasn't ended, but we are still connected.

'Zara? Can you hear me?'

Still no response. Maybe the Bluetooth headband isn't connected properly, or I've got the microphone on mute.

'Zara?'

I freeze when I hear the sound of a mechanical child's toy laughing down the line. And in that instant, I know for a fact: he's back.

8

BEFORE

Wednesday, 6 December 2023, National Sports Centre, Crystal Palace, London

Molly takes two painkillers as she heads to the gym, hoping they'll do something to dull the constant ache in her lower back. Dr Jürgen Oppenheimer has sent several messages, which she's chosen not to respond to, hoping he'll subtly get the message that she's not interested in his help or attention.

She strips out of her tracksuit and undertakes the stretches her physio has proposed, holding onto the pain and twinges, reminding herself that nothing good ever came easy. She plugs in her earbuds, opens the Spotify app on her phone, and starts the treadmill. As she steps onto it, and slowly builds up her speed, she catches sight of herself in the floor-to-ceiling mirrors on the wall closest to her. The skin around her surgical scar resembles a banana skin.

If she could go back and change just one moment of her life it would be to ask for help moving that bloody couch.

No, she decides instantly; if she could change one thing, it would be to answer her mam's final call. Not that Molly had known it would be the last time her mam would phone. The worst part is it wasn't like Molly was doing anything important at the time. She'd just got home after completing a half marathon and all she'd wanted was a long, hot soak in the bath. She'd intended to phone her mam back afterwards, but had forgotten, and only remembered the following morning, when the doctor phoned and broke the news.

In many ways, that's why she's so determined to get her career back on track – literally as well as figuratively – and get her race time under the qualifying requirement. It has now been eight weeks since she last raced, and most of the elite runners in her category are posting times below the two hour twenty minutes mark – nine minutes faster than her own personal best. It's possible the Olympic Committee could lower the qualifying time ahead of next April's London Marathon, and if they do, Molly is going to be in trouble.

'Penny for them?' a voice says, and Molly starts as she sees Thea staring back at her in front of the machine.

Molly pulls out one of the earbuds, but doesn't stop running. 'Oh, hey, I didn't hear you come in.'

Thea removes her own tracksuit top and bottoms and hops onto the treadmill beside Molly. 'It's good to see you running again. How's the back?'

Molly bites down against the pain. 'Getting better every day. And how's everything with you?'

'Well, my mum is still a nightmare, but that's another story. My coach has said I don't need to run the London Marathon as I already qualified with a two-nineteen in Berlin earlier this year, but I said I wanted to do it to provide you with some moral support.'

'You were incredible, and third place was incredible.' Molly streamed her friend's performance in the Berlin Marathon from her hospital bed.

'Thanks. My coach reckons I can get it below two-nineteen, but I figured you'd benefit from your own personal pace setter. I want my friend in Paris with me.'

That means a lot to Molly, and she finds another gear to shift into, the painkillers finally kicking in.

'Have you heard of a German physio called Dr Jürgen Oppenheimer?' she asks.

Thea shakes her head. 'Nope. Who is he?'

'I don't know much more about him, other than he used to work with the German Olympic squad. He messaged me on Instagram and offered to assess my injury. He said he thought I was being pushed too hard here and could make my back worse. Has he ever messaged you?'

'I don't have Insta, I'm afraid. My agent says I should do more on socials to help raise my profile and earn money from endorsements, but my mum would hit the roof if I started posting seminude photos online. I'm not allowed to do anything that would tarnish my clean girl persona.'

Molly's cheeks flare, but she knows Thea isn't passing judgement.

'I wish I didn't have to endorse shit, but my agent insists, and it's the only way I can afford to be down here at the moment. If I can qualify for the squad, the committee will give me a bursary to help, but until then I'm on my own.'

'Do you need me to lend you a bit of cash?'

Molly shakes her head vehemently. 'No, I'm not here with a pity pot. I appreciate the offer, but I'm coping, just about.' She pauses, uncertain whether to keep speaking. 'It's just... I don't know... this guy's messages started friendly enough, but more recently they've become... I don't know, maybe I'm just misreading them.'

'Show me,' Thea says, offering out a hand, so Molly unlocks her phone and passes it over.

Thea reads the messages, her eyes widening with each one, before passing the phone back. 'What a creep! I'd delete these and block him if I were you.'

'You think?'

'That is exactly why my mum won't let me use social media. You've no idea who is out there watching you.'

'Yeah, but he's legit. I Googled him and he's a real person. I even checked his profile picture and it matches what I found online.'

Thea asks to look at the phone again, and Molly hands it back. 'My brother, Seb, has Insta, and showed me a few tricks,' she explains while tapping the screen. 'The guy who's messaging you only has like a dozen followers, which is a red flag in itself, and none of those that follow him are anything to do with athletics, which seems a bit weird. He's following several hundred people, but...' she scoffs, 'they all have one thing in common: young, pretty, and female.' She quietens as she taps away again. 'And furthermore, there is another profile for a Dr Jürgen Oppenheimer, with the same profile picture and several thousand followers, including half the German Athletics team. I think you've got yourself a scammer there, Molly, and you'd be wise to block him ASAP.'

She passes the phone back, and increases the resistance on her machine.

Molly stares down at the real Jürgen Oppenheimer, angry at herself for not finding this sooner.

'My autistic brother is awful at socialising, but really into tech and gadgets, and cyber security and stuff,' Thea continues. 'It's Seb's doomsday view of the internet that influences my mum so much. You need to be careful; there's no way of ever really knowing who anyone is online.'

Molly deletes the messages and blocks the fake-Oppenheimer, embarrassed that she didn't do it sooner, and feeling dirty that she'd even contemplated responding to his messages. What troubles her more is who else is out there now, watching her posts.

9

NOW

21 April 2024, Woolwich, London – Mile 3

The mechanical laughter echoes through the Bluetooth headband, like one of those cymbal-bashing monkeys; the kind that can be wound up and then left to bash, laugh and occasionally flip over. The shoe shop in Dumbarton used to have one in its window and I can remember pleading with Mam to buy me one, but she refused, stating I would soon grow tired of its antics.

I look down at my watch again, but the number still shows as withheld, so I have no way of knowing who is doing this to me, nor any means of phoning them back. I stab my finger at my watch to end the call. I'm angry, but also terrified. He has my number, but I don't know how he could have obtained it, and that puts him another step closer to me.

My arms and legs are continuing to pump but I'm not conscious of how that's happening. My body must be on autopilot, as somehow I'm managing to still run in a straight line, even though there are multiple internal monologues vying for airtime in my mind. My mind is a fog of questions.

My eyes scan the few people lining the road, focusing on each face, searching at first for the puffy cheeks of Otto Bistras, but if he is watching me now, I can't locate him. I look next for anyone paying me undue attention. If he does have someone working with him, then maybe that person placed the call. There's a woman puffing on a cigarette, a dressing gown pulled tightly around her, but there's no sign she's holding a phone. Our eyes meet and she continues to stare at me as I run past, but I can't see how or why she would mean me any threat.

The next person – a man in small spectacles – stands proudly behind two children. The boy can only be about seven and the girl a few years older. They are waving small Union Jack flags, but again there's no trace of a phone. If I had to guess, I'd say they probably live in the large semi-detached house that dominates behind them.

I continue to look at the faces of the residents who have stepped out to cheer for the cameras, but I'm in no position to know which of them could be partnered with Otto, if any.

Although DC Zara Freeman never formally said it to my face, I don't think she agreed with my belief that Otto isn't the only person to cause me trouble since my move to London. Whenever I've mentioned it, she didn't outwardly dismiss the idea, but as far as I'm aware she's never taken any definitive steps to investigate who that person could be either. Maybe my expectations of the young detective, overwhelmed with work in a city as crime packed as London, were too high. Even when I presented her with indisputable proof that Otto had been at my flat, she wasn't willing to drop everything and deliver the justice I deserved. How many times has she answered my recent calls and listened to my complaints just because she's too polite to ignore me?

'Molly?'

Thea's concerned voice snaps my mind back to the course. I no longer know where we are. The surroundings aren't familiar, and if it weren't for the crowd ahead of me, I wouldn't have a clue which way we should be headed. I'm not even sure what mile we're on now.

'You're pale as a sheet,' Thea continues.

I do feel light-headed, but my arms and legs don't relent, and I'm grateful that muscle memory has taken control, as the way I'm feeling, I'm not even sure I could walk in a straight line.

'Are you feeling ill? Do you want me to call a race steward?'

I don't know how to answer. What would I even say to them? I think my stalker is back because I heard a cackling monkey? Even I wouldn't believe me. Nobody knows how stressful these last five months have been. Always looking over my shoulder; a never-ending sense that I'm being watched; someone going out of their way to make life that little bit more difficult, just because they can. I can't remember the last time I felt truly safe in my surroundings, and it isn't fair. I should feel confident going wherever I want whenever I want, and to lose that fundamental freedom is soul-sapping.

'I'm calling a steward,' Thea states, and I just about manage to grab at her arm as she starts to veer closer to the pavement.

'No,' is the only word I can squeeze past the lump in my throat. I shake my head for added emphasis.

'You don't look well,' she says, her brow so low I can barely make out the whites of her eyes.

'I'm fine,' I just about muster, but there's no certainty in the tone.

'You don't look fine. Is it your leg? If you're injured, you could do untold damage if you keep running.'

To be honest, I'd totally forgotten about my misplaced step on the speedbump and the ensuing pain. I certainly can't feel the twinge in my calf any more, but that's probably because my brain is too busy processing everything else.

'I told you: I'm fine,' I tell her, when I'm anything but.

Maybe she's right and I should go and speak to a race steward. I don't feel safe being out here in the open, knowing he's out there somewhere watching; if not *him* then his partner. The sensible thing would just be to stop running. I could feign an injury to save face. There'd be no shame in withdrawing due to a muscle strain. I could phone Finn and tell him the calf muscle has gone again, or better still that I'm experiencing pain in my back; given I didn't even think I'd make it this far last year, I could easily bow out gracefully. The only reason I've kept going throughout this campaign of terror is the dream of representing my country one last time; going out in a blaze of glory. But I'm not the only one with that dream, and I wouldn't be the first to fail to achieve it at the last knockings. If I had given up when the surgeon told me he would have to operate, Otto Bistras would never have found me, and I wouldn't be so scared of everything now.

I'd probably be back in Dumbarton where the greatest danger is catching a cold. Maybe I'd have found something new to do with my life; less exhilarating, but safer nonetheless. I try to picture a life without racing, but all I can see is a heartbroken girl who would be glued to the television watching the race unfold, filled with regret.

From the moment I finished the last games in fourth, narrowly missing out on the bronze, I've been transfixed on making it to Paris. *Everything* I have done has been leading towards that target, and I've had to force myself to wear blinkers to stay on that path. I have come too far to throw all of that away, haven't I?

When I look up next, I realise Thea is no longer beside me. At first, I think she's run on ahead to join Kat, or has taken matters into her own hands and gone to speak to one of the race stewards, but then I spot her beanie hat at the front of the pack, and realise I have dropped back amongst the straggler group. I don't even remember the others passing me by, but here I am, a good hundred or so yards behind the middle pack.

A road sign indicates that the Woolwich military barracks is up ahead. This will later be the section of the course where the various start points will merge, but thankfully I don't have to worry about competing against more runners as they haven't started yet. I can make out the barracks building, so long and unwelcoming; how I could do with such a fortress to protect me from them.

It would be so easy for me just to wave down one of the stewards, and tell them I need to withdraw. I pass one holding a sign advising that there is a water station coming up in a few hundred metres, but my legs continue to move me onwards. If I had phoned Finn when I stumbled over that speed bump, he probably would have told me to stop, rather than risking a more serious injury; after all, what's the point in qualifying, only to then be ruled out through injury?

And maybe that's exactly what they want you to do.

The thought drives to the front of my mind from nowhere. This whole time I've been unable to explain, nor understand exactly what Bistras (and his potential partner) hope to achieve from what they are doing. Is it just to feel some kind of power over me: letting me know they can get at me at any time, with me powerless to prevent them? It seems a lot of effort to go to for something so insignificant. But what if that's how it started, and now the intention is to exercise that power by causing me to give up on the one thing more precious to me than anything else: my dream?

The thought gathers weight in my mind the more I think about it.

Why send me the card, other than to inform me that they're still out there? Why leave blue orchids – Mam's favourite – other than to tell me they know more about me than I them? Why leave both outside my hotel room other than to tell me they can get to me at any time, any place?

They want me on edge, because if my mind is filled with fear and doubt, I won't be on my game in the race of my life. If I phone Finn now, or approach one of the stewards, then they win. If I voluntarily give up on my dream, I will relinquish all control.

I cannot let that happen.

I can't believe I've fallen so far behind Thea and Kat. I look back to Thea's beanie hat, and she's already so far ahead I'm going to have to work hard just to catch up. And every faster step is going to cut into my reserve tank later. But as far as I'm concerned, if I fail to hit the qualifying time, I might as well not finish the race. If I can't get back to Thea and Kat, I have no chance of getting anywhere near that time, especially as heavy rain starts to fall. And the longer I stay back here, the harder it will be to catch up.

I bite down, and put my eyes to the road, summoning all my willpower, beginning to edge closer. The rain is thumping hard against my face and top, and it isn't long until my vest is soaked through and I am having to brush my sodden fringe out of my eyes. These are far from clement conditions, particularly when I have so much time to make up, but I push harder, summoning all my strength to make my arms pump faster, my legs bounce quicker. Down and then up; down and then up.

I pass the two runners at the back of the middle pack, and I can't tell if they're deliberately hanging back, waiting to make their move, or striving just to keep up with those immediately ahead of them. But it doesn't matter; they are not my priority.

I have to circle wide to get past the next row, and it's like the rain is coming from below as each of us splash through surface puddles. It's hard enough running a marathon without having to do it in wet socks and shoes, and I can already feel my toes starting to chafe, despite the petroleum jelly I smeared on them after I got out of the shower this morning.

I'm forced wide again as I catch a stray elbow to my left, but I can see Thea's bobble hat barely a stone's throw away, and I know I'm making progress.

I lower my head because the rain is pelting my face and clawing at my eyes, but still I push myself to get ahead. I shouldn't be putting myself under this additional strain, but I have found new motivation for completing this race: defying my stalkers. I can almost picture them watching on and pulling their hair out as I make my way up the pack.

You won't defeat me today!

But suddenly I hear the screech of brakes and the sound of a man yelling, and as I look up, I see the onrushing camera on the back of the motorbike hurtling towards me.

10

BEFORE

Saturday, 23 December 2023, Streatham, London

Aunt Rachel's Christmas card hangs from the fridge magnet as a constant reminder of where Molly could be now, if she wasn't so stubborn. The card stands out as it's the only one she's received, and the message within – inviting her to join the rest of the family for Christmas – weighs heavy on her mind. Her mam and aunt hadn't spoken in years after a falling out that neither chose to explain, reflected in her aunt's reluctance to attend her sister's funeral service. She hadn't hung around for the wake, giving Molly no time to ask for help with moving everything out of the house. Rachel had said Molly could come and stay 'for a few days' while she got herself back on her feet, but hadn't offered any emotional or financial support afterwards.

The invitation to stay isn't even that, technically. All it says is:

Would be lovely to see you at Christmas if you're up this way.

But Molly has no reason to catch three trains to North Wales with no guarantee of accommodation, and sitting on a train for that long certainly won't aid her recovery.

Last night was the first when she didn't wake in excruciating pain following an unconscious twist, and even the bruising is barely visible. For the first time in months, she finally feels as though things are starting to slot back into place. Her physio and coach have even suggested she can get back on the track properly in early January, and she's been saving her endorsement money to treat herself to some new spiked trainers so she can make the most of her track time.

Mam would probably turn in her grave if she could see the lack of festive decoration in the pokey one-bedroom flat. Christmas was always such a lavish affair with trees in every room, decorations pinned to the ceiling, and tinsel adorning every picture frame. By contrast, Molly's cheap, undecorated, foot-high artificial tree from a market stall is paltry. It isn't the cost of buying decorations, but it's the storage once she gets out of this flat.

She sees her phone vibrating on the bed, but is reluctant to pick it up. The situation with the fake-Oppenheimer has escalated, and Jamie has told her to sort it out as it's upsetting her sponsors. After she blocked fake-Oppenheimer, he started commenting on her posts, warning others that 'she's nothing but a prick tease' and how she led him on 'for commercial reasons'. She's contacted the site administrators to report his behaviour, but they've taken no action. Last week, fake-Oppenheimer started posting images of her face superimposed on other photos endorsing brands of her promoters' rivals.

What is wrong with this guy?

The vibrating ends, but Jamie immediately phones back, and he isn't going to stop, so she groans audibly before answering it.

'He's at it again,' is the first thing Jamie says. 'Have you looked at your account? He's got friends reposting his shit now too. You need to get a handle on this, Molly.'

'What the hell do you expect me to do about it? I've reported him countless times, but he just sets up new accounts.'

'I've reported him too, but I'm getting it in the ear from everywhere! I almost sorted you a deal with Reebok, but they're now having second thoughts because of the scandal surrounding you. Reputation is everything in this business.'

'But what do you want me to do about it? Close my account?'

'God, no. You might as well give up and move back to Scotland if you do that.' He lets out a pained sigh. 'I'm sorry, I know this isn't your fault, and I'm sorry to take it out on you. You need to keep your socials live if you want to keep earning, but we've got to get this guy to stop.'

'I'm open to suggestions; blocking and reporting hasn't worked.'

Jamie doesn't answer for what feels like an age, but when he does, it's clear he's been trying to pluck up the courage. 'You need to make peace with the guy. Okay? Send him a message, apologise for any miscommunication, and if necessary offer to send him a signed photo or something.'

Her mouth drops open. 'You've got to be kidding me.'

'What's the problem? It's not like I'm asking you to sleep with the guy. Just flatter his ego a bit, and hopefully he'll stop.'

'I bet you wouldn't be telling your male clients to do that!'

She doesn't mean to snap, but can't ignore the feeling of double standards.

'This is nothing to do with gender bias. It's my job to manage your commercial interests, right? Well, right now, all potential investors in your brand are getting cold feet because this scumbag – whoever he is – is messing things up. Throw him a bone, and

then tell him you're so busy with training that you're taking a
break from socials until after the marathon.'

'And if that doesn't work?'

He doesn't answer at first, and when he speaks again, his voice
is quieter; more strained. 'Please just give it a go. If you can get him
to stop with all these shitty posts, then the sky's the limit as far as
future endorsements go.'

He ends the call with her promising to try, but it's another hour
before she can squash her anger enough to open the app. She
searches for fake-Oppenheimer's account and unblocks him.

> **23 Dec, 17:59**
> Hey, just wanted to say sorry I've not replied sooner. Been so
> busy at the track that I've barely looked at my phone in weeks.

She can't be sure he's still using this account, as she's certain he's
the same person who's set up other accounts and been messaging her.
She has no proof it is the same person, but the timing of the messages
– coming moments after she's blocked the latest – seems too coinci-
dental. She tried to report his campaign to the police, but it isn't 999-
worthy, and when she searched for police contact details online, there
was nothing she could find to deal with this form of cyber bullying.

He doesn't respond, and she's dreading Jamie checking up on
her, so she taps out another message.

> **23 Dec, 18:36**
> My back is feeling much better now. In fact, my physio reckons
> I should be able to get back on the track soon. I guess your
> concern was misplaced.

He still doesn't respond, so she drops her phone on the bed

and microwaves a packet of rice, stirring it in a bowl as steam swirls around her face. She spots her screen light up, and with a sense of dread, approaches the desk, placing the bowl of rice down.

> 23 Dec, 18:43
> Oh, hey, that's great news about your back. You must be so excited to be returning to training. I know I'm looking forward to seeing you back in action.

Her skin crawls as she reads it, but is she now just reading it as sinister because of the other posts, which she doesn't know for certain are his?

> 23 Dec, 18:45
> I genuinely can't wait. Running is what I feel I was born to do, so it's been tough not being able to do it. Thanks for your continued support.

> 23 Dec, 18:46
> Always happy to support a fellow sportsperson. And please don't lie to me, Molly. I've seen you posting various adverts for products, so don't say you've been too busy to message.

Her brow furrows at the cheek of the message. How dare he accuse her of lying when she's been doing anything to avoid him? She's about to reply with that very message, when she thinks about what Jamie said about her keeping him onside.

> 23 Dec, 18:51
> Oh, no that's my agent who posts most of that stuff. I don't

have time, so he has access to my account and permission to
post adverts on my behalf. I wouldn't lie to a fan.

23 Dec, 18:52
I'm more than a fan, Molly. I think you're one of the smartest
and prettiest people I've ever met. Sorry, this must sound so
trite, but I really feel like we have a connection. Do you feel it
too? I know if we actually met in person, you'd realise I'm not
just some weirdo, hiding behind an avatar.

She doesn't respond, turning the phone face down instead,
and ignores the rice, her appetite vanishing in an instant. How
much more of this bullshit does Jamie expect her to put up with?

23 Dec, 18:54
I know I could make you happy if you'd give me a chance. I'm
fairly well paid, so you wouldn't have to flaunt yourself the way
you do.

Her thumb hovers over the 'block' button, but then Jamie's
voice plays loudly in her head: throw him a bone, and then tell
him you're so busy with training that you're taking a break from
socials until after the marathon.
She's about to type her response when he messages again.

23 Dec, 18:57
I'm not far from Crystal Palace now. Why don't you let me take
you out for a drink or some dinner? Or I could come to your
flat?

Her eyes widen at the possibility he somehow – impossibly –
knows where she lives.

23 Dec, 18:58
That's sweet, but actually I'm not at home. I'm away visiting my
aunt.

23 Dec, 18:59
Oh, what a shame. Not to worry. Maybe we can make a date
for after Christmas instead? I know plenty of restaurants where
we won't be disturbed by paparazzi.

23 Dec, 19:03
Thanks, but actually my coach has said I need to be really strict
with my routine in the run-up to the marathon. Lots of early
nights and a strict diet to be at my best. I'm sure you under-
stand. I really do appreciate the kind offer though.

Her stomach turns as she presses send, and then she locks her
phone so she won't have to see his response. Grabbing her sports
bag, she fills it with handfuls of clothes, and pulls the Christmas
card off the fridge. There's no way she wants to spend another
moment in this flat with him out there maybe searching for her
address. She grabs the envelope of cash she'd been saving for the
running spikes, and heads outside, hailing the first taxi to take her
to King's Cross.

11

NOW

21 April 2024, Charlton, London – Mile 4

I brace for impact, but something grips the inside of my elbow at the last second, and pulls me out of the motorbike's path, and when I look to my left I'm relieved to see Thea beside me. I look back towards where the motorbike has now had to mount the kerb in order to avoid the collision that I must have inadvertently instigated while trying to run past the last row of ladies. I offer an apologetic smile as the pale-faced cameraman stares back, but they should never have been that close to me in the first place. I'm all for the BBC wanting to broadcast the race, but that shouldn't come at the expense of the safety of the runners, especially in rainy conditions like this.

The droplets continue to splash up from the ground, and as I look towards the thick blanket of grey overhead, it doesn't look as though it will let up any time soon. It is so hard to see with the wind blowing the droplets towards us, and I envy every one of the people watching the race unfold from the dry warmth of their homes.

'Are you okay?' Thea pants, slowly lessening her grip on my arm.

Has there ever been a more complex question in my life? I don't know how to answer. My mind is all over the place, I have totally blown the carefully orchestrated plan Finn and I created, and there are still another twenty-plus miles between me and my dream. How do I even begin to answer?

'Thanks for catching me,' I say, hoping she doesn't realise I'm deliberately avoiding answering.

'That's what friends are for,' she says, forcing a smile, but I can still see the concern in her eyes.

Kat and the pack of runners ahead of us are just passing the rehydration station which has been set up where the course nears The Valley stadium, where Charlton Athletic play football. This is where Finn suggested he leave me an energy drink. Although there is free water and sports drinks every couple of miles for runners, the elite competitors generally have their own supplies along the route to help optimise pace and energy levels. And God knows I could do with refreshment right now. The occasions where I've already had to catch up have taken a toll, and I'm going to need all the additional energy I can consume if I'm to make it to the end of the race, let alone hit the required qualifying time.

I can imagine Finn must be pulling his hair out if he's keeping track of my lap times and progress. He's worked so hard to get me in any kind of state to compete today, and the fear of letting him down is almost as overwhelming as it is for letting myself down. I could phone him and let him know what's happened and why I've been so off the pace, but I don't want him to worry more.

The motorbike is back alongside us and I keep a watchful eye on the direction it's headed, as I don't want us to cross paths again.

He is still dangerously close if you ask me, but it is a narrower road, so it's inevitable that we're closer. It's only when the sight of the camera mounting begins to blur that I realise just how light-headed I'm feeling. I accidentally bash into Thea as I try to correct myself, and I swiftly apologise. My legs feel so heavy, and every contact with the wet road feels like I'm trying to run through treacle. Something is wrong, but it's all I can do to keep the rain out of my face and one foot in front of the other; I have no capacity for figuring out what's happening.

'You're pale as a sheet,' Thea warns me, but her voice sounds so far away.

I don't resist when she grabs my arm and pulls me towards the left of the road, forcing me to slow my pace in the process. Several others overtake, and I'm powerless to understand how they can still have so much energy left.

What is wrong with me?

'I think your blood sugar is low,' Thea says in an empathetic tone. 'You need sugar and fast.'

I don't argue. I've felt the consequences of hypoglycaemia before, and it certainly explains the light-headedness and lethargy. Thea is leading us towards the rehydration station, which is essentially a portable table, covered in a fluorescent yellow tablecloth, with each runners' named receptacle on top.

'What does your bottle look like?' she asks.

I can picture the tall, black plastic bottle with gold stars, but when I try to describe it to Thea, my lips flap but no sound emerges.

The protocol is for runners to slow enough to collect their bottle, taking it with them and consuming their drink of choice, before throwing it into one of the designated bin liners being held by race stewards at the side of the road. Because each elite runners' bottle has their name on it, it's easy for these bottles to then be returned to the coaches.

Thea and I have now dropped back to the rear of the second pack, and I can't tell if that's her intention because she's worried about me, or whether it's my lack of coordination acting as a drain. What I do know is I can barely keep my legs moving, and that if I don't get an energy boost soon, I'm just going to collapse.

'What does your bottle look like?' Thea is asking again, and it snaps my eyes to the table that is coming towards us.

I stare at each bottle in turn, looking for the gold stars, but I don't see it. I must be in a worse state than I feared. I start again, looking from one bottle to the next, but it isn't there. We've now reached the table and stopped, as I scan each of the bottles.

Where the hell is it?

I look up at the Mile 4 marker being held by one of the race stewards, and I'm sure this is where Finn and I agreed he'd leave the bottle. The rehydration schedule is key when seriously competing in this event, and we carefully mapped out exactly where and when I would take on more fluids.

I can see Thea has located her bottle, and is taking a long drink from it, while glancing at the rest of the pack who are edging further away with every delayed second. I don't want to be the reason she doesn't finish the race.

'You go on,' I slur, as I start handling the dozen or so bottles that remain on the table, struggling to read each name, searching for my own, and coming up empty-handed.

But as much as I can see the sadness in Thea's eyes, she doesn't leave my side, checking each bottle a second time.

Could Finn have made a mistake and forgotten to leave it?

I could phone him and check, but right now, I can't even remember how to make a call using my watch. There is a normal station with bottles of water coming up in a mile, but water isn't going to be enough to get me going again.

'Is there a problem?' the woman in the luminous tabard asks behind the table.

'Where's my bottle?' I ask, but she looks back at me like I'm speaking a foreign language.

'She can't find her bottle,' Thea explains on my behalf.

The stragglers have turned onto the road and will be upon us in under a minute, which means both Thea and I are going to need to run faster just to get back to where we were when I nearly collided with that motorbike.

Has someone taken my bottle?

The thought hits me square between the eyes. If my stalker wants me out of the race, what better way to hinder my progress than by restricting my access to fluids? But in order to do that he – or they – would need to have got close enough to the table in order to take it. But surely this woman in the tabard would have stopped anyone trying to interfere with the bottles?

Unless she's working with them?

I stare at her face, trying to work out whether I've seen her before. She must be in her late sixties or early seventies, her fringe white as snow and the crown of her head light grey; her glasses are misted up and peppered with raindrops; moderately overweight based on her frame, but nothing particularly stands out as familiar.

Her face blurs as my eyes grow heavier, and it's as if my body is ready to wave a white flag, when Thea thrusts something into my hand.

'Drink,' she shouts, and I obey without even looking at what she's given me.

The liquid is sweet and coarse, and releases a rush of endorphins in my head; it's like I've swallowed a rainbow, and it's suddenly filling my body with sparkles. I don't stop drinking until the bottle is empty, and although my legs and arms still feel like dead-weights, I can already sense my mind creating new connections and telling me to get moving.

It's only when I look down at the bottle that I realise it's black with gold stars and the letters of my name stare back at me from the adhesive label.

'It was under the table,' Thea says, draining the rest of her bottle. 'It must have got knocked, fallen off and rolled under,' she says, pointing at a corner of the fluorescent tablecloth. 'Are you okay to start running again?'

I look around the crowd behind the barriers, looking for the Lithuanian Otto Bistras, but there is only a sea of faces. Is Thea right and the bottle was accidentally knocked to the floor and simply rolled beneath the table? Surely that's more reasonable than the prospect that my stalker did it deliberately.

Thea is grabbing at my hand and dragging me as the straggler pack comes closer. I stop resisting and break into a jog. I can feel the lactic acid funnelling through every muscle in my legs and arms, but push the pain to the back of my mind, while I try to process just how much time has been lost.

'You go on,' I tell Thea gratefully. 'Don't wait for me.'

She looks pained by the choice, but I nod encouragingly, promising I'll up my pace when the glucose takes effect. My personal guilt eases a fraction when she nods and slowly begins to accelerate away. Although she has already qualified for Paris, I know she wants to beat her personal best time today, and I don't want to be responsible for her missing out.

I need to be completing a mile of the course every five and a half minutes to hit the qualifying time, and we must have been at the rehydration station for at least a couple of minutes, so I'm going to have to complete at least four miles in five-minute splits, or shave off time every mile until the end of the course, but that is going to take an enormous effort.

I focus on my breathing, willing my body to process the sugar as quickly as possible, and finally feel my legs and feet starting to recover as there is a break in the rain. I am soaked through, and am desperate for fresh socks and trainers, but with Finn nowhere in sight, that isn't an option. But I can feel my energy levels rising, and it's all the motivation I need to slowly increase my pace, keeping a watchful eye on Thea, using her as my pace setter.

I start at the sound of a ringing phone through my headband. I don't even want to look at my watch, already anticipating who's on the other end.

12

BEFORE

Putting her head down, and tightening her grip on the handlebars, Molly pushes through the wall of fatigue and pumps her legs faster on the exercise bike. The display shows her speed notch a level higher, but it isn't enough. A large droplet of sweat crashes against the display, and she quickly wipes it with her hand, increasing the resistance in the pedals as she does.

'It's all about optimising your legs,' her coach Finn has been telling her, but he wouldn't be happy if he knew she was still here now, putting in extra miles.

It's almost eight o'clock, and the cleaner will be round to wipe down the equipment soon. She shouldn't still be here, but nobody seems to have noticed, and so she continues to pound the exercise bike, knowing that every extra metre of stamina she can harness now will pay dividends on race day. All her competitors will have other competitions under their belts, but the London Marathon will be Molly's first competitive event in ten months. No amount of practice and gym work will have her as conditioned as the competition, but it's the best she can manage, and so she's determined to make the most of every bonus minute she can grab.

It's not the only reason she's still training when everyone else has packed in for the day. These facilities are secure, with cameras constantly watching who's coming and going and the benefit of on-site security guards. He can't get her here.

The trip to Snowdonia over Christmas was long, but ultimately worthwhile. She switched off her phone the moment the taxi dropped her at her Aunt Rachel's cottage, and she kept it off the whole time she was there. A break from the outside world was exactly what she needed: no social media pressure; no Googling random facts; no watching cat videos; no explaining to friends why she didn't want to come out.

Molly's cousins were very welcoming, and after an initial awkward ten minutes while Rachel made up a spare bed in one of the boys' rooms, Molly felt like she managed to settle. Rachel didn't go into specific details about what had caused such a rift between her and Molly's mam, but she did talk of her regret at not reconnecting before she passed. Molly helped prepare the sprouts and potatoes on Christmas morning, attended mass at the local church – something she hadn't done since leaving home – and gorged and danced and chatted with the others. It was the most relaxing three-day break she'd ever taken. But then came the day when she needed to return to her dingy flat in South London, and with it, the prospect of running into *him* again.

She turned off her messages on Instagram, hoping that cutting him off at source would send a clear message that she wouldn't put up with his abuse. And after a chat with Thea, she learned how to switch off comments on her posts too. She thought that would be enough, but he continued to tag her in drivel, until Thea learned from her brother, Seb, how to stop people tagging her as well. Jamie seemed happy that her account was back on track and secured her a lucrative promotion with a new moisturising cream company.

But stopping *his* ability to contact her through that platform has left her vulnerable to attacks by other methods. She has been receiving phone calls from withheld numbers at odd times, and although she refuses to answer them and give him the chance to rile her further, she's certain he's the one behind them. Her phone has rung several times during the night, waking her, but she has stopped that now by putting her phone on airplane mode when it's time to sleep, and ignoring the calls during the day. She has switched her phone to silent, and disabled the vibrate function so, unless she is physically using her phone when he calls, she isn't aware of it until afterwards.

Changing her phone number hasn't helped, because somehow he's managed to get hold of her new number as well, and continues to bombard her. Ideally, she would just give up her phone completely, but she needs to be able to speak to Finn and Jamie, and she has no other means of doing so.

Molly starts as someone touches her arm, and she flings herself from the bike, landing in a crumpled heap on the hard floor.

'Oh, shit, are you okay?' Thea's high-pitched voice yelps, as she hurries round the bike to help Molly back to her feet. 'I tried calling your name from the door, but you didn't hear me, I guess.'

Molly's heart is racing. In that split second, she genuinely believed he had managed to bypass site security and got to her. Her breathing is heavy, and it takes several attempts to settle her nerves and find a steady rhythm. Thea is wearing a sparkly dress and knee-high boots, her makeup subtle but emphasising her cheekbones.

'I was just on my way out with some of the others,' she explains, as she fetches Molly a drink of water. 'Wondered if you could tear yourself away for long enough to join us?'

The thought of being able to forget about everything else is so appealing, but she is exhausted, and just desperate for sleep. And she doesn't trust that he isn't out there right now, waiting to get her alone.

'I can't tonight,' Molly lies, smiling apologetically, 'I have plans already.'

Thea does a lousy job of hiding her disappointment. 'You've been training in London for two months, and you haven't hung out with any of the team so far. The other girls are a real laugh; I think you'd like them.'

Molly knows that a core part of Team GB's historic successes has been the team spirit generated by the athletes, and Thea is right that she's done nothing to ingratiate herself with the others. She's seen several around this complex, and has nodded a hello, but little else. Her sole focus has been on earning her spot on the plane to Paris, but she knows she's going to have to step up her social skills as well.

'Maybe next time,' Molly says. 'I should be getting showered and changed myself. You have fun, and we can chat more tomorrow. Maybe we could all meet for lunch or a smoothie or something?'

Thea's face brightens. 'Sounds like a plan. You'd better grab your stuff, though, now. Security are doing the rounds ahead of closing up for the night.'

Molly had hoped to grab a shower before leaving, but throws on her tracksuit top and bottoms, and her fleece-lined coat over the top. The two of them leave the facility together, and Molly watches on enviously as Thea makes her way towards the nearest tube station, with no evident paranoia about who could be out here watching.

Molly pulls the straps of her bag over her shoulders and walks quickly along the shortest route back to her flat, trying to ignore every sudden sound – a door slamming, an empty can being kicked, a cat howling – and just focus on her destination. But the thought of being alone in her flat, with only a kickable door to protect her, suddenly seems too little, and she stops at a pizzeria around the corner from home. Bad carbs and fatty cheese are against her diet plan, but she craves something to release endorphins so orders a small pepperoni pizza. Inside the safety of the restaurant, it's loud with only a couple of vacant tables, and she allows herself to disappear into the background. When the pizza arrives, she's already salivating and feels no guilt as she bites into the crisp crust.

'Telephone call,' the Italian waiter informs her when she's nearly finished her first slice.

'For me?' she asks, wiping grease from around her lips and chin.

'Sì, you are Molly Fitzhume, athlete, yes?'

'Um, yes, but nobody knows I'm here.'

'He say he is your coach, Finn.'

Molly follows him through the restaurant and to the bar where a telephone handset is upturned. He leaves her.

'Hello? Finn? How did you know I—'

She doesn't have the chance to finish her sentence as she hears the sound of a mechanical child's toy laughing down the line.

'Who is this? What do you want from me?'

Still the toy laughs, and that's when the realisation hits her: he knows she's here; he's watching her now.

13

NOW

21 April 2024, Charlton, London – Mile 5

The phone continues to ring through the headband, each beat jarring. I don't want to keep running away from fate, so I tap the earpiece.

'Who are you?' I shout, no longer caring who else hears me. 'What do you want from me?'

'Molly? It's me,' comes Finn's reply, and my heart skips a beat as relief floods through my body. I look at my watch and see his name on the screen. 'Has something happened? You sound... on edge.'

My eyes sting with the threat of tears, but I fix my stare on the road ahead, and refuse to cave.

'He's here, Finn,' I say, my voice breaking under the strain.

'He who? What are you talking about?'

'My stalker.'

He sighs audibly. 'He's in prison, Molly.'

'He isn't working alone,' I tell him as firmly as I can. 'He phoned me, and then he messed with my bottle at the drink station.'

'Wait, what? You saw him?'

I grind my teeth. 'No, but my bottle wasn't on the table. Thea found it on the floor, like someone had hidden it from me on purpose.'

'But you've taken on fluids, right? You can't run the race without rehydrating.'

'I know, I know. I finished the drink and I'm running again.'

'What do you mean your bottle wasn't on the table? I put it there myself.'

'That's what I'm saying. It wasn't there. I think... I think someone purposely hid it from me.'

'Why would someone do that?'

'Because he's trying to mess with me. He wants me to know that he's here; that he's watching me. It's the same shit he's been doing for the last five months.'

I haven't shared all of the details with Finn, and although he is aware of some of the abusive messages I've received, I don't think he realises just how serious this is.

'He isn't here, Molly. Okay? He is in prison.'

'No, he has a partner: they're messing with—'

'Stop, Molly,' Finn cuts me off. 'I'm sorry, but the time for excuses is past.'

'I'm not making excuses,' I snap back. 'He's here.'

'No, he isn't. At least not physically.'

'What's that supposed to mean? You think I'm making this up?'

'No, but it's understandable that your paranoia is causing you to see and feel things that aren't real.'

'You think I imagined someone hiding my bottle? Ask Thea if you don't believe me. She'll confirm I'm not making this up.'

'I'm not saying you're making it up, Molly, but that maybe you're letting your fears get the better of you. You're in the middle of a televised race that is being broadcast globally. He's not going to harm you in front of all these cameras. Do you really think the man who's been hiding in the shadows for all this time is going to suddenly show himself in front of the world?'

'He phoned me,' I shout back.

'He phoned you? Today? What did he say?'

I never told Finn about the call from the laughing monkey, and I don't know how to explain it now.

'He didn't say anything, but I know it was him. The flowers at my room, the phone call and then hiding my bottle... *He's here*, Finn.'

I sense that nothing I say will convince him, which is why I need to get hold of DC Freeman. I'm about to ask Finn if he's spoken to her, when his next line throws me.

'If you're not up to the challenge, then you need to withdraw from the race.'

My mouth drops open at the suggestion. 'I'll make the time back.'

'Your times are way off. I've been placing your bottles at the tables where we agreed, so I haven't been tracking your timings. I figured you'd be fine maintaining a steady pace for the first few miles, but you're several minutes behind. Are you injured?'

I don't want to tell him about the twinge in my calf. 'Looking for my bottle cost me a lot of time, but I can make it up.'

'You'd better. I had to fight to get you this shot today. Do you understand? Gloria Hutchinson was ready to have you permanently excommunicated from Team GB, and I had to beg her to give you a second chance. Are you listening to me? It isn't just *your* reputation that's at stake today. If you don't qualify, it's both of our careers over. I don't know how I can make myself any clearer.'

My last meeting with Gloria Hutchinson was awkward, but I didn't realise Finn had to fight to keep my place in today's race.

'I'm not going to let you down, Finn.' I barely get the words out before I feel the tears escape. I wipe my eyes. Now is not the time for self-pity.

'Good, see that you don't. You're going to need to increase your pace to get back to those ahead of you. Kat is already two and a half minutes ahead, and she's the one you need to get ahead of. Right?'

That means she's almost half a mile ahead of me, and that's a lot to make up, but I know I can do it, so long as nothing else goes wrong.

'Looking at her current lap times, Kat is pushing herself today, but she usually drops off the pace after ten miles, so you need to get within touching distance by that point if you're to stand any chance of getting past her.'

'Have you managed to get hold of Detective Freeman?'

His lack of immediate answer tells me he hasn't, and given his attitude to what I've told him about my stalker being here, I can't even be sure he's been trying to phone her like I asked.

'No, not yet. Let me worry about keeping you safe. You just need to focus on the race and closing that gap. Okay?'

I confirm I will, and hang up. It wasn't exactly the pep talk I needed, but he is right that finishing ahead of Kat is the priority. The last spot in the team will go to one of us, and if she crosses the finish line before me, it won't matter how fast I've run. There is no prize for second place today.

The remaining shakiness from the low blood sugar has passed, and although my mouth is feeling dry, I feel re-energised. Two and a half minutes is a lot of time to make up, but I have five miles in which to do it, and then it will be a straight race until the finish between Kat and me. I have to believe I'm capable.

The rain is yet to return, and the thick blanket of cloud is starting to thin out as I make progress along the road. There are fewer people cheering at this section of the course, but the smidgen of applause keeps my legs pumping. Once I pass the six-mile marker I will go by the Cutty Sark and will be almost a quarter of the way through the race. At this point in the marathon I should be further ahead. I lower my face, and push harder again.

I grimace at a stabbing pain in my lower back, and pull up almost immediately. For the briefest of moments, I actually think someone has plunged a dagger into my hip, but as I move my hand to the pain, there is nothing there, but the ache.

Not now.

I try to start moving again, a gentle jog rather than the virtual sprint I was doing moments before, but the pain is almost over-whelming. I can't afford to be stationary, and do my best to hobble forwards, stretching my torso in different directions to try to iden-tify exactly which muscle group is sending pain signals to my brain. I haven't felt a pain this intense since the day I collapsed under the weight of moving the sofa, but on that day I couldn't even stand, let alone keep moving forwards. I continue to stretch as I jog along the course, and I do my best to ignore the horrified stares of those cheering from the sidelines. I don't want to think about how odd I must look with the shapes I'm pulling.

The pain begins to subside, and because I don't know if or when it may return, I push myself harder, swallowing the gap between myself and the runner ahead of me. At first I assume it's Thea, but there's no beanie hat and this runner has blonde hair instead of dark brown, which means Thea must have already over-taken her. Maybe she's already caught up to Kat in the front pack. In fact, it wouldn't surprise me if Kat slows to allow Thea to catch up now that I'm no longer on the scene. She's certainly made no secret of how much she despises me.

I shouldn't be jealous. They've known each other longer, but since I arrived in London in November, I've felt like a spare wheel. Thea has been welcoming, but I don't really know any of the rest of the team. I suppose part of that is my fault for not being more sociable. But between training, physio and recovery, I've had no time to be social. So I shouldn't be surprised that I've not been welcomed with open arms.

If I was in Kat's shoes, I probably wouldn't act any differently, though I'd like to think I wouldn't be so openly rude to her face. She feels threatened by me, which I suppose is a compliment in some way, and it has served to push me harder, despite all the setbacks. There's a part of me that would enjoy usurping her place in the GB team.

But what if I do manage to defeat her today and secure that final place? How are the other athletes going to react to me joining the party so late? What if Kat has other close friends in the group who go out of their way to make me feel unwelcome as well? Can I ever become part of a team that has been competing together for so long? Do I have any right to crowbar myself in at this late stage?

I'm sickened by the feelings of self-pity and inwardly cringe. To hell with the rest of them! I don't need their support to realise my dreams. And I've survived this long on my own, what's a few months more of isolation if it means I get to taste gold in Paris?

Finn is right: the only person holding me back right now is myself. If I want to be on that plane in July, then I have to prove to myself that I deserve it. I'll do what Finn has asked and I'll get Thea and Kat within my sights, but I'll hang back. I'll let them think they've got the best of me, and then when they least expect it, I'll call upon my reserves, and give everything I've got to reach the finish line first.

14

BEFORE

Friday, 12 January 2024, Marylebone, London

'Coming up on tonight's *The One Show*, we'll be talking to the farmer who refuses to adhere to British Summer Time because he says it confuses his cattle,' presenter Matt Baker tells the camera, with a sincere look.

'We'll also be speaking to the octogenarian whose viral TikTok videos have seen her on the verge of landing the number one spot in the UK's download charts,' presenter Alex Scott adds, smiling with genuine excitement.

'But before all that,' Matt continues, 'with only a hundred days to go until this year's London Marathon, a lot of you out there will be cranking up the miles ahead of one of the world's toughest races. And tonight, we've got one of the UK's brightest running stars here to share her journey with us. Molly Fitzhume was milliseconds from taking bronze at 2021's Olympic Games in

Tokyo, and she's now determined to go for gold in Paris this summer.'

Molly feels heat rise to her cheeks as the light on top of the camera pointing at her switches to red. She forces herself to smile at the two presenters who've already been so welcoming backstage, and have done their best to allay her obvious nerves at her first live television appearance in over a year. She can't help thinking that fake-Oppenheimer is glued to his screen, watching. She tries to shake that troublesome thought away, and then realises Alex has asked a question she didn't hear. There is just dead air while Molly tries to figure out what the first question was supposed to be.

She reaches for the small glass of water on the table and takes a sip, desperately trying to buy time. She's about to ask Alex to repeat the question when she sees the reflection of the autocue in her glass, and her mind tries to reverse the text.

'It's lovely to be here,' Molly quickly says, realising it was a welcome, rather than a specific question.

She didn't want to come on the show. Jamie thinks raising her profile on television will curry favour with the Olympic Committee as well as potential lucrative sponsors ahead of the marathon itself. And of course it will help fix the damage caused by fake-Oppenheimer's Instagram campaign. Since blocking all comments and closing her inbox, she hasn't heard a peep from him, to her relief, but she's now spending as much time at the track and gym as physically possible, in case he's watching her flat. The endorsements are paying well, but not well enough to move somewhere new.

Alex stares past Molly into the camera behind her. 'Everybody knows that training for a marathon is a mammoth task, but for poor Molly, a broken back has more than hampered her preparations. Only three months ago, she was laid up in hospital, unable to walk, her Olympic dreams in tatters.' She pauses to allow the gravity of the situation to sink in.

Against Molly's wishes, Jamie exaggerated the severity of the injury when speaking to *The One Show*'s researcher, to invoke more empathy with the audience. Molly desperately wants to correct the host, but bites down on her lip.

'But Molly has battled back, and is in training once again, and is set to compete in this year's London Marathon. So, Molly, how's training going? And more importantly, how is your back coping under the pressure?'

The light on Molly's camera turns red again. 'My back is getting stronger every day, and so far is standing up to the punishing schedule of stretches and extended runs.'

She tries to smile, despite the glaring heat of the overhead lights. Jamie suggested she wear a cocktail dress for added glamour, but she refused. She'd only appear if she could be comfortable, and so she's wearing a clean tracksuit top and bottoms, but she regrets choosing something so warm. She's certain the cameras must be picking up on the sweat flooding her hairline, and she prays the mascara applied by the makeup artist isn't running.

'Your decision to compete so soon after the injury is inspiring,' Matt picks up, 'but there is a reason why you need to make it to race day, isn't there?'

Molly nods, pleased she'd been shown a copy of the likely questions before they'd gone on air, giving her time to prepare her responses. 'That's right, Matt. The marathon represents my last chance to prove that I'm ready and able to compete in Paris this summer.'

'But you haven't just got to complete the marathon, have you? You've got to finish within a certain timeframe?'

Molly strains her smile wider, as if it's no additional pressure.

'To qualify for consideration, I have to finish inside two hours and thirty minutes.'

Alex suddenly touches her earpiece. 'Actually, the Olympic Committee have today announced the qualifying time has dropped to two hours and twenty-eight minutes now.'

Molly's smile evaporates in an instant. Jamie had said there was something he needed to talk to her about later, but he hadn't wanted to disrupt her performance on the show. She can't see him anywhere behind the cameras, and takes another sip of water to try to compose herself before answering the question. She's never run under two hours twenty-eight before, and this news is like a dagger to the heart, but she's also aware she's not the only Team GB runner who'll be affected by this change of time.

'The Committee bases qualifying times on the average finish times of competitive runners across the globe,' Molly says, as casually as she can manage, 'and yes, you're right, it has reduced today, I forgot.'

Alex and Matt continue to fire questions at her for a further four minutes, and the responses get easier, but she's relieved when the hosts turn to face the central camera and introduce a pre-recorded wildlife segment with Chris Packham.

'You did great,' Alex whispers, leaning forwards, and smiling encouragingly. 'I remember how nervous I was the first night I hosted this. You came across as very natural.'

Molly thanks her, but is now just desperate to get back to her dressing room, and to wash the makeup from her face. The sound man disconnects her microphone, and one of the runners leads her from the stage, through the cameras and seated producers, and out to her dressing room, where a hastily printed sign of her name has been stuck to the door. Her shoulders finally relax as she closes the door and leans against the back of it.

There's still no sign of Jamie, and when she checks her phone she sees a message from him, saying he had to dash away but will stop by to see her tomorrow. A second message arrives, apologising for not mentioning the qualifying time reduction. Finn must have known about the impending change, but he also neglected to tell her when they spoke earlier today.

Why do all the men in her life underestimate her ability to roll with bad news? The time reduction is not ideal under the circumstances, but it provides added motivation to keep going, and if anything, to push herself further. Realistically, if she wants to secure a podium finish in Paris, she's going to need to get her time closer to two hours twenty-eight anyway. There's nothing she can do to change the committee's decision, so there's no point in wasting energy worrying about it.

She crosses to the dressing table and yanks out two wet wipes, which she rubs over her eyelids, cheeks and chin. She throws them into the wastepaper bin beside the table, but then catches sight of a square white cardboard box in the large mirror's reflection. The box is sitting on the armchair in the far corner of the room, and a large red bow is neatly tied around it.

A present from Jamie?

Molly steps across to the chair, unable to keep the smile forming on her lips as she searches for a card to check who the gift is from. Finding none, she slides the bow from the box, and lifts the lid, expecting to see a cake inside. Instead, she sees the pair of running spikes she'd been trying to save for before Christmas. It has to be a gift from Finn, as nobody else knew she was so desperate to get this particular pair. Lifting one out, she turns it over in her hands, marvelling as the overhead light glistens off each perfectly poised spike.

This is too much, but it's just the boost she needs after a challenging few weeks. She wants to know exactly who to thank, so she continues to search inside the box, eventually finding a small envelope inside the other shoe. Opening it, she's confused by the printed message:

I'M RIGHT BEHIND YOU.
SEE YOU AFTER THE SHOW.
xxx

There's no name on the card, and she can't see anything to highlight which company delivered it. Unless of course it was Jamie who'd brought it here himself, but she doesn't understand what the message could mean. She's just about to return the shoe to the box, when she sees something colourful poking out beneath the white tissue paper beneath the other shoe. Pushing it to one side, she pulls out the colourful item, now realising it's a book of some sort. She doesn't recognise the title – *Right Behind You: The Story of the Coaches and Medical Professionals Who Train Athletes* – but it's when she sees the author's name that her mouth drops: Dr Jürgen Oppenheimer.

She knows it's a message from *him*, but the worst part is that *he* brought it here tonight. He was in her dressing room.

15

NOW

21 April 2024, Greenwich, London – Mile 6

The road narrows on the approach that will eventually pass around the Cutty Sark and the Greenwich Maritime Museum. I remember Mam bringing me here when I was a child. We came down to London so she could visit a friend from college who'd recently married and settled in Ealing. She brought me into central London on a sightseeing tour, taking in Big Ben, the Houses of Parliament, Oxford Street and then to see the Prime Meridian Line here in Greenwich.

'Do you know what this is?' she asked, pointing down at the metal track cut into the surrounding concrete.

I stared blankly back at her, and then she proceeded to explain that the line represents the historic Prime Meridian of the World and how every place on earth was measured in terms of its distance east or west from this line.

'If you stand with one foot on one side and the other on the left, you are perfectly in the middle of east and west, according to the Prime Meridian Line,' she added, but must have seen the look of disinterest in my eyes, as we then went and bought ice cream cones.

I never would have thought that some twenty or so years later I would be charging towards that line, hunting down my competition. If she was here now, I've no doubt Mam would be telling me to stop feeling sorry for myself and to push harder. I can almost hear her voice telling me that anything can be accomplished with a bit of time and effort. I miss her little idioms.

I sense it will take more than a little time and effort to figure out why someone has made it their goal to terrorise me. But time is exactly what I have – or at least another hour and forty minutes – to figure out who is behind it. I can either wait for them to strike again, or I can start using my brain. And I know exactly who can help me.

Raising my left wrist, I twirl the dial on my watch until I find Zara's name and hit the dial icon. I hear the line ringing through my headband and am expecting the answerphone to once again cut in, when there's a click.

'Hello?'

'Zara? Can you hear me?'

'Molly? Is that you?'

She's finally answered, but she doesn't sound too pleased to hear from me.

'Sorry, did I wake you?' I ask, panting as I keep my eyes on the road ahead.

'What? No, you didn't wake me. I haven't been to bed yet. Where are you? You sound exhausted.'

'I'm running,' I pant, trying to keep my answers short to conserve as much energy as possible.

'Okay, well, can we maybe catch up when you've finished running? I'm a bit tied—'

'He's back,' I blurt as I approach the next line of supporters cheering from behind the erected railings.

'Sorry? Say that again. The signal is terrible down here.'

'He's back. Otto. He's watching me now.'

I can almost hear the frown in her voice. 'You think Otto is watching you now? Impossible unless you're phoning from Stuttgart. Where are you?'

'Greenwich,' I pant. 'It's marathon day.'

When she speaks again, I can't tell if the incredulity is because I'm calling from the course, or because she didn't realise what day it is. 'You're competing in the London Marathon right now?'

'Yep. I need you to meet me here.'

'I can't meet you right now, Molly. I'm on a task force, and it's all hands on deck.'

I can only hope that's the reason why she hasn't been answering my calls up to now. Better that than the prospect that she's been ignoring me; I shouldn't have been so judgemental.

'Please, Zara. He's here. Now. Somewhere.'

'Hold on a second,' she says, and there's a muffled sound like the phone has been pressed against her top. She returns a minute later. 'Right, I'm outside now. You said something about someone watching you.'

'There were flowers outside my hotel room this morning. Blue orchids, my mam's favourite. And there was a card. A card like he left at Broadcasting House back in January. Same font and language. He's back.'

'That's impossible, Molly. Otto Bistras is incarcerated in Germany. You know that.'

'I told you before: I think he has someone helping him. They hand-delivered the flowers to my room. They knew I'd be there.

They knew the blue orchids were Mam's favourite. They want me to know they're watching me now.'

'When did all of this happen?'

'This morning. I was leaving for the race and heard noises in the corridor. Then when I opened the door, the box was outside. They knew I was there.'

'Where were you?'

'The Clarendon Hotel in Blackheath.'

'Was the card signed?'

'No, it said: "I'm right behind you; see you at the race." That was how he phrased the message at the television studios. Do you remember? He left a card and a book in the box with the new running spikes.'

'I remember, I remember, but Otto Bistras can't have delivered the flowers to you today.'

'No, but his accomplice could.'

'There is no evidence that Bistras was working with anyone, and in cases like this, stalkers don't usually have accomplices. Part of the psychology of what they do is because they want to exert power over an individual; it isn't something they tend to share; it would kind of ruin the point.'

'You're wrong, Zara. I can't tell you why, but I am *certain* there is someone else involved. There have been too many unexplained things happening since he was sent to prison.'

I've kept a diary of all the moments when something has felt off, and I've shared each of the dates, times and locations with Detective Freeman. That feeling like I'm being watched when I emerge from my flat in the morning; the sense that someone is following me when I return at night. Things being moved when I'm at the track, and yet there is no CCTV showing anyone haunting me. If I was truly paranoid, I'd say there was a ghost after me, but I don't believe in paranormal events. But I can understand

Zara's scepticism. She very much sees the world as black and white; things are either right or wrong, and she won't be persuaded otherwise. I guess that's what makes her so good at her job.

'And you're sure nobody else could have left the flowers. I mean, the message you said was left on the card isn't exactly threatening. If anything, it sounds supportive. Isn't it possible that the flowers could have been sent by one of your fellow athletes, or your agent perhaps?'

I grab a bottle of water from the table as I pass, and take a long drink, before emptying the rest of the drink onto the road and hurling the bottle towards the plastic bag one of the race stewards is holding.

'Thea and my agent Jamie were the only people who knew I was staying at The Clarendon last night, but they didn't send the flowers. Jamie's not that considerate. And my coach Finn didn't send them either, before you ask.'

I know I shouldn't snap at her – it isn't her fault – but I'm frustrated that nobody seems to be taking me seriously today. Finn and Thea also seemed to suggest this is all in my head, when I know this is more than just paranoia.

'He phoned me as well,' I add.

'He phoned you? Otto?'

'Yes, him... or whoever he's working with.'

'You spoke to them?'

'No, they phoned from a withheld number. I thought it was you, so I answered the call, but all I heard was this mechanical laughing voice. Do you remember me telling you something similar happened when I was at an Italian restaurant months ago?'

'Sure,' she says, but sounds vague.

'Well, it was exactly the same laughing voice. It reminded me of one of those wind-up monkeys that bash cymbals together. If it wasn't him or someone associated with him, then who was it? What logical reason is there for someone to phone my mobile and play such a voice down the line?'

I pause, waiting to hear if she dares to formulate a response, but there's silence.

'It's *him*, Zara. He's back and he wants me to know about it.'

There is a blast of static as she sighs into the phone. 'Okay, let's work on the hypothesis that Otto or some acquaintance is behind these two incidents. We know that Otto is in prison, so he can't have delivered something to your room, but that doesn't mean he didn't arrange for someone to deliver the flowers. Even though access to mobile phones and the internet is restricted in prisons, I've seen enough examples of prisoners sneaking in devices and continuing their operations, so it isn't too big a stretch to think that's what he's done, *if* he is the one behind it. But the biggest question I have is why.'

'He wants me to know that he's not given up on ruining my life.'

'Yeah, maybe, but he's behind bars. He can't get to you now. So, apart from a bit of emotional torture, he's not a threat to you. The flowers were in poor taste, but not life threatening, and you can block calls from withheld numbers, so if you block him he's not going to be able to contact you again. I realise this isn't easy for you, and I am so sorry that he's targeted you, but ultimately, he can't get to you. You're safe, Molly.'

'He interfered with my drink bottle as well.'

'Wait, he did what to your bottle?'

'He hid it so I couldn't boost my energy. My friend found it hidden under the table. That's why I know he is here – or at least someone is here – and they want to make me suffer. I know I sound paranoid, but what if I'm right? What if everything he's been doing until now was just a taste of things to come? What if he's been building to this moment all along, and now I'm trapped inside his twisted game?'

I can see the Cutty Sark on the horizon. Mam was so proud to take me around the ship. 'It was built in Dumbarton, just like you,' she said, smiling. 'She was one of the fastest ships in her time; could outrun all her sister ships, even in the poorest conditions.'

'You should speak to the race stewards,' Zara says. 'If you don't feel safe, then you should withdraw. I'm sure the stewards can escort you to the nearest police officer where you'll be safe.'

'I'm not withdrawing,' I say defiantly, staring up at the mast as I swallow the gap to the bend in the course that will take me within touching distance of the ship. 'I have to finish the race or I won't make the Olympic squad.'

'But if you're right, Molly, then you're not safe continuing. Your safety is paramount.'

'But what if that's precisely what he's hoping for? I'm not giving in.'

'So what do you expect me to do? I can't come and protect you. I'm not a bodyguard; I wouldn't last five minutes in a foot race.'

'No, but you have contacts in Germany, right? Or at least, you can find out who the arresting team were?'

'Yes, but how are they going to help?'

'Find out from them whether Bistras has any known associates. I mean, when he was in London, did he meet with anyone, or was he staying with anyone? We need to narrow down who's helping him.'

'Okay, I'll see what I can do. In the meantime, you stay safe. If you see him or anyone who is a threat, get to safety. I'll call you back when I know more.'

16

BEFORE

Molly pounds the pavement, as she races from Broadcasting House in Marylebone to the only place that offers any kind of safety. Water splashes up from the puddles she tears though, soaking the cuffs of her tracksuit bottoms, but she doesn't care; she just wants to put as much distance between herself and the TV studios as possible.

Carrying the large white cardboard box isn't making her journey any easier, but she didn't know what else to do. As soon as she saw the real Jürgen Oppenheimer's book beneath the trainers, she knew it was a message from her stalker. Nobody else could have been so cruel. She thought cutting his access from her socials would be enough to put him off, but now he's back, and the fact that he left the gift in her dressing room means he wants her to know he's in the country. Not only that, but he knows her schedule and can get to her anywhere.

She shivers as these thoughts race through her mind. She no longer cares about the rain, nor the fact the box is getting heavier as the cardboard soaks it up.

She should have asked one of the runners on the show about who left the box, and how they were able to get access to her dressing room. She should have demanded someone phone the police and examine the scene, search for fingerprints, and check the security camera footage to prove he was there. She should have demanded the police take her into protective custody, but at the time none of that went through her head. She had only one thought: get out!

If he managed to get into her dressing room, then by proxy, he managed to get access to the TV studios, which meant he knew she would be there. And she had no way of knowing that he wasn't still there in the studios watching her reaction to the present. Her fight or flight instinct took over, and she fled.

Most troubling to Molly now is how he knew that she wanted this particular pair of running spikes. As far as she knows, she hasn't shared that information with anyone but her agent and coach, and even then only in passing. But neither Jamie nor Finn would have hunted down a copy of Oppenheimer's book and left it hidden in the box. So how could he have found out? She doesn't remember posting about it online, but what's the alternative? That he's been close this whole time, eavesdropping on conversations? Or worse still: he's managed to plant some kind of surveillance software in her flat or on her phone.

It's a relief when she sees the university's halls of residence at the end of the street. She should have warned Thea that she was coming over, but she hasn't stopped running since the studio. It's possible Thea won't even be home, but with other students milling about the large four-storey building, at least there's safety in numbers.

Molly stops when she reaches the communal entrance to the building, sheltering beneath the overhang, and desperately trying to get her breath back. She's no idea how far she's run, but would estimate five to six miles in less than clement conditions. The cardboard box is now misshapen from the weather and from Molly's struggle to carry it without dropping it. Her phone is zipped into the pocket of her dripping tracksuit bottoms, so she searches the panel beside the door for Thea's name, and stabs the buzzer with her nose.

She stares out into the dark street behind her, unable to escape the feeling she's being watched. There are cars parked on the street, but she can't tell if the shadowy figures behind the wheels are real, or just the overhanging trees creating optical illusions. What if he followed her from the studios? She was too busy running to notice if anyone was trailing. She didn't hear footsteps, but what if he was tracking slowly in a car?

She stabs the intercom again, and it buzzes seconds later.

'Hello?'

'Thea, thank God. It's Molly, can you let me up?'

'I'll be right down.'

Molly pushes herself further under the doorway, keeping her eyes peeled on the street, looking for any sudden movements, or for anyone acting strangely. It's hard to concentrate as the smell of marijuana hangs in the air, and lively noise is echoing from a row of open windows on the top floor.

Thea bangs her knuckle against the glass door, and ushers Molly to step back so she can push the door open and allow her in.

'You brought me a cake?' she asks once they're both inside, staring down at the box.

Molly shakes her head, trying to gather her thoughts. 'It's from *him*.'

Thea doesn't understand. 'Him who? Someone sent a cake for me?'

A clatter against the front door causes Molly to jump and she stare daggers at the two girls, laughing hysterically, barely able to stand straight enough to get the key in the door. Thea takes pity and opens it for them. The stale smell of wine on their breath assaults Molly's nostrils, and she takes a subconscious step backwards to allow them to pass.

'What's she doing here?' the taller of the two students asks, glaring at Molly.

Molly doesn't recognise her at first; squeezed into a sequined dress that does nothing to hide the muscular strength of her arms and legs. She can't imagine how she could have offended the girl.

'She's here to see me,' Thea says. 'Nothing to do with either of you.'

The girl doesn't move on, a look of pure hatred now contorting her face as she stares Molly down. 'You think you can come to my place and act like it's your own? You've got another think coming, girl.'

Thea grabs Molly's arm, and leads her up the stairs to the second floor and into a room. When the door is closed, Molly finally feels able to relax a little, and lowers the box to the table. The room is bigger than her own, with a double bed against one wall and fitted wardrobes across from it. There is a small kitchen area with a fridge, sink, and microwave, near the door. She imagines Thea isn't paying nearly as much for the space as the university students receiving subsidises for their accommodation do.

'Sorry about Kat,' Thea says, crossing to the sink and filling the kettle.

'That was Kat Campbell?' Molly says rhetorically as she connects the name and face. 'What's her problem with me?'

'She sees you as a threat, I guess. She took the last place in the

Olympic distance running squad, until you put yourself forward. I think she's worried that you'll qualify in a faster time than her, and she'll lose her spot. I'm sure that's all it is. Don't let it trouble you.'

Molly has been studying the qualifying times of the rest of the elite women runners in the squad, and from memory, Kat Campbell completed Berlin in just over two hours twenty-nine, so she'll need to compete in the London Marathon too now.

'She thinks I'm after her place in the team?'

'Exactly. There's only four spots for Paris, and Kat has the slowest qualified time so far, so you are a genuine threat to her place, especially after they lowered the qualifying time today. My spot is already safe, but I'm competing as a practice and to set the pace for the two of you. Probably best to stay out of each other's way for now.' Thea makes tea, before nodding at the sodden box. 'So, are you going to tell me who sent me cake? I hope it's chocolate.'

The talk of the race meant Molly had momentarily forgotten about her reason for coming. She lifts the lid and shows Thea the trainers.

'These were left in my dressing room when I was at Broadcasting House.'

'Nice! A gift from the show's producers?'

Molly slowly shakes her head. 'I think they were left by him: the stalker.'

Thea frowns in confusion. 'You mean the weirdo who was sending you all those messages weeks ago?'

'I blocked him online, and now I think he's coming for me in real life.'

Thea still doesn't look convinced. 'How... Why do you think they're from him?'

Molly pulls out the book and passes it over. 'This was the name on the profile when he first messaged. Do you remember? You showed me that he was using a fake profile?'

Thea turns the book over in her hands, and fans the pages, before handing it back. 'Crikey. And the book was in the box too?'

Molly nods.

'No way, man. Ooh, that's creepy!' She shudders.

'Exactly! Not only did he know where I'd be, he followed me there. It's messed up, but now I'm terrified he's waiting at my flat; that's why I ran here. I appreciate it's a lot to ask, but is there any way—'

'Hey, listen, no sweat, you're free to crash here for the night; so long as you don't mind sharing a bed.'

Molly's shoulders relax a fraction. 'Thank you.'

'What are friends for, right? Have you reported him to the police?'

'I was panicked, and I ran. I can't prove it's him, or even who *he* really is.'

'That's their job. Honestly, you need to tell the police that you have a stalker and that your life is in genuine danger. This isn't something you can handle on your own.'

Molly knows she's right, but isn't even certain what she can tell the police.

'I'm happy to come with you if it would help,' Thea offers.

Molly's eyes fill with gratitude, and she hugs her friend.

'We'll go first thing tomorrow,' Thea says. 'Right now, I think we need something stronger than tea. Sit down while I go and get some wine from the local off licence. Don't worry, you're perfectly safe in here.'

Thea pulls on a coat and grabs her purse before Molly has the chance to argue, disappearing through the door. Molly strips out of her wet tracksuit, hangs the top and bottom on the warm radiator beside the bed, hoping they'll dry enough before Thea makes it back. She knows she should phone Jamie to tell him what happened, but she doesn't want to worry him unnecessarily, so she sends him a message instead, double-checking that he didn't leave the box in her dressing room. The message doesn't send due to low signal, and standing by the window doesn't improve the signal strength.

Moving to the door, Molly opens it a crack, before freezing as she hears voices in the corridor.

'You best not be plotting my downfall with that bitch,' Kat's voice echoes.

'Don't be ridiculous,' Thea whispers back. 'Her being here has nothing to do with running or the squad. Okay? She's just a bit shaken up by something in her personal life.'

'Well, you'd better tell your new bestie to watch her back; ain't no skanky bitch stealing my seat on that plane. I'll do whatever it takes to get to Paris.'

17

NOW

21 April 2024, Greenwich, London – Mile 7

The Cutty Sark looms closer, the shiny dark paint contrasting perfectly with the blanket of cloud blocking out London's other historic landmarks on the horizon. What I would give to be able to board her now, and just sail far away. Away from the pressures of professional racing; away from the stresses and strains of muscle groups most don't even know exist; away from seedy older men and incels who think they have the right to obsess over me; away from the additional stress and pressure I inflict on myself in some subconscious guilt about not being there for my mam when she needed me most.

Her death, whilst unexpected, shouldn't have been a total surprise. Although I spoke to her at least once a week, I hadn't realised she was keeping things from me. She occasionally mentioned having colds, but she didn't tell me about the sudden pain that developed in her calf. A pain that she had booked an appointment to discuss with her GP, but that nobody realised was a blood clot, which moved to her heart a day before her appointment. I wasn't to know that this was going to happen, but I'd like to think that if she'd mentioned the cramping pain, I would have suggested a more urgent appointment, or that I would have jetted home to check up on her. In truth, it was easier checking up on her over the phone, rather than returning to Dumbarton. Deep down, I probably knew that she wasn't telling me everything. It was an unwritten rule between us that we would try not to make the other worry unnecessarily: I wouldn't tell her about my financial struggles and poor track performance, and she would only raise things she was genuinely worried about.

I'm angry at myself for not making more of an effort to see her. It's a lame excuse to blame her fussing and old-fashioned attitude whenever I did visit, because all mams become like that. Are you eating enough? Are you drinking too much? You should wrap up or you'll catch a cold. You look tired, are you getting enough sleep?

I avoided going home because I didn't want her to see how much I was struggling. Back then, I was training hard, but was arrogant enough to see myself as almost invincible. I thought my body could handle the late-night parties, competing despite hangovers, and that nothing would stop me. The irony that Mam passing directly led to my falling off that pedestal isn't lost on me.

I blamed her fussing for me not wanting to return home as often, when in truth, I didn't want a critical eye being cast on me, because then that would mean I'd see how foolhardy I was being.

I miss her every day. Grief isn't a feeling that diminishes over time. I've read it can become easier when we are able to put enough measures in place to handle the pain, but it never goes away; just becomes easier to manage. My grief has the added side portion of guilt because I wasn't there when she died. And in fact, my last words to her were mumbled under my breath after she'd started in on why I didn't have 'a nice boy' to look after me. She meant well, and her fussing was driven by concern and love.

If she was still here today, I probably wouldn't have told her about the campaign of hate Bistras and his counterpart have cast my way, because I wouldn't have wanted her to worry. She'd have probably told me to move back home and throw my phone in the bin, and maybe that would have been the best thing to do. Or better still, she would have scrimped and saved her pension and hired a bodyguard to keep me safe so I could keep striving towards my dream.

I would give anything right now to hear her voice.

The cheering is louder here; the crowd penned in like sheep behind railings covered in advertising. The road twists and bends around the Cutty Sark, so it's impossible to see how far ahead the twelve other runners are. I've put in a huge effort to run faster and my last two miles have definitely been under the five-minute mark. I knew I was capable of completing miles that fast, but it isn't sustainable, and I can already feel it taking its toll. I'm starting to feel light-headed again, and I will have to take on more glucose as soon as possible. But I know there is a table with sugary gel packs coming up not long after this section of the race. They weren't in the schedule I agreed with Finn, but given I've not stuck to the rest of the plan up to now, I'm just going to have to make it up from this point anyway.

Someone is ringing a bell as I hit the first bend, but I am trying to put the cheering crowd out of my mind and just focus on keeping my pace fast. If I can keep at this rate for at least another mile, I'll soon have Thea and Kat in my sights. That is, assuming they haven't accelerated as well. I can't think about that now. They both had racing schedules – we all did – that were based on running at a consistent speed. I'd be shocked if they've deviated from that.

Passing around the bow of the ship, I keep my head down, not even raising a hand to acknowledge the cheering and calls of my name.

'Go on, Molly!'

'You've got this.'

'I'm right behind you.'

My blood chills at this last shout, and my head snaps up, but there are so many people it's impossible to see from where within the crowd the shout came from. Splashes of cold rain are peppering the ground once again, and many within the crowd have erected umbrellas, making it even more difficult to discern one face from another.

I race around the next bend, and the crowd and railings continue as we meet the shuttered shops, bars and cafés of Greenwich town centre.

'We love you, Molly.'

'You're the best!'

I briefly glance up as I pull around the next bend, hearing the familiar rumble of a motorbike, and realise I can see the back of the second pack. It's all the motivation I need to find another gear, and I stretch myself to close the gap. No obvious sign of Thea or Kat, but they can't be much further ahead of this group. I am renewed with faith that my dream is still within touching distance; I just hope my body doesn't give up on me before the finish line.

I grimace as a drop of rain catches me direct in the eye, and I eagerly brush it away with my knuckles, but the stinging is so much that I have to close my eye. I wipe at it with sweaty fingers, but that only makes the sting worse. I need to keep up my pace, but with one arm raised, I'm losing momentum. Keeping the eye closed, I try to rediscover my rhythm.

The last couple of runners are now directly ahead of me, and I am going to have to time it right to get around them, but I am conscious of the motorbike up and to the right. I don't want a repeat of what happened earlier. If it hadn't been for Thea, that motorbike would have taken me out. And when I look at the cameraman, I see it is the same one as before. I can only hope his rider has learned their lesson.

The homemade cardboard signs are looking sodden through the rain, and just beyond the motorbike I see a pair of bespectacled eyes staring back at me. There is something alarmingly familiar about the man's face, but I can't place where I've seen it before. He is positioned on the next corner, but he has no interest in the pack of runners ahead of me who are now taking the bend directly in front of him.

I prise my closed eye open, and try to focus on where I know that face from. Did I see him earlier in the race? I don't think I know the man, and yet there is something so recognisable about his appearance. His beard is long, a deep maroon nest of curls, and the grey anorak covering his shoulders looks so out of place amongst the vibrant colours of the other hats and coats of the spectators immediately around him.

And he is still staring directly at me.

Is that Bistras's partner?

I need to get around these runners, but I don't want to get any closer to him than is necessary.

Why is he staring at me so intently?

And then the world slows. He briefly looks down, unzips his anorak, and begins to pull apart the sides. Even the falling raindrops seem to slow as I see him reaching into the inside pocket of the coat. He has gripped something, and I'm getting closer; maybe only twenty metres separate us now. His elbow starts to rise as he withdraws his hand, his fingers wrapped around something small and black.

He continues to pull out the item, and my eyes begin to widen, my mouth slowly dropping open as I realise what he is clutching.

Finn's words echo in my mind: *He's not going to harm you in front of all these cameras.*

But what if that's precisely what he *is* planning? How many assassinations of American presidents have been attempted in front of a streaming camera? Some of them do it for the fame and publicity. What if that's what Bistras and his counterpart want too? What if everything that's happened before has been building to this?

I want to be anywhere but running through Greenwich in this pouring rain, and it isn't just my own safety I'm fearful for now, but that of my fellow runners. I dart my body to the left, keeping my head low, desperately hoping I can hide behind the jostling bodies ahead of me. I don't want to see him holding the gun and grinning at me, so I keep my eyes averted, yelling for those around me to get down and take cover.

I don't realise how close I am to my fellow competitors, until my shoulders are crashing into their elbows, and we all lose balance, barely able to keep upright. But just as I'm expecting to hear the sound of gunfire, instead there's a whistle, and race stewards are barrelling towards us.

'What the hell is wrong with you?' I hear the woman next to me yelling, and I straighten, pointing over to the man in the grey anorak, but he isn't there. Or at least, I don't see him at first, but then I do catch sight of his square spectacles, and see that he has now erected a black travel umbrella above his head.

There is no sign of the gun that I'm sure I saw him removing from inside his coat.

I stare at him for what feels like an eternity, until I realise the other runners have started up again, and I'm the only one not moving.

I grab for two glucose gel packs as I pass by the table, and tear into them, hoping my panicked reaction doesn't face further scrutiny from the race adjudicators later on.

18

BEFORE

Saturday, 13 January 2024, Brixton, London

Molly wakes, shivering, unfamiliar with her surroundings at first, before the weight of the cloud hanging over her head lifts enough to remind her she crashed at Thea's last night. Although they agreed to share the bed, Molly has lost the battle for the duvet, and it's her exposed legs causing her shakes. Rather than pulling it back, she dresses quickly, and boils the kettle.

She's sitting at the table with two steaming mugs of tea when Thea finally wakes.

'You sleep okay?' she asks, stretching her arms over her head and stifling a yawn.

'Like a log,' Molly lies, to protect her friend's feelings.

'You don't half fidget at night,' Thea continues, yawning again. 'Oh, and when you called out in the middle of the night, I thought I was going to have a heart attack.'

'I called out? For who?'

Thea stands and continues to stretch her limbs as she moves about the room. 'I don't know. It was all gobbledygook to me. Were you having a nightmare?'

Molly doesn't recall a night terror, but given the stress she's feeling as a result of fake-Oppenheimer, and then finding the trainers in her dressing room, she understands it's highly possible it's affecting her sleep.

It's not yet eight o'clock, but Molly is desperate to get to the police station to report what happened yesterday. In the back of her mind, she's conscious that there's probably not a lot the police can do, but she doesn't want to keep burying her head in the sand and pretending it's not happening. As Thea said last night when she opened the bottle of wine, 'What if it escalates into something worse?'

Molly hasn't mentioned what she overheard Kat say at the door, as she shouldn't have been listening in, but she's now more aware of how the other athletes in Team GB are perceiving her. They've always seemed such a friendly bunch when interviewed on television, but she can understand why there might be animosity towards someone threatening to break up the band. She doesn't want to let any of that worry her at the moment; her focus needs to be on getting faster, not on making friends.

Thea joins her at the table and Molly slides the mug of tea across to her. If Thea is suffering a similar level of hangover to her, she isn't showing it. Thankfully, they stopped at the one bottle, but it's the first alcohol Molly has had since her mam's funeral, and her body is no longer conditioned to handle it. She now hates the feeling of losing control of her mind and body.

'I usually have ingredients to make a breakfast smoothie,' Thea tells her, 'but today is shopping day. I can offer you a bowl of cereal.'

'That's okay, I'll pick up something later.'

The truth is Molly has no appetite for food right now. She just wants to get this guy reported and get back to training. At least last night's five-mile run from the studio counts towards building up stamina for the race.

Thea showers quickly while Molly dresses in her now dry tracksuit and they head out. The cardboard box is now bent out of shape, having become wet and then dried, but it's still a struggle to manhandle it to Brixton Police Station, which Google says is the closest to Thea's halls of residence. Molly keeps her eyes peeled the whole way, wondering if fake-Oppenheimer could be in one of the moving cars, or hiding behind every corner.

Thea tags along, even though Molly knows she's disrupting her own training schedule. When she tells her she can cope on her own, it's only because she doesn't want to be a nuisance, but Thea waves away her protests.

Brixton Police Station is three storeys high, with the entrance in the lower left corner, emblazoned with Metropolitan Police signs, and for the first time in ages, Molly feels safe. He wouldn't be stupid enough to follow them in here.

The young officer behind the windowed desk smiles as they approach and asks how he can help. Molly's mouth is so dry and she doesn't know what to say. She's never been in a police station before, nor had any brushes with the law, but suddenly feels as though the officer can read her mind and will somehow find out about something she's done wrong in the past.

'She wants to report a stalker,' Thea says matter-of-factly when she sees her floundering.

The officer's smile transforms to empathetic concern, as if a switch has been flicked in his head. He proceeds to ask questions about the identity of the stalker, and what has happened. With Thea's coercion, Molly is able to share the details, and he asks them to wait while he goes to find someone to take a formal statement. There are benches against the wall where they sit, but they're hard and wooden, and uncomfortable. Molly starts to pace as the tension builds in her gut, fearing they won't believe her story, or will see it as attention seeking.

Minutes later, a woman in jeans and a polo shirt approaches, introducing herself as Detective Constable Zara Freeman. She must be in her late thirties or early forties, judging by the crow's feet near her eyes. She has jet-black braided hair, and leads them to a room beside the front desk, closing the door behind them. Sunlight shines through the large window, in stark contrast to last night's storm. She offers them both a hot drink, but Molly settles for water, which the detective pours from the water cooler in the room. There are two medium-sized sofas in the corner beneath the window, and Freeman encourages them to sit together, while she sits to the side.

'There are cameras in the room,' Freeman advises, pointing to two LEDs in opposite sides of the ceiling, 'and we will record everything you say to help me write the statement for you. Okay? Nobody will see these recordings unless we're able to go to trial. This interview isn't under caution, but you're encouraged to speak honestly and openly. Okay?'

Molly nods, and the detective asks them to introduce themselves for the purposes of the recording. Molly then proceeds to fill her in on the last two months of unwarranted behaviour.

'Can I see the messages he sent?' Freeman asks when Molly has finished.

Molly unlocks her phone and opens the app.

'I don't understand,' Freeman says, showing Molly the screen. 'All I can see are some messages from before Christmas where you seem to be apologising to him.'

Molly looks at the screen. 'That was my agent's doing. He said I should apologise to try to get the guy to stop.'

'With all due respect – and don't get me wrong, I am on your side, but – these messages here could easily be interpreted as a guy trying to chat you up; I'm not seeing anything particularly sinister.'

'That's because she deleted the rest,' Thea chimes in.

'I thought blocking him would send the right message, but then he set up new accounts and tried messaging again. I blocked and deleted all of them.'

Freeman hands her the phone back. 'Obviously, that's not ideal. If he makes contact again, please keep the messages, or screenshot them before you delete or block. Okay?'

Molly nods, angry at herself for not considering this sooner. 'What about the running shoes, though? He was in my dressing room last night.'

'This is potentially something I can follow up on. I will contact Broadcasting House and ask to review their security camera footage. Leaving a gift isn't technically a crime, but it may help identify the culprit.'

'Are you going to dust the shoes and box for fingerprints?' Thea asks.

Freeman considers the battered box. 'I'm going to assume you've handled the trainers yourself?'

Molly nods.

'Then I don't think there's any benefit to having them checked for fingerprints if I'm honest. It's an expensive request, and historically in cases like this, the perpetrator often wears gloves anyway. I'm not diminishing the gravity of your situation, but I don't think it will aid your case.'

Freeman takes photos of the shoes, box, and book.

'It's up to you whether you choose to use the trainers or not. You said they were ones you wanted, so in my book it would be crazy to throw them away, but I would also understand you not wanting to use them because of who they're from.'

Molly has no intention of giving him the benefit of seeing her using his gift, but she'd rather donate them to another athlete than throw them away.

'I'm worried he knows where I live,' Molly says, her voice breaking as the fear takes hold. 'What if he comes for me at home?'

Freeman reaches into her pocket and hands over a business card. 'This has my number on it, and if you think he's nearby, phone me. If I don't answer and you believe you're in danger, you can phone 999. Okay?'

Molly accepts the card, but doesn't feel any sense of satisfaction.

'It would also help if you started keeping a diary of any interactions you have with him. For example, if he sends a message, keep a log of it. If he leaves any more gifts at places you frequent, again make a note. We take stalking cases very seriously, and I promise I will do all I can to find and stop the person responsible.' She fixes Molly with a sincere stare. 'I will write up this interview and email a copy of it to you. If you're happy with it, you can then sign it digitally and return it to me. In the meantime, take care of yourself.'

She stands to show them out.

'What if he's at my flat waiting for me now?' Molly says, reaching for the detective's arm.

Freeman looks back at her. 'How about I give you both a lift home now, just to check the coast is clear? Would that help?'

Molly is grateful for the offer, and when they arrive back, there are no parked cars or unfamiliar faces hanging about outside the building.

'You might want to ask your landlord whether he'd consider installing some security cameras,' Freeman suggests as she stares at the drab building. 'He's not obliged to, but it might provide all of his tenants with a greater feeling of security.'

Molly says she will, and decides to ask Jamie to have a word with him for her. Exiting the car, she takes a deep breath before heading inside the building with Thea, hurrying to her room and locking the door behind them.

19

NOW

21 April 2024, Deptford, London – Mile 8

I've swallowed both glucose gel packs and discarded the packets, but the fatigue is heavy in my legs and head. I feel like I've already been running for hours, and yet my watch tells me it's only been forty or so minutes since we set off from Greenwich Park, and we're not even halfway through the competition. I've pushed myself too hard, and I'm already starting to feel the effects of it. Running too fast early on is one of the criminal mistakes to make as a marathon runner, and I know that. God knows Finn has drilled it into me often enough since we started working together. It's naïve to keep telling myself that I'll have time to slow and recharge before the final stint. The truth is, because of all the catching up, my body is likely to shut down sooner, and I'm going to be suffering before we even reach the halfway marker.

And yet, despite knowing this, I don't relent. I've come too far to give up, and whilst catching up with Thea and Kat remains a possibility, I have to keep believing I can beat them to the finish; or at least I can beat Kat. I wince at a cramping in my gut, but don't let it put me off; probably just a reaction to downing the two gel packs. I try to push the pain from my mind.

Putting my head down, I circle around the runners ahead of me, and make a half-hearted attempt at a sprint to close the distance between me, Thea's beanie hat, and Kat's hot-pink vest top. The two of them are at the front of the second pack of runners. Several hundred yards ahead of them are the leading pack – the five women who are genuinely competing to win the marathon overall. These are the true elite athletes, the ones who compete to win at every major marathon. None of them are British, and if I was to compete against them in Paris, I'd have no chance, but thankfully their attention is elsewhere. And thankfully for me, they aren't my competition.

One of the motorbikes has hung back and is filming Thea and Kat, and I can just imagine how the commentary team for the broadcaster are praising their efforts. I wonder if they're also questioning my peculiar race tactics. I can only hope they didn't capture the near collision with the cameraman, nor my panic at the spectator raising an umbrella that I mistook for a gun. The last thing I need is to give Gloria Hutchinson any more reason to keep me from joining Team GB. I keep a watchful gaze on the bike as I make it past the next row of runners.

I nod at Thea as I fall into line with her and Kat, and adjust my pace to match them stride for stride. This is how I hoped today would be: the three of us in a line until the final mile, at which point I planned to leave them in my wake. But that theory was based on having a reserve of energy that is already drained. I don't offer any greeting as I'm too focused on just keeping one foot moving ahead of the other, and besides, they are not engaged in conversation with each other. All I can hear is the consistent rhythm of our breathing, as our trainers slap the tarmac. And it's only now I realise I still haven't started my playlist of music. Maybe that's why my other senses seem so heightened today. I've become so accustomed to music drowning out the background that running without feels so alien.

The rain has eased off now, and the blanket of cloud is starting to part in the distance. I can actually see blue sky, and there is just a hint of sunshine poking through gaps in the cloud. The temperature is rising, and I just have to hope it doesn't creep up too much. It's one thing to be battling against rain on a slippery course, but it's another to be running in hot temperatures. I will have to increase my water intake if it gets too warm out here.

I see Kat tilt her head and fire a glare in my direction. I offer an apologetic smile, but before I can say anything, her eyes are back on the road, and she accelerates forwards. I don't have the energy to chase after her, and I'm grateful that Thea maintains her pace with me. I really wish I knew what I'd done to upset Kat. All the animosity I've experienced has been unwarranted as far as I'm concerned. Maybe I harmed her in a previous life.

I think back to our first encounter, the night of my appearance on *The One Show*. She glared at me with a look of such hatred: *You think you can come to my place and act like it's your own? You've got another think coming, girl.*

Thea passed it off as Kat being worried I would qualify in a quicker time than her, and that her animosity was purely driven by concern for her place in the squad, but what if it was something more than that? Despite my own history with Team GB, this is the first time I've been in competition with Kat Campbell. She's almost a decade younger than me, and if she continues to train hard, she should have a bright future ahead of her.

Kat's voice echoes in my mind again: *You'd better tell your new bestie to watch her back... I'll do whatever it takes to get to Paris.*

The breath catches in my throat as my brain processes the threat.

I shake my head quickly. No, I'm being ridiculous: there's no way Kat can be behind what's been going on.

And yet, as much as I try to dismiss the possibility... She has all the motivation for wanting to see me fail today. She qualified for the Olympic squad based on her time in Berlin months ago. That time was higher than the new qualifying time, but that will only come into play if there are other challengers who beat her two hours twenty-nine pace. If I don't hit the qualifying target today, then they'll have no choice but to take Kat, regardless of where she finishes today. She just has to do better than me, which explains why she keeps pushing herself forwards whenever I appear.

But could that fear have driven her to do more?

I can't be sure whether Kat would know about Otto Bistras specifically, but she must have seen some of the targeted abuse I received when he was posting negative comments about me. Even if she doesn't follow me online, British athletics is a small pond, and there's every chance my social media will have been the topic of conversation in the locker room at some point. Thea definitely knows what I've been through and could easily have mentioned it to others, without realising the consequences. Heck, they live on the same floor, and have known each other for longer. That whispered conversation I overheard in the corridor between them could have started because Thea mentioned the real reason I was staying over that night.

What if in some twisted way, Kat decided to bring Bistras's threat back to the forefront of my mind on race day to put me off?

She could have had the flowers delivered to my hotel room this morning, or may even have placed them there herself. I remember now there was a strange scratching sound at my door; what if that was her too? All it would have taken was for Thea to have mentioned the message in the card in passing, and Kat would have been armed with the means of getting inside my head. My drink bottle winding up on the floor beneath the table could also have been engineered by her. In the bustle of her collecting her own, who's to say she didn't bump the table, or swipe at mine, sending it crashing to the floor?

Bile fills in my stomach as I imagine her doing just that. The steward in her tabard could have been looking the other way or distracted by the number of athletes hunting for their bottles. Would she have seen if Kat had tampered with the table? Had Thea not found the bottle, there's no way I could have continued; I was totally out of it.

But Kat must have thought there was a possibility that I'd find alternative energy, and so couldn't solely rely on that working. Plus, she'd have no way of knowing just how far behind I would have been at that point, so she'd need a contingency. Which could explain the phone call and the laughing voice. I haven't seen if she has a phone on her today, but maybe she does?

I'm not convinced by the argument, but for all I know she could have someone on the outside helping to put doubt in my mind. I never told Thea about the laughing voice calling before, so I don't know how Kat would have found out about it. Nor do I know how Kat could have known blue orchids were Mam's favourite flower. And I'm not sure how she would have found out that I was staying at The Clarendon Hotel last night.

As much as Kat would benefit from me failing today, there are too many questions about her ability to pull off everything that's happened so far.

But if not Kat, then who? No matter how hard I think about it, it always comes back to Bistras and whoever is helping him. I should chase up Zara. Convincing her that Bistras has an accomplice is my best method of stopping him.

'You need to stop pushing yourself,' I hear Thea pant beside me. 'I know how much Paris means to you, but you need to take care of yourself as well.'

'I'm doing great,' I lie.

'Picking up a significant injury or failing to finish will be far worse than not hitting the qualifying time.'

I know her heart is in the right place, but that's easy for her to say when her place on the plane is already guaranteed. If our roles were reversed, I'm sure she'd be doing everything she can to qualify.

'I'm not pushing myself,' I lie again. 'Don't worry: I've got plenty of miles left in me yet.'

I want to cringe at the deceit. I sound like the novice runner competing in their first marathon who doesn't realise the effort it takes just to finish. There's a reason the tortoise beats the hare, and I'm wilfully ignoring that and all the advice I've ever received, in the hope that somehow I'll be the exception to the rule, when I know there are no exceptions.

My stomach turns again, and it's all I can do to stop myself yelping at the stabbing pain in my gut. It isn't a stitch, but something doesn't feel right. It isn't my blood sugar; the gel packs have dealt with that hurdle, and it isn't dehydration because I have taken on water.

The nine-mile marker is approaching, with the residential development at Surrey Quays on the horizon. But I can't concentrate on it as my stomach cramps, and I cut across Thea to the kerb. The crowd has dissipated and it's a relief that nobody is going to see what is about to happen. I can't afford to stop running, but I also can't escape the inevitability of what's about to come.

I keep moving forwards but Thea and the rest are already piling past me, and as soon as I'm alone, I double over and expel the contents of my stomach across the road.

20

BEFORE

Friday, 26 January 2024, Streatham, London

Molly has spent the last thirty minutes pacing backwards and forwards in her tiny flat, telling herself she can go through with tonight. Finn has said it's just a meal out for the runners, coaches, and medics, and that it's another opportunity for her to show the Olympic Committee how serious she is about qualifying. She is wearing a gold, sparkly mini dress and heels, but she's never felt so out of her depth. Finn said to pull out all the stops, and she's even spent twenty minutes making up her face. But she doesn't want to go, and she's trying to think of an excuse to bail that won't sound like she's disinterested.

In truth, a night out is probably the perfect distraction she needs, but she can't stop thinking about the laughing robotic voice on the phone. She has dialled and cancelled the call to Finn a dozen times, because she can't think of a good reason. Feigning illness would be easiest, but she has a 10K park run tomorrow morning and can't afford to give them any reason to exclude her.

Thea has been banging on at her to make more of an effort with the other runners, and that the only way to win over the likes of Kat is to show them that she doesn't mean them any harm. So when this dinner was mooted, Thea begged her to come along, and even loaned her the dress and heels. Molly has been telling herself to make more of an effort to be sociable, but her limited efforts at the track haven't worked. If the members of the Olympic Committee sense any kind of hostility between the competitors, they might think twice before considering her potential qualifying time. She has little choice but to make an appearance tonight, and that's what's making her anxious now.

DC Freeman from Brixton Police Station has been no help in tracking down fake-Oppenheimer, despite the screenshots of messages Molly has been sending her. And although Freeman managed to review the security camera footage at the television studios, all it uncovered was that the cardboard box had been left by a member of cleaning staff. When interviewed, the man admitted to being paid fifty pounds cash to deliver the box, by a man he'd never met before and whom he was unable to adequately describe. Apparently, there are a lot of men who fit the description 'average height, average build, and wearing a baseball cap'.

He continues to message her, even though she refuses to acknowledge or respond, but they have no way of tracing him, or so they say. It has reached the point where Molly no longer logs into her Instagram account. Instead, she has granted Jamie full access, and he posts on her behalf to keep the sponsors happy. It is no way to live her life.

She starts at a knock at the door, and when she dares to look through the peephole, she's relieved to see Thea smiling back at her.

'Damn, girl, you're looking hot,' is all Thea says as she grabs Molly's hand and drags her down to the waiting taxi.

Molly keeps her eyes peeled on the road around them. There's a figure in a helmet sitting astride a moped, staring back at her. She can't tell if he is actually staring at her or in their general direction – she can't even if tell he's a real delivery driver. She's about to ask Thea what she thinks when the taxi pulls away. Molly turns to watch the bike out of the back window, but he doesn't begin following them, and she eventually turns back to face the front. But at the second set of traffic lights they arrive at, she sees a moped pull up beside them, the figure dressed all in black against the night sky, but she can't be sure it's the same one. She desperately wants to go back to her flat and lock herself inside, but she dare not risk being alone.

The taxi pulls to the right at the lights, and a few minutes later is pulling up at the restaurant. Molly looks all around as she stumbles from the car, but there is no sign of the rider.

Thea pulls her over to where Finn and several other runners are waiting to go in. Finn pecks her cheek to a chorus of woos before he blushes, and tells her she looks incredible. Molly is barely listening, instead using the reflection of the restaurant's windows to watch the passing pedestrians.

'What's she doin' here?' Kat calls out, marching over and invading the space between Finn and Molly. 'It's supposed to be for the team only.'

'And there's a very strong chance Molly will be rejoining the team soon, so I invited her to join us,' Finn retorts back, unintimidated by Kat's height and attitude.

The restaurant is fancier than Molly is used to, and she's relieved when Finn leans over and tells her to pick whatever she wants as the dinner is already paid for. Molly allows herself to relax, having opted for a chair beside the wall so nobody can watch her from behind. She orders a cheese and basil soufflé to begin and a Malaysian monkfish and coconut curry for her main, and devours them both. She notes that the other runners all choose soft drinks and is pleased to follow the trend. And for an hour she allows her mind to forget the messages, and the constant paranoia, and actually has a good time. Being seated between Finn and Thea helps, and they introduce her to a physio called Tommy who is sitting across the table from her. He has dark eyes and a chiselled jaw, and has so many funny stories about unnamed athletes that he has her in stitches.

After dinner, when everyone is back outside, booking Ubers, Thea pulls Molly to one side and tells her Kat is going to take them to a club where the management is discreet, and where they can properly unwind. Molly has no desire to go along with them, until she sees that everyone else has already gone and she'll have to wait alone for a taxi home. Kat says the club isn't far, and when she sees Molly lurking with the group, doesn't attempt to omit her.

The club is so loud inside, and with smoke pumping out near the stage, Molly soon becomes disorientated. She follows Thea to the bar, where Kat orders drinks, which are slowly passed down to each girl. Molly tries to tell Thea that she doesn't want anything alcoholic, but it's impossible to hear voices over the loud music. She regrets the decision to tag along, and is relieved when they move to a segregated part of the club where it's marginally quieter.

'I ordered you a Diet Coke,' Thea shouts over the din. 'You fancy a dance in a bit?'

She doesn't really want to dance, but she hates the idea of being left on her own even more, so when Kat and the others leave the area to hit the dancefloor, she follows. They dance to several songs, but Molly doesn't appreciate being bumped into by people, and can't stop looking at the faces of those coming in and out of the darkness in case *he's* amongst them. She eventually heads back to the segregated area, determining it's safer to be there than in a crowd, and sips on her drink through a straw. She doesn't notice the slightly different taste, and panics when she begins to feel light-headed. There are too many people in the club, and she can no longer see her friends. She stands, and stumbles from the raised stage, in search of Thea, but can't find her amongst the jiving bodies, and eventually heads for the exit, hoping fresh air will clear the fog from her mind.

She stumbles from the club in darkness, but the sound of car horns and screeching tyres is almost as bad as the music inside. She unlocks her phone, and tries to concentrate on the screen, but the images and words blur and rotate, and she has no way of figuring which app to use to book a taxi. She falls several times, scraping her knees on the pavement, but rejects all offers of help from passers-by, despite becoming more convinced that he's out here watching. She can barely see straight, but one thought pounds at the fog in her head: run.

21

NOW

21 April 2024, Surrey Quays, London – Mile 9

My body shakes as the burning liquid erupts from my mouth, and the retching is like someone's dragging an enormous pipe cleaner up and down my oesophagus. Doubled over, I can't keep my legs and arms from shaking as the vomit is expelled from my body, splashing against the concrete kerb, flecks landing on the side of my well-worn white trainers.

I can only think of one time I've felt more embarrassed – a college trip away to Carlisle and the remains of Hadrian's Wall, when one of my hostel roommates snuck a bottle of her mam's vodka into our room. We did shots until the early hours and had massive hangovers the following morning at breakfast, and the smell of black pudding had me racing to the toilets. The teachers must have put two and two together, and letters went home to our parents warning of the dangers of binge drinking.

And yet this is so much worse. Mam won't be receiving a letter on this occasion, but the whole world can see what's happening. I wish a hole would open in the road and swallow me up.

The pain is unbearable, and in my periphery, I can see something bright hurrying towards me. Thank God there are no spectators at this spot in the road. The bright yellow blob comes closer, and when I have a momentary respite from the retching see that the bright coat belongs to one of the race stewards who is asking if I'm okay, and proffering an unopened bottle of water. I'm about to tell him I'll be fine when a fresh bout of retching begins, but at least this time it's dry, although it doesn't make it any easier to bear. I can see the racing pack getting further and further away, and it's like they're carrying my dream with them.

I accept the bottle of water and take a long drink, the cool liquid easing the burning sensation somewhat. The steward is telling me to take slow sips, but I ignore his advice, and drain most of the bottle in one go. He's about my height, with aged, dry skin that sags around his cheeks. He is bald at the crown, his remaining dark grey hair forming a kind of nest above his ears. He asks me if I need him to call for medical attention, but I shake my head.

Vomiting after a marathon is quite commonplace amongst runners, and can often be the result of a digestive system shutdown. A marathon has an extreme impact on the human body, and forces oxygen-rich blood cells to essential areas only, which can have a negative impact on the stomach and other digestive organs. This is why training for marathons in the right way is key. But I know that and I have been so careful with my food and liquid consumption during training that this shouldn't be happening now.

Dehydration can be a secondary cause, but it hasn't been too hot today, and I've been taking on fluids where Finn and I had predetermined, so I don't think it can be that either. I had a banana and granola bar for breakfast, and avoided the offer of fruit juice so my body shouldn't be having a reaction to too much acid.

So what else can be causing this?

I take another slug of the water and rinse my mouth before spitting it onto the floor, nodding apologetically at the steward, who takes an unsteady step backwards. I hand him the empty bottle, and even though my whole chest and hips ache, I take several steps back onto the course. The straggler pack have just turned the bend in the road, so thankfully none of them witnessed my digestive pyrotechnics. But it won't take them long to catch me up if I don't get going again.

I really should message Finn and tell him what's happened, but I don't want him to force me to withdraw. I know I can still complete the course, and I'm not prepared to turn my back on all the years of training, and months of trying to get back to where I was. My mind won't let me give up on my dream. If I don't keep going, I will always wonder what could have been. Mam used to tell me to never allow regret to spoil the future.

'It's the things we don't do that lead to regret,' she would say whenever I was showing reluctance to try new things. If she hadn't encouraged me to try my hardest at cross-country at school, I wouldn't be living this life now. If she was here now, I am sure she would tell me to keep running.

'Every passing second is another chance to turn it all around,' was another of her favourite sayings, and I recite the words over and over in my mind now, willing my legs to move quicker, transitioning from jog into run, and then into acceleration.

Deep down, I know that the likeliest reason for my being sick in the road is probably a consequence of the way I've been pushing myself today. Had I maintained the slow and steady tortoise approach, I would be further ahead, and wouldn't be feeling so awful. But not pushing myself and failing to qualify will be as sore as throwing the towel in now. I have to try. Otto and his counterpart are desperate for me to fail, and I don't want to give them the satisfaction.

What if they poisoned you?

I don't know where the thought comes from, but it slams into my head, and I'm suddenly replaying everything that's happened in my mind's eye. They couldn't have poisoned the banana and granola bars, and the bottles of water I've consumed so far have all been sealed, but my rehydration bottle wasn't.

The idea is so ridiculous that I almost burst out laughing. It's one thing for someone to hide my bottle, but to have unscrewed the lid and dropped something inside without being seen or stopped is just too farfetched.

And yet I can't totally dismiss the idea.

But how could Otto and his accomplice get close enough to do something like that? And what could they mix into my drink to cause vomiting but be odourless and tasteless?

I recall the night of the club when everything felt off, and I know now what caused that, but this isn't the same feeling. I was away with the fairies as I raced through the streets of London like a headless chicken, but now my mind is more focused.

The headband erupts with noise, and when I glance at my watch I see it is a withheld number, so I ignore it, refusing to be drawn into Bistras's game any more. If he thinks I'm going to fall for the same trick again, he's got another think coming. I know he's out there, and I don't need a laughing, robotic voice to remind me. I decline the call with a stab at the watch.

Although my kidneys feel as though they've been kicked, the post-vomit adrenaline is doing wonders for the rest of me. I feel renewed somehow, as if what has just happened has given me a second wind.

I can't waste this feeling.

Looking up, I concentrate on the pack ahead of me. I only need to consistently run a few seconds faster than them and I will soon make back the time. I don't know where Kat is ahead of them, but I just need to take baby steps. We're not even halfway through the marathon yet, and if Finn is right, she'll be starting to tire soon anyway. I just need to be close enough to hunt her down for the final mile.

This feeling of positivity is what I've been missing all race, and I can't help thinking that Mam is with me now, spurring me on with her little phrases embedded deep in my memory banks. I have been chasing everyone all race and look where it's got me so far. It's time to take ownership of my race, and to stop worrying about the hurdles I've already overcome.

Another table with glucose gel packs is coming up, and despite it not being long since I took on more energy, given what just happened, I don't think it will do any harm, so I grab one as I'm passing and squeeze half the contents into my mouth, but swallow it slowly as I maintain a steady pace. Surrey Quays is now long behind me, and I appear to be in another residential area. Houses stand both sides of the road, and a smattering of supporters applaud as I pass by. I give a small wave to a little girl in a wheel-chair who is applauding louder than those surrounding her.

The rumble of an engine passes me and the camera is pointing at me again. I try not to think about it, and just look ahead, focused on the runners that I am steadily catching. But there's something off about the cameraman. Curiosity gets the better of me, and when I look up, I realise he isn't actually holding his camera up. Instead, it's resting on his lap, but he is staring at me. His Aviators have mirror lenses, and sparkle. I have no doubt he's the same cameraman I nearly crashed into earlier, but I don't understand why he's just staring like that. Surely, if the two of them are this close it's because they've been told to film my progress, and yet the camera is pointed to the side, away from me.

I study his face longer. He's wearing a motorcycle helmet, so I can't see what colour his hair is. He is slightly overweight, and the lines around his mouth suggest he's on the older side, but I can't say exactly how old. I can't put my finger on it, but something isn't right.

I'm about to call out to him and demand to know what he wants, when the rider accelerates and they soon turn off down a side road. I can't see where they go as I pass the turn.

Bistras enjoyed watching me suffer. His campaign of online posts was designed to embarrass and hurt me, and he revelled in setting up new accounts to send me his messages of hate. Would he go so far as to film me struggling today as well? This whole time I've been thinking that my near collision with that particular rider and cameraman was as a result of my clumsiness, but what if it wasn't? What if – like everything else – it was designed to try to put me off?

And what if he's been hiding in plain sight this whole time?

I flick at my watch until I see my recent calls list and dial Detective Freeman's number.

It connects on the third ring.

'I need you to do me another favour,' I tell her, before she has a chance to speak. 'Can you find out how many cameramen have been deployed on motorbikes to film today's race?'

'Hey, Molly, now's really not a good time. I'm in the middle of—'

'I think he's here now, and if not Bistras, then someone who's working for him. There's a particular rider and cameraman that keeps getting too close to me.'

'You've seen Bistras on a motorbike?'

'No, at least I don't think so. I can't tell if it's him beneath the helmet or not. But something is off.'

'If you're worried about someone stalking you at the race, you need to report it immediately.'

'I thought that's what I was doing.'

'But I'm not there. As I told you before: I'm tied up in a developing case here. I'm part of a team looking for a missing child.'

'Please, Zara. I don't have anyone else. Can you just try and find out who this cameraman is? If he's legit, then there's nothing else you have to do.'

I relay the motorbike's registration number to her.

'I'll see what I can do, but you need to get to safety just in case. No race is worth risking your life over.'

'Just find out who's doing this to me. Bistras is not working alone. I need you, Zara. Please?'

22

BEFORE

Friday, 26 January 2024, Poplar, London

Neon lights race past in a blur. Breathless, Molly knows she can't stop running. Shadows come and go, as if stretching to catch her; their points like fingers scratching at her back. She can hear footsteps behind her, echoing off shuttered shop fronts, and the brickwork of low bridges. She can barely keep hold of the stilettos in her hands, as she pumps her arms, willing herself to stay upright, almost tumbling over several times.

Car horns blare in the near distance, but she ignores them, and continues to try to put distance between herself and *him*. Her feet splash through puddles, showering her once glittery dress with streaks of mud, but she doesn't care. Still she continues, adrenaline substituted for air and sense.

He must have spiked her drink; that's the only reason her head feels so out of it right now. He must have spiked it, knowing she'd freak and run. Yes, that has to be what happened. She didn't have any alcohol with dinner, and Thea ordered her a Diet Coke, so he must have slipped it in before Kat brought it back from the bar. And now he's chasing her.

Turning round the next bend, she stops abruptly, not expecting to collide with a wired fence, covered in raindrops that leap on to her dress and skin. She has no idea where she is, and can only see the fence courtesy of a streetlight the other side of the wire. Her breaths come in quick, sharp bursts, and they manage to drown out all other noise. She feels so dizzy that she can't keep upright, and rolls into the fence, bashing her thigh on the rough pavement.

She stares back along the narrow road she came down, listening out for his footsteps, certain he will come round the bend next. She needs to stand and try to get over the fence, but she has no energy left; she's at his mercy, and there is nothing she can do to protect herself. She cranes her head left and right, searching for anywhere she might be able to hide out of sight, but it's all open: just the brick wall of the tall building to her right, and the street he's racing along.

'Get up,' she tells herself quietly, but her muscles don't obey.

Still she waits and watches the bend in the road, waiting for him to emerge, but he is eking out every last second of tension. He wants her at his mercy.

'Get up,' she says again, this time through gritted teeth, willing her body to find a defensive position.

Her trembling hand touches loose gravel on the pavement, and she pushes her weight into it, her second hand finding the sharp ends of the fence. Slowly, counting to three, she presses into her hands, using all her willpower to slide her knees beneath her body, slowly straightening, until she's back on her feet, clinging to the intertwined wire squares of the fence. Her legs are failing under the weight of lactic acid burn, but she maintains her balance. Her breathing finally begins to slow, despite the continued racing of her heart. She can no longer hear the echo of footsteps but refuses to accept that she might have managed to lose her pursuer. He could be around that corner now, composing himself, while he waits to move in to attack.

She is so light-headed, and her eyelids so heavy that it's a struggle to stay on her feet. She can no longer even feel the rain, and curling up here for a few minutes would give her the boost she needs to keep going, but that could be exactly what he's waiting for; he wants her out of it so she can't put up a fight.

She decides she needs to keep running. Turning to look at the fence, she cranes her head upwards, trying to estimate the fence's height, wondering whether she can scale it, but she can't even see the top; it's as if it has disappeared into the low cloud of the night sky. It's a dead-end, and the only way out is back the way she came.

Taking a deep breath, she pushes herself off the relative safety net of the fence, but her legs aren't ready to run yet, and she stumbles forwards, holding out her arms for balance, until she makes it to the sodden brickwork of the building. The wet moss tickles her cheek as she leans into it, but she dares to poke her nose around the edge of the brickwork, scanning every dark corner, searching for his hiding place.

But wherever he is, he's well hidden.

She jerks as she realises her eyes are closed and she's sliding down the wall. What the hell did he slip into her drink? She just wants to sleep, but she needs to focus.

Call Thea, a thought bursts through the mud in her mind, and she fiddles with the catch of her clutch bag, until she pulls out her phone.

She unlocks the screen with her thumb and sees a list of missed calls from Thea and Finn. They've been calling nonstop, and she doesn't know who to phone first. Thea's name appears on the screen as she calls again, and Molly answers, putting the phone to her ear, and whispering, 'Help me.'

'Molly? Is that you? Oh, thank God. Where are you?'

'Help me, Thea,' she whispers again, but she can't be certain any sound is coming out of her mouth, as her lips struggle to form the words.

'I'm here, Molly. Where are you? Are you still in the club?'

'No,' she replies, the vowel extended.

'You're not in the club. Okay? Are you on your way home?'

'No.'

'How are you feeling? Are you okay? I think... I *know* someone slipped something into your drink. I need to find you ASAP.'

Could Thea have seen fake-Oppenheimer at the club and put two and two together?

'Tell me where you are, Molly, and I'll come to you now.'

Molly looks back over to the fence, conscious that he is still hiding somewhere in the darkness. She doesn't want to draw attention to the fact she's now seeking help.

'Don't know where I am,' she replies slowly, her voice so deep in her ears.

'Oh, Jesus. Did you leave the club?'

'Yes.'

'Oh, no. Right, which way did you go when you left?'

'I ran.'

'Of course you did, but did you run right or left?'

Molly desperately tries to remember but it's like a black hole in her head is swallowing up her most recent memories. 'Don't know.'

'Shit! Okay, well, what can you see? Are there any road signs, or famous landmarks in sight?'

'There's a fence,' Molly says, her tired eyes struggling to stay open as her head lolls one way and then the other.

'You have your phone, though? I want you to stare at your screen and open Google Maps. It should tell you where you are.'

Molly lowers the phone, and opens the app as directed. The tiny words on the screen blur and dance before her eyes. 'Marron Street,' she shouts, but isn't certain that's what it says.

'Okay, I don't know where that is. Can you zoom out and tell me if there are any London Underground tube stations near you? Use your fingers and pinch outwards until you see a tube sign.'

Molly fiddles with the screen. 'East India.'

'You're kidding! That's bloody miles away! Okay, listen, this is what we're going to do. You make your way to the East India station and wait for me. I will make my way there somehow. Okay? I'm coming to get you. Keep your phone on. And if you find a policeman or PCSO, tell them what happened, and get them to call me.'

'I think my stalker followed me,' Molly says into the phone. 'I think he's hiding.'

She frowns at the phone when there's no response.

'Did you hear me, Thea? I think fake-Oppenheimer is here.'

She continues to stare at the phone, and finally realises that Thea has already hung up, meaning Molly's on her own again to fight him off. Taking a deep breath, she flings herself around the corner, clinging to the wet brickwork for protection, but the street appears to be empty. She takes tentative steps forwards, keeping the wall close to her fingertips, but if he's hiding, she can't find him. She's certain she didn't imagine the echo of his footsteps, but no longer trusts her senses. Staring back down at her phone, she presses on the DLR station icon, and it offers her directions. She realises now she is no longer carrying her shoes, but doesn't care, and focuses on the screen, following the blue dot as it moves steadily closer to the destination.

She freezes at the sound of a glass bottle being kicked. Was she wrong to assume he was no longer following her? She continues slowly towards the end of the road, straining to hear the faintest of sounds, and then she hears them: footsteps – behind her, getting closer. She doesn't hesitate to break into a run, no longer looking at the phone screen.

23

NOW

21 April 2024, Rotherhithe, London – Mile 10

I start as my phone rings through the headband again, but when I see it is withheld again, I quickly reject the call through my watch. If I ignore him, he can't affect me. Yes, I know he's out there and trying to put me off, but it's good to be able to exert some control of my own.

I won't let him get the better of me again.

The withheld number rings back almost immediately, and I decline it again. I wonder which of us will get bored of this merry-go-round first.

The pack is still just ahead, and I could have caught back up with them by now, but I've reduced my pace. I've spotted Kat has already dropped back to Thea, and based on the ten-mile marker that's coming up and the timer on my watch, they are both on course to finish close to the qualifying time, assuming they maintain this pace. Finn warned me that Kat would slow after the tenth mile, so I need to just bide my time. If I show my hand too early, Kat will see and increase her pace again.

We're running through a residential estate again, so the applause is less. The houses here look newly built, certainly within the last twenty or so years. Houses filled with families and love. Maybe some of them are proud that the marathon passes along their road; maybe some of them hate the disruption. But how many of them realise the importance a day like today plays in runners' lives? And I don't just mean someone like me trying to qualify for the Olympics. My motivation for doing this is totally selfish, but there are thousands of others who are putting themselves through one of the most gruelling activities for the benefit of others. Those running for charities and great causes wouldn't be able to do so without the closing of roads through the Greater London area.

In the distance I can hear the sound of bagpipes, and it fills me with huge pride. Although I'm here representing Great Britain, I am the only elite runner born north of the border, and I sometimes forget the significance of that. There have been some huge Scots athletes – legends in their own right – and whilst I can't hold myself up with such luminaries, I have an obligation to inspire those future Scots stars.

The bagpipes reach a crescendo and I spot the piper decked out in traditional Highland dress. His tartan kilt is made up of reds and golds and greens, the sporran worn proudly. The rhythm of 'Mull of Kintyre' grows louder as I near, and I see now he isn't alone. Five ladies of varying ages are dressed in velvet jackets and tartan, and are performing a choreographed routine. My heart swells as I see them, and even more so when they turn their backs and I see my name spelled out on the backs of their jackets. My hand shoots to my mouth as I struggle to contain my emotion. I wave at them all, and blow kisses in thanks. On any normal day I would stop and pose for a photo with them, but my mind is elsewhere.

The large trees lining the streets are bringing some welcome shelter from the direct sunlight overhead, now that the rain clouds have moved on. The sky is so blue that it's hard to remember the downpour that's already been and gone. It really is turning into a beautiful day, the kind that should be spent with friendship groups in gardens, making lifelong memories. The rapidly rising temperature is not ideal for distance running. Finn and I were aware that it could be a warm day, but the threat of storms has made it difficult to predict exactly what I would face today. We had plans for cool, wet weather, and we had plans for dry, warm weather, but it's hard to formulate a strategy to cope with both.

I need to check in with Finn to see if he knows whether the rain will return or whether we should now be switching to our hot day strategy.

My watch buzzes on my arm to indicate I've received a message, but when I try to read it, I'm told I need to read it on my phone. Not ideal, but I adjust the Velcro strap on my left forearm, so the screen is facing inwards, and tilt my head so I can read it. My eyes widen when I see a still image of me doubled over on the side of the course. The caption below reads:

Was it something you ate?

Instinctively I scan the road and pavements around me, looking for anyone who might be holding a camera and filming me, but of course it was more than a mile back when I was retching, so whoever snapped the image could be well gone by now.

I look back at my phone again, trying to work out where the photographer would have been standing to capture the image. Embarrassingly, they've managed to capture the exact moment I expelled the contents of my stomach, the brownish-green liquid resembling a waterfall as it leaves my lips. The image has been taken from behind, as I can see my right buttock and leg front and centre, which means they must have been across the road from where the incident took place. I don't remember any runners passing by at that moment, as Thea and the rest of the group had already torn past before I started retching.

It must have been one of the spectators.

But I remember feeling relieved at the time that it happened in an area where there weren't any spectators.

Does that mean he was in one of the houses on that side of the road?

I don't know how he could have known I would definitely throw up, and in that particular spot of all places. Unless he did actually slip something into my drink and then just had to watch and wait.

As unlikely as that seems, I have no other way of explaining how he could have captured the picture. I glance around me again. Up ahead I can see a motorbike and cameraman focusing on the group Thea and Kat are leading, but the licence plate is different to the one I recited to Zara, so I don't think it's the one that's been trying to put me off.

I think back. The bike *did* appear from behind me after I'd finished being sick. Could he have snapped the photograph and waited until now to send it? Should I forward it to Zara? Maybe the police would have a means of finding out who took it or where they were standing at the time. I don't know if that's possible, but it's worth a try, I suppose.

Another buzzing and a fresh message replaces the image of me retching on my phone's screen.

YOU SHOULD HAVE TAKEN THE HINT AND LEFT THE RACE.

I'M RIGHT BEHIND YOU, BUT YOU WON'T SEE ME COMING.

xxx

I look over my shoulder, half-expecting to see the motorbike and cameraman with the mirrored Aviators, but the road is clear, save for the Highlander with the bagpipes.

Ahead of me there are spectators applauding, not ringed in by fences as this isn't one of the official spectator stands. He could be any one of the people gathered in jackets, and clapping, and I wouldn't know. I scour their hands for phones and recording equipment, but most are just enjoying the spectacle.

Where are you? Why are you doing this to me?

I wish I knew how I could block his messages, but I'd need to stop and search for the answers online. I could switch off my phone, but in doing so, I'd also be cutting myself off from Finn and Zara. And what would happen if Bistras or his counterpart suddenly appeared from nowhere? I'd need to be able to get hold of Zara immediately. No, switching off the phone is not a solution.

I find Zara's number and call her. If she has any lingering doubts about what I've told her about Bistras being here today (whether in person or through another), then this message *proves* that I'm not just being paranoid. She needs to come and help me.

The answerphone cuts in, and I sigh in frustration.

'He keeps phoning me, and now he's sending messages,' I stutter between pained breaths. 'I will forward what he's sent, but you need to do something. He's here and he means me harm.'

My pace has slowed while I fiddle with my phone and try to send the two messages to Zara. I can see the group still ahead; I can't allow myself to fall too far behind.

A group of spectators is gathered on a footbridge going over the road. They are holding painted signs, cheering on the runners, and I spot one that reads:

WE'RE BEHIND YOU!

I try to see who's holding the sign, looking for Bistras's bulk, but the sign is between the fingers of two children who can't be much older than seven. The boy is wearing a West Ham football shirt, and the little girl is dressed as Supergirl. Still, I scan the bridge, looking to see if *he's* there, and has drafted them into his sick game.

My watch and phone vibrate, and I don't want to look in case he's sent something else, but I need to know whether it's Zara replying. My eyes dart from the cardboard sign to my watch and back again.

Where are you?

Reluctantly, I dismiss the children on the bridge, and bring my gaze back to the phone's screen. A photograph of Otto Bistras slowly appears in pixelated form, and my pulse quickens. But it isn't just a photograph of him. As the image continues to download, despite the poor phone signal, I see now it appears to be some kind of screenshot. No, in fact, it looks more like the front of a newspaper. A bold headline stands out, but it's in a language I don't recognise, and I don't understand what it means, other than it must have something to do with Bistras. Now that it's fully downloaded, I can see it is in fact his mugshot, so maybe the newspaper is just confirming his sentencing.

Another buzz from the same withheld number. It looks like a duplicate image of the newspaper front sheet, only this time, the headline has changed. The image has the same mugshot, but emblazoned in large font above his face are four words that make my blood run cold:

CONVICTED STALKER ESCAPES CUSTODY

24

BEFORE

Saturday, 27 January 2024, Brixton, London

Molly wakes with a start, her heart racing, the last memory being her running through the dark and sodden streets of east London, with her stalker gaining on her every step. She bolts upright, surprised to see Thea in the small kitchen area, making breakfast. Molly has no recollection of how she ended up in Thea's flat again.

'Morning,' Thea calls over. 'There's tea on the table, and some painkillers for what I'm imagining is a very sore head.'

Molly hasn't noticed the headache, until Thea mentions it, and now it's like a wrecking ball is slamming into the side of her face. She barely makes it to the small bathroom before expelling the contents of her stomach. Waves of intense, lava-like heat roar up her throat, and she retches until there's nothing but air. Thea hangs nearby, keeping Molly's shoulder-length hair away from the seat, and offering words of comfort.

When the nausea passes, Thea helps Molly to the table, and

slides the mug of tea across to her, before opening a packet of shop-bought brioche rolls.

'You need some dirty carbs and rehydrating,' Thea says. 'What can you remember about last night?'

Molly doesn't want to remember anything, but the sense of paranoia is overwhelming, and despite her efforts to forget, all she can remember is the feeling of being chased.

'I strapped up your hand as best as I could,' Thea continues, 'but I don't think there's any lasting damage.'

Molly looks down at her right hand, only now seeing the brown plasters, and significant taping over her palm. She doesn't remember injuring her hand.

'When I found you, your hand was like something out of a horror movie. Blood everywhere. I thought I'd have to take you to the hospital for stitches. But when I got you back here and washed it, I managed to stop the flow. You were pretty out of it, so I thought it best to let you sleep it off.'

A flash of memory fires in Molly's mind: being slumped against the wet wire fence, and a sharp pain in her hand when she caught it on the lower spikes when trying to stand. She'd had no idea it was bleeding, though.

'I think the dress might be unrecoverable, but worth trying to get it dry-cleaned just in case. Your feet were in a bit of a state as well. Running barefoot over London's cracked pavements will do that to you, though. If I were you, I'd tell Jamie you're unwell and need a couple of days' rest.'

Molly looks down at the small scabbing lacerations on both soles of her feet, again with no recollection about how they got hurt.

'I'm sorry I lost your shoes.'

Thea waves away the loss as no big deal.

'What happened to me?' Molly asks groggily. 'I'm sure *he* was there, following me, and I felt uneasy in the club. I was just desperate to get away.'

Thea looks down at her own hands and takes a sip of her tea. 'Your drink was spiked,' she says quietly.

Flashes of last night's paranoia appear in Molly's head, and she's surprised she hadn't made the connection before. Someone in the club slipping something into her unguarded drink makes so much sense. Does that mean he was in the club? She shivers at the thought.

'When we got to the club, I ordered you a Diet Coke, which is what you were given.' Thea pauses. 'I left you in the VIP area, and when I came back, you'd vanished. I tried looking for you on the dancefloor, in case I'd missed you, but nobody knew where you were. I tried phoning and messaging, but you didn't answer. I was starting to worry, and genuinely wondered whether you and Finn had hooked up.'

'Wait, you thought I'd gone off with Finn?'

'Sure. Everyone knows he's got a bit of a thing for you, and then there was that awkward moment when you arrived at the restaurant, so it's pretty clear you like him too, so...'

'I don't fancy Finn. He's just my coach. That's all there is to it.'

Thea holds her hands up in surrender. 'Okay, okay. Anyway, he said he hadn't seen you, but would try and phone. I was really starting to worry and one of the girls said they thought they'd seen you heading for the exit, so I went outside, but it was raining, and I couldn't find you.' She pauses again. 'And then one of the girls told me what they'd done, and I knew I had to find you.'

'Wait, who did what to me?'

Thea's sigh turns into a pained groan. 'Some of the girls thought you were too... too uptight, and one of them thought if they could loosen you up a bit, you'd be more sociable.'

'No, it was *him*. *He* did this to me.'

'I'm afraid not. One of the girls slipped some ketamine powder into your drink before they passed it to me. I swear I had no idea until later in the night.'

But Molly is sure he was there. She could feel him watching, and she could hear him chasing her. Couldn't she?

'I Googled the effects straight away. Ketamine increases heart rate and blood pressure, and can make you confused, agitated, and disconnected from reality. Sound familiar? Apparently, it affects memory and can even make you hallucinate. The worst part is, because it's a type of anaesthetic, it can prevent you from realising you've injured yourself, which is probably how you were able to keep running despite the pain in your feet. I'm so sorry; it was me who convinced you to come to the club, but had I known what they were planning, I would have kept a better watch over you, or made sure you got home safely.'

One of them did this to her. One of the professional athletes had deliberately slipped something into her drink which had led to one of the most terrifying experiences of her life.

'Who did it?' Molly asks through gritted teeth. 'I'm going to report them.'

'Please don't. The girl in question is so sorry, and she said she didn't put a lot in your drink. She thought it would just loosen you up a bit. It was a mistake, but she doesn't deserve to lose her chance at the games.'

'Who was it, Thea?'

'I'm not going to tell you, because that wouldn't be fair on her.'

Molly thinks through the girls who were in the club, and one name leaps out. 'It was Kat, wasn't it? I know how much she hates me and wants me out of contention.'

'No, it wasn't Kat, but I'm not going to answer any more questions. The important thing is you are okay, and that no serious harm came of it.'

'No serious harm? Are you fucking kidding me? Anything could have happened to me last night. I'm lucky I wasn't sexually assaulted or run over.'

'I know all of that, and I understand why you're angry – I would be too – but nothing good will come from you reporting it.'

'She – Kat or whoever it is – deserves to be kicked out of the sport for this. Hell, they deserve to face criminal charges.'

'She didn't mean any harm, I swear to you. If you report it, we could all be in trouble for breaking curfew and going to the club. Do you really want us *all* booted off the team?'

'They won't do that. A severe reprimand maybe, but they won't kick you off the team.'

'If they become aware that we were out clubbing and that alcohol and drugs were involved, they'll demand we all take drug tests, and... it wouldn't be good for several of us.'

She looks away, her cheeks reddening.

Molly's mind slowly connects the dots. 'You took something last night as well?'

'I sometimes take something to help me get to sleep. I've done it for years. Ever since... that doesn't matter right now. It's nothing serious, and it doesn't benefit my race performance in any way, but I don't need it leaking to the press; it would be frowned upon by the committee. Do you remember what happened to Caroline Hoebeck?'

I shake my head, unfamiliar with the name.

'She was in the national championship finals with me five years ago, and failed a test after the event. They kicked her out of British Athletics and she's never competed since. They want us all clean as whistles. You know that.' She reaches across and rests her hands on Molly's. 'Please, don't ruin this for everyone else.'

Molly pulls her hands away, a fresh wave of nausea bubbling in her gut.

'When I found you,' Thea continues, 'you were in a bad way. You kept talking about your stalker and begged me to bring you here rather than your place. You said he knows where you live and that you don't feel safe. Why don't you just find new digs?'

'I can't afford to move.'

'Aren't you getting financial support from UK Athletics?'

'I will if I qualify for a recognised event – such as the games – but until then I'm on my own.'

'Oh, shit, that's too bad. I'd say you could move in here, but I don't think the university would be happy with that.'

'I'm sure he's always there – when I leave home and return every day.'

'What has that detective said about it?'

'The police don't know who he is, and I don't know what he looks like, and there's nothing they can do until one of those questions is answered.'

'You should put up some cameras.'

'My agent asked the landlord, but he said he won't.'

'So?' Thea pulls a face. 'Just do it yourself.'

'And how would I do that? I'm not savvy enough to set up a surveillance system.'

'Oh, please, it's really not that difficult. Not these days. Practically half the population has cameras in their doorbells. In fact, I tell you what, I reckon Seb could sort it for you.'

Molly is grateful that Thea doesn't think she's making a mountain out of a molehill.

'Your brother Seb?'

'Sure. I mean, he talks like a robot, but he managed to rebuild the toaster when he was like two. He's a tech genius and could probably fit some temporary cameras to give you reassurance. I'll speak to him today.'

If Molly can identify fake-Oppenheimer, then Detective

Freeman will have to take action against him. She wonders whether he's sent any more messages while she's been out of it.

'Where's my phone?'

'It was out of juice, so I put it on charge. It's over by the bed.'

Molly collects the phone and switches it on, but the first message she sees isn't one she's expecting.

'What's wrong?' Thea asks. 'You look like you've seen a ghost.'

'It's Finn. He says I'm late for a meeting at the track, but it's Saturday, right? I don't remember having a meeting scheduled today.'

She checks her calendar and now sees a pending invitation, but it was only sent this morning. Dressing quickly in a tracksuit that Thea lends her, she tries to ignore the ache in her head and gut as she jogs to the track. She desperately hopes her bad start to the day isn't about to get worse.

25

NOW

21 April 2024, Rotherhithe, London – Mile 11

My eyes remain glued to my phone screen. I don't recognise the name of the newspaper – something German presumably – but that is definitely Otto's face, and if the translation is correct, then he is no longer in prison. Does Zara know he's escaped? She hasn't responded to my request to look into his whereabouts, but now I know. My biggest fear has been realised: he's here, and he won't stop.

I look around the course uneasily, actually turning in a circle as I study the few faces at the side of the road, scanning and dismissing each.

This is it: the moment when I should just abandon the race and my dreams. Not only is he here, but he wants me to *know* he is here. I'm the reason he was arrested in London, and that indirectly led to his capture in Germany, so he must hold me responsible. I return to the image of the newspaper, and try to zoom in to see the date it was printed, but it's still too small to read. But if this isn't new, then he will have had days – maybe even weeks – to make his way over here and plan his revenge. He wouldn't have been able to travel with his own passport, but something tells me a man who's managed to create so many alternative identities online wouldn't struggle to find fake travel documents as well.

Where are you?

Despite the global audience watching today's race, I've never felt so alone. There is no motorbike or cameraman in my immediate vicinity; they're busy with the two packs of runners ahead of me, and the stragglers some distance back. If I want to feel safer, I'm going to have to run with one of the groups.

Forwarding the messages to Zara, I right my course, and plough ahead, more determined than ever to catch up with the group Thea and Kat are leading. But my eyes don't leave the sides of the road. As each new spectator appears, I study their appearance, searching, but failing to find him.

Would he really just be out here in person?

He has thrived by remaining in the shadows. Always a step ahead of me in this twisted game of his. He wants me to know he's watching, but part of the power kick must be keeping me in the dark.

Beyond a row of blue portable toilet cubicles, I spot a larger figure in a long, beige raincoat. He has his back to me, and the German Shepherd at his side is straining and barking at the group ahead. My heart skips, and I splutter as the air catches in my throat.

Is this him? Is this the moment he plans to strike?

I look for any cut ways where I can circumvent him, but we are on a straight road, tall fences separating the pathway from whatever lies beyond. My only way past him is to run, and all I can do is hug the opposite side of the road to keep as great a distance as possible.

The dog quietens, but then it spots me and strains to bark in my direction as well. The owner is hunched over, saying something to the animal so I can't see his face. I keep my eyes glued to them, and I finally pass, my head turning, waiting for the moment of recognition. The figure begins to straighten, and I continue to watch, looking for any kind of weapon. But then the figure looks over to me, and I'm embarrassed to see a made-up face and a large chest straining in the raincoat. The woman gives me a curious look, as if she's trying to determine if she recognises me, but I don't hang around for her to make the connection.

I try phoning Zara again, but this time I don't leave a message. I can't see if she's received the images yet, let alone looked at them. I know she'll tell me to withdraw, as she said earlier, and now I'm genuinely considering it. I've worked so hard to keep going despite everything Bistras has done to me, but maybe I'm just making matters worse. Had I conceded and met him for that drink last year, maybe none of this would have happened. Or had I just stopped training and returned to Scotland, maybe he would have moved on to another target. Maybe in some twisted way, he thinks I'm enjoying this level of attention, when nothing could be further from the truth.

I've caught up with the pack, which brings some relief to know I'm no longer on my own, not that I know any of them well enough to ask for help; apart from Thea, of course. I don't think I would have survived this long without her help. But I don't want to take advantage of her kindness. She has her own race to run and doesn't need to know the finer details of what is happening. If I can run next to her, I'll feel safer; at least until Zara returns my call, or comes to help.

There's no sign of Kat when I fall in line with Thea. She offers a surprised, but friendly nod in my direction, her cheeks red with the exertion of maintaining her pace. I dread to think how my own face must look right now. I have overdone it today, and if I appear even half as tired as my body feels, then I must look a right state. But appearance is the last thing on my mind.

'Where's Kat?' I ask, unable to spot her pink vest top in the pack of runners some distance ahead.

'Toilet,' Thea puffs back.

Loo breaks are a necessary evil during a marathon, particularly if you don't get the right balance when taking on additional fluids. It's why Finn and I planned strategies for multiple race conditions. A full bladder in a race isn't something that should be ignored as it's an unnecessary distraction, which can slow speed and cause other complications. The best advice is to stop when the urge strikes, and make up the time. I don't need to stop, because in truth I probably haven't taken on enough fluids to replace what I've lost through my additional exertions. I'm grateful that the next rehydration station is nearly upon us.

The course here follows the bend in the Thames as it approaches the Rotherhithe Tunnel. We've just passed the domineering site of Canary Wharf across the river, and we will pass closer to those skyscrapers between miles fifteen and sixteen, such is the circuitous route the marathon follows. The cool breeze blowing from the water is a welcome relief, but the temperature is continuing to rise dramatically, and that is going to have a major impact on the speed each of us can maintain going into the second half of the race.

I don't want to admit how pleased I am that Kat is now behind us. She will have to exert herself to catch up, and that plays into my hands perfectly. And if Finn was right about her pace tailing off, all I need to do is maintain my current speed and keep her behind me.

I glance back over my shoulder but there's still no sign of her pink vest.

'What are you looking for?' Thea asks.

'Kat,' I admit.

'She really isn't as bad as you make out, you know.'

'I'm not the one with the problem,' I say, more defensive than I expect. 'She's had it in for me since day one.'

'I think if you gave her a chance, you might actually like her. You're taking this rivalry thing too far.'

Does she really think I'm the cause of the animosity?

'She's made no secret of how much she despises me. And we both know it's possible she was the one who spiked my drink that night at the club.'

'There you go again: I told you she had nothing to do with that.'

'Yeah, but you won't tell me who *was* responsible. And Kat had most to gain from freaking me out. It wouldn't surprise me if she was the one who knocked my bottle to the floor at the first rehydration station.'

'You need to chill out, yeah? Kat is my friend as well, and I won't have you badmouthing her. Besides, she wouldn't do something like that.'

'No? You were the one who told me she's scared I'm going to take her place on the plane to Paris.'

'Yes, she is, but she wouldn't resort to putting you in danger. There's a lot you don't know about her. She's had a harder life than you can ever imagine.'

'That doesn't mean she can mess up my chances.'

'You don't understand.'

'Explain it to me then.'

Thea sighs, and checks over her shoulder, as if ensuring Kat isn't within earshot. 'She and her mother were abused by her stepfather for years until Social Services came to their rescue. Getting to the Olympics would mean so much to Kat and her mum, and that's why she's so intent on making it through.'

It's true I don't know anything of Kat's background, but that doesn't give her the right to make life more difficult for me.

We cross to the right of the road where the next table of bottles are lined up, and at first I can't find my bottle again, and suspect Bistras's hand at work, but then I do spot it near the back of the table, and grab it with my left hand, slowing long enough to allow Thea to grab her bottle. And then we continue to lead the second group of runners. I try not to think about the fact that my bottle was still in place, given that Kat is now behind us. I don't want to think poorly of her, even though she does of me.

I pull open the sports lid with my teeth, and suck on the end, but only taste dry air. Confused, I pull on the lid again and this time tilt the bottle so gravity can push the drink into my mouth, but still nothing emerges. I lower and shake the bottle, curious to know if there is some kind of blockage, but the bottle is too light, and I don't feel any liquid swishing about inside. My shoulders tense, and I shake it again, finally unscrewing the lid, and staring into the empty bottle with disbelief.

How can it be empty?

Sniffing the rim, I recognise the unmistakeable sticky sweetness of what the bottle once contained, but someone has either already drunk the contents, or more likely, tipped them away. I throw the bottle to the side of the road and scream out in frustration.

'What's going on?' Thea asks, concerned by my outburst.

'My bottle is empty,' I say, fighting against the sting of tears forming at the corner of my eyes.

It must be Bistras.

There's no other explanation for what must have happened.

Finn wouldn't have left an empty bottle at the table, so someone – Bistras or his crony – must have got there first and emptied it. I need to phone Finn and find out if he can get me an urgent replacement.

I feel something cold press against my arm.

'Here, have some of mine,' Thea says, and I see that she is holding out her own bottle.

'I can't. You need it,' I say dismissively.

She presses the bottle more firmly. 'Please. I don't need it all, and I don't want you collapsing again. Drink.'

I don't argue, accepting the bottle, and pressing it against my lips, taking big gulps, before handing it back.

'Finish it,' she tells me.

I do, and hurl it to the grass verge.

'Thank you, Thea.'

'No worries. I can't believe your coach would have left an empty bottle.'

Neither can I.

26

BEFORE

Saturday, 27 January 2024, National Sports Centre, Crystal Palace, London

Molly is breathless and in dire need of water when she makes it to the track, and her scarred feet are in agony. Thea was right; she should have just reported she was not well enough to come in, especially for an unscheduled meeting. She knows she can't afford to take a day's rest, but there's a danger she'll do more damage than good if she hits the track or gym today. Her stomach is empty, but she has no appetite for food.

She heads to Finn's office, but there's no answer when she knocks, and when she depresses the handle finds the door is locked. She's about to phone him, when he comes around the corner, and throws up his arms in disbelief.

'Where the hell have you been?'

She's surprised by the frustration in his tone. 'I was at Thea's place. My phone died last night and it's only just back up and running. Listen, do we have to do this today? I was ill this morning, and—'

'I bet you were!'

Her brow knots. 'What's that supposed to mean?'

'We don't have time for this. We're late, and if you want my advice, I think you should lay off how bad your hangover is, and beg for forgiveness. Where's your agent?'

'Jamie? I have no idea.'

'He was invited this morning as well.' He scans the surrounding area, before shaking his head. 'Never mind, we'll just have to start without him.'

She's about to ask what he means, but he storms off, and she has to hobble to keep up with him. They head up the stairs to the first floor, and along the walkway to the large office at the end. Finn knocks twice, and then heads inside, holding the door open for Molly. It's only as she passes that she sees the name on the door, and realises something is very wrong.

'I found her,' Finn declares brightly.

Molly has never formally met the woman behind the desk, but her reputation precedes her. Gloria Hutchinson was appointed new Head of the Olympic Committee following Great Britain's abysmal performance at the 1996 Atlanta games. After we finished in thirty-sixth, below countries like Algeria and Kazakhstan, she was brought in to revolutionise the nation's approach to competitive athletics. Stern-faced, she is rumoured to take no prisoners. And judging by the glare she gives when Molly enters the room, she hasn't invited her in for a pep talk.

'Well?' she says, removing her glasses and widening her eyes.

Molly looks to Finn, but his head is bowed.

'Um, I'm sorry I'm late,' Molly begins. 'I wasn't aware of the meeting as my phone was off. Had I known, I would have been here much sooner.'

Gloria glances at Finn's bowed head, before glaring back at Molly again. 'Well? Are you going to explain yourself?'

Molly senses there's something they know that she doesn't, but she dare not ask, hoping instead they'll reveal their secret. Whatever it is, it's not good news. She immediately thinks of fake-Oppenheimer, and dreads what further mess he's caused now.

'Um, listen, this guy, I've reported him to the police, I've blocked him from my socials, and yet he continues to be a nuisance. I'm at my wits' end with him.'

The confusion ruffling Gloria's eyebrows suggests she isn't talking about fake-Oppenheimer.

'You're blaming last night's embarrassment on your stalker?'

How can Gloria know about the ketamine-spiked drink? Unless one of the other girls has mentioned it, Molly can't imagine how it would have come to her attention.

Molly is about to ask her to clarify, when Gloria turns and slides an iPad across the desk. Molly skim reads the headline, but it's the photograph of her on all fours that fills her soul with dread. The camera's flash reflects in the sequins of her dress, but it's the dead eyes and slurred lips and her general state of disrepair that paints the worst picture.

'READY, STEADY, TUMBLE' reads the headline, with the article implying that Molly was seen exiting the nightclub in a clearly inebriated state.

'Do you think this kind of behaviour is appropriate?' Gloria grizzles.

'No,' Molly mouths, but the word sticks in her throat.

'I expect better from all Team GB athletes. This is the kind of thing British sport has been trying to distance itself from. You are supposed to be an elite distance runner, Molly, and what kind of example does this set for the future Team GB athletes? The culture of binge drinking and late-night partying brings our reputation into disrepute.'

'I wasn't drunk,' Molly fires back, but remembers Thea's warning about drug tests, and knows she needs to tread carefully, which isn't easy to do with her head pounding.

There is a small fridge containing bottles of mineral water in the corner behind Gloria's desk, and Molly would give anything for the offer of one.

'Oh, please, I've seen plenty of drunk athletes before, and you can't tell me you're not under the influence in this image. And judging by the state of you this morning – pupils dilated, bags under your eyes – you're clearly feeling the effects of last night's antics.' She slides the glasses back onto her nose. 'You leave me no choice but to suspend you from the association with immediate effect.'

Molly's mouth drops. 'No, you can't do that.'

'I can and I am. What you fail to understand, Miss Fitzhume, is that it is my responsibility to protect the reputation of the association, and if I don't act now, it sends out the wrong message. I'm sorry. Once the dust has settled, you may reapply for membership, but I will expect to see a fresh leaf turned over, and proof that your injury nightmare is behind you.'

'Please, Gloria,' Finn speaks up, finally daring to make eye contact. 'Molly has been training so hard, and she's on target to meet the qualifying time in the marathon. She made a mistake and she's very sorry.' He looks at Molly, as he says this, ushering her to concur.

'I wasn't the only one in the club last night,' Molly says instead, instantly regretting the statement.

'Oh, really, and who else was there?'

Molly buttons her lips, not wanting to get the rest of the girls – especially Thea – into trouble.

Gloria slides off her glasses again, and places them face down on the desk. When she finally speaks, her voice is calmer, almost empathetic. 'I understand the importance of letting off steam from time to time. The pressure on modern sportspeople these days is intense, with every Tom, Dick and Harry carrying camera phones, but that's why you need to be conscious of who's watching and how you're behaving at all times. I don't take issue with the team going dancing after last night's dinner, but there are no images of *them* stumbling out of the club, off their faces, in the early hours. That is the art of discretion; something you could do with learning.'

'Please don't kick her out,' Finn tries again. 'You want our elite distance runners to have a chance in Paris, and Molly is one of our best. With the progress she's been making, she has the potential to be a real contender for a medal. She did wrong, and she's sorry, and she won't let it happen again, will you, Molly?'

Molly is close to telling Gloria Hutchinson where she can shove her association, for blaming her for something that wasn't her fault, but she knows better than to cut off her nose to spite her face.

Molly bites down hard on her cheek. 'I am sorry for what happened, and I promise it won't happen again. Please don't snatch away my dream.'

A knock at the door is followed by Jamie entering and offering profuse apologies for his own poor timekeeping, blaming traffic. 'Molly has been under a huge amount of stress, and I have prepared a public statement that we can release, including an apology to you, the team and the whole association.' He passes a sheet of paper to Gloria. 'And you have my word that nothing like this will ever happen again, if you'll show her mercy.'

Molly doesn't like Jamie apologising on her behalf, but doesn't say anything when Gloria hands him the sheet of paper back, with a swift nod.

'Very well. Consider this your final verbal warning, Molly. Any further behaviour that brings our reputation into disrepute will see you permanently excluded from competitive events. Am I making myself clear?'

Molly wants to tell her that she is the victim of an unkind prank, but holds her tongue, and follows Jamie out of the office, down to the canteen where he buys a coffee for himself and a water for her. She quietly explains to him what happened, and he tells her she made the right call in keeping quiet.

'Listen, I had an idea about how you could get your stalker to focus on someone else,' he says after a minute. 'We post a photo of you snuggling up with some handsome guy.'

Molly frowns. 'And how will that help?'

'If he thinks you're loved up, he'll realise he has no chance of dating you, and can turn his attention elsewhere.'

'And who am I supposed to snuggle up with? I have no interest – or time for that matter – to start a relationship with some guy just to discourage some sycophant.'

'It doesn't have to be a real relationship; just implied. The picture could be something intimate with your coach for all I care.'

'With Finn? Are you for real?'

'Why not? He's sweet on you, and if you explained why you wanted the picture, I'm sure he'd be supportive.'

This is the second time this morning someone has suggested that Finn might have a crush on her, but she's never considered it before now. She doesn't see it, personally – not that she isn't also attracted to him. But the last thing she wants is to give Gloria Hutchinson another reason to get rid of her.

27

NOW

21 April 2024, Bermondsey, London – Mile 12

The Bluetooth headband erupts to life just as we're passing through a set of bollards, and I almost lose my footing. At first, I'm expecting to see Zara's name on my watch screen, and I almost decline the call from Jamie, but then figure he wouldn't be calling without good reason.

'How's my favourite client getting on? I just got home and tuned in. You must be nearly halfway through now, right?'

'Not quite.'

'Oh, well, you're doing great from what I can see. Decent split times, and getting plenty of coverage on the BBC as well, which is exactly what we need.'

I shouldn't be surprised that Jamie is measuring my progress in terms of minutes on screen, but I resist the urge to tell him I am less concerned about image, given Bistras's antics. I glance at Thea, whose head is down as she continues to work her arms and legs in perfect harmony.

'I'm doing my best,' I tell him, conscious that he's blocking the line and potentially preventing Zara from getting through. 'I'd better go—'

'Before you go, do me a favour, will you? Smile more.'

My brow furrows at the request.

'Ooh, no, don't do that. No frowning. A nice bright smile, please.'

'I am smiling,' I lie.

'I'm watching you right now, Molly, and that is not smiling. You look like you've got trapped wind.'

My head shoots up, and I see that there is a motorbike and cameraman directly ahead of us, the camera pointing in our direction.

'You can see me now?'

'Yes, and I need you to look like you're enjoying yourself.'

'Enjoying myself? I'm running a marathon!'

'I know, I know, but this is your dream and passion, and you need to show the viewing public that. I'm not expecting you to beam like you're advertising toothpaste, but show that determination and enthusiasm for what you're doing. Don't forget: all that clobber you're wearing has been gifted by your sponsors, and they don't want it to look like you're not supremely comfortable in the gear. There's every chance they'll want to license footage from today to use in future advertising campaigns.'

I fix my eyes on the camera, and do my best to smile, but hear Jamie gagging down the line.

'Can't you make it look a bit more... *natural*? I appreciate it's an endurance event, but try and relax a bit more. We need you to create a good impression. The world is watching, and this is what it's like in the big leagues. You want to make good money, then you need to put on a performance. It isn't just about completing the race – not for you – you need to show what it means. It isn't about where you place, it's the style you emanate that will bring the big players to the table. Nike. Adidas. Reebok. I have potential contracts in my inbox, depending on how today goes. I shouldn't need to remind you of what that could mean for you going forwards.'

Heat rushes to my face, and I feel like a child being chastised for talking at the back of class.

What it means for *us*, is more like it, but I don't call him out on it at this point, as I have bigger fish to fry.

'I'm trying my best,' I say instead. 'The thing is... I think my stalker is back, and they've been messaging again.'

'Really? I haven't seen anything on your Insta.'

'They're phoning and messaging me directly.'

'Oh my God, this is perfect! So you're in touch with them right now?'

I don't like the excitement in his tone, and am reluctant to go into the full details with him.

'They keep phoning, yes.'

'And have you reported it to the police or the race stewards?' He gasps. 'Oh, God, you're not thinking about withdrawing from the race, are you?'

'Not unless my life is in danger, but he may not give me the choice.'

'How likely is that, though? Has he threatened you? Do you need me to do anything?'

I can picture him at home right now, probably stretched out on his sofa with a glass of juice and a croissant. Not exactly a knight in shining armour.

'I've reported it to the police, and they are searching for him now. He's sending threatening messages, but so far that's all – I think – but I don't know how or when he might escalate.'

'Oh, my, I hadn't realised; explains your resting bitch face, though...' He trails off. 'Listen, keep your chin up. I'm sure the police will act in your best interests, but if you need anything from me, then just call.'

Thea is looking over with concern.

'Just my agent,' I mouth, and offer a weak smile, which does little to ease her worried frown. Maybe she's now wondering whether her own life could be in danger if she continues to run beside me.

'Actually, you could do me a favour,' I say as his previous words repeat in my head. 'Can you check my Insta messages for anything new or suspicious?'

'Sure.'

The line goes quiet while I presume he logs into the account to check. My head feels so heavy having to process all this additional stress on top of the remaining fifteen or so miles that lie ahead of me. The road here is coned and taped off, preventing traffic from interfering with the event. Small cheers and applause sound as we pass each small, bespoke group of supporters; some are standing, others sitting in camping chairs. There's another row of portable toilet cubicles as well, and suddenly I'm conscious of the possibility that Kat might be gaining on us at last. I do my best to look back over my shoulder but all I can see are the swaying fists and shoulders of those runners directly behind me. I don't see a pink vest top, but that doesn't mean she isn't gaining. I need to keep her behind me, no matter the cost.

'Right,' I hear Jamie say, 'I'm in your Insta now, but there's nothing new in here, but then we blocked new requests from unknown sources if you remember?'

'Wait! What? When did you do that?'

'I don't know, a few weeks ago. You were getting bombarded, so I amended your settings so nobody else could message unless you'd already started following their account.'

'You didn't tell me you'd done that.'

'Didn't I? I'm sure I did. Anyway, that's better than all the abuse you were receiving?'

'When did you change it? How long ago?'

I try to remember exactly when Zara told me Bistras had been captured, but the memory is just out of reach. I'd assumed the messages had stopped because he'd been arrested, but what if his being arrested and the messages stopping was merely a coincidence? It was never proved for certain that he was the one sending all of the abusive messages. Some, yes, but I can't hand-on-heart say I know for certain he sent all of them.

'I don't know. It was a few weeks ago. I could see how much they were getting to you, so I switched it off. You never mentioned it, so I assumed you realised what I'd done.'

What if someone else was behind some of the abuse I was receiving, but we missed it because Jamie stopped their ability to reach me? No wonder Zara thinks the possibility of an accomplice is all in my head.

'Anyway, you can tell the world about all of that tomorrow morning.'

My shoulders tense. 'Why would I do that?'

'Okay,' he says giddily, 'I was going to save the surprise until after the race, but I'm too excited. The producers at *Good Morning Britain* have invited you to be a guest on tomorrow morning's show! How exciting is that?'

It feels like the rug has been pulled from beneath my feet, and I don't know how to react.

'Obviously, they'll talk to you about today's race and the Olympics, and all that, but they're really interested in hearing your story about this stalker and the nightmare he's put you through. They're doing an hour-long slot on cyber bullying and the dangers of social media for teens and children, especially with the summer holidays rapidly approaching. Kids with phones and tablets are being exposed to social media and they want to use your story as a cautionary tale, and to provide advice to viewers on how to handle it.'

I shake my head in disbelief, but I can't find the words to tell him how horrific this sounds to me.

'Once you've told them your story, they want to open the phone lines and have you field some calls from worried viewers – parents, teens who've experienced similar – so you can share your experience and knowledge. It's going to do wonders for raising your profile. Your appearance on *The One Show* was good, but *GMB* has a bigger audience, and I know you're going to smash it. If we do this in the right way, you'll have the biggest brands falling over themselves to make you their summer poster girl ahead of the Olympics. And sports brands are just the start. We could be looking at lucrative contracts for energy drinks, snack bars, and even cosmetics.'

My anger boils to the surface. 'Why would you do this to me? I don't want the world to know what he's put me through. Because of him I'm scared of my own shadow most of the time. I don't feel safe being out by myself, regardless of how light or dark it is outside. There have been nights when I haven't been able to sleep because I was scared that he was going to break into my flat. There have been nights when I have cried myself to sleep.'

'And that's precisely why you need to tell your story. You're not the only person experiencing these kinds of issues, but you could be the spokesperson for the masses.'

'Can you hear yourself? I don't want you cashing in on what he's done to me.'

'With all due respect, Molly, I'm not trying to *cash in* on your trauma. Cyber bullying is a major issue that isn't discussed enough in the public eye. There will be thousands of young people out there experiencing similar abuse and feeling like there's nowhere for them to turn. By talking about your own plight, you can show them they're not alone and that even one of the biggest names in sport can be targeted.'

I end the call before I say something I might later regret, but I can't get over the sickening taste in my mouth. I don't doubt there's some truth in Jamie's last statement, but I don't buy his claim that he's set up the interview because it's in the public interest and morally right.

I look up at the camera ahead of me, but my eyes widen as a new thought strikes: *could Jamie have engineered my stalker's return for commercial gain?*

28

BEFORE

Saturday, 24 February 2024, Streatham, London

'Who is it?' Molly calls through the door, desperately wishing she had a peep hole to identify the person who'd woken her with their knocking.

'It's Thea. I brought my brother to install your doorbell.'

Molly throws open the door, and pulls Thea into an embrace, her heart thundering so fast in her chest that she's certain Thea will be able to feel it.

'Molly, this is Seb,' Thea says when she finally breaks free of the impromptu hug.

Seb is a good foot taller than the two of them, his hair gelled into a dark side-parting, and his square-rimmed glasses plain and practical. Molly thrusts out a hand, but Seb stares down at it without shaking it, lifting the box into the air instead.

'Where do you want it fitting?'

Thea places a delicate arm around his shoulders.

'You'll have to forgive my brother. Charm and communication aren't his areas of strength. Why don't we head inside for a cup of tea and leave him to it?'

Thea takes Molly's hand and the two head inside. Molly grabs at the stray clothes from the floor, trying to subtly tidy. When Thea said she would bring her brother around at the weekend, Molly had assumed she'd meant in the afternoon, and would have made more of an effort to make the tiny flat appear less cluttered.

Seb enters, studying the door jamb meticulously, before dragging in a large rucksack Molly hadn't earlier noticed. He plonks the bag on the table, unzips it and extracts an electric drill, hammer, and screwdriver.

'Where do you want the bell?'

Molly eases past him and points roughly at the door frame. He raises his glasses to see where she is pointing, stooping to examine the wall opposite.

'If we put it on this side instead, you'll have a better view of the whole corridor,' he says, pointing at the opposite side of the frame. 'Is that okay? Thea said you're worried about men coming and going.'

Molly frowns at the suggestion. 'Well, yeah, sort of.'

He nods without making eye contact.

'There are some real monsters out there. Did you know the overall crime rate in City of London last year was 819 crimes per 1,000 people? The most common crime is theft, with 1,963 offences during the year, but that doesn't include those offences not reported to the police. I'm always warning Thea that she needs to be more careful when she's—'

'Sorry, he's really into statistics,' Thea says, rushing over and pulling Molly away. 'But he's a real sweetheart, and would do anything for me.'

'I need your phone,' he says, following them and holding out his hand.

'What did we say about saying please and thank you, Seb?'

'I need your phone, please,' he says, avoiding eye contact. 'There's an app I need to install so you'll be able to see who comes and goes.'

Molly unlocks the device and hands it to him, relieved to have an expert on her side.

* * *

Molly is late getting to the track, because Seb insisted on showing her a number of safety apps that would help her should she be out alone and come face to face with an attacker. Despite Thea trying to cajole him out with eye rolls, he insisted that should she have any problems, he would be happy to return and adjust the settings. He'd warned her that the app would buzz every time someone came near the door, but she hadn't realised just how often that would be. In the thirty minutes since she started her warm-up, her phone must have vibrated a dozen times, all of which were her neighbours coming and going along the corridor.

With just over eight weeks until the marathon, Molly is now regularly completing twenty-mile stints every two days, with plenty of rest and recuperation in between. Her coach has her using the swimming pool to work on breathing exercises and muscle stretches, but she's always happiest when she's back on the track, monitoring her times.

Thankfully, there's been no sign of the cold snap meteorologists have been predicting for the last couple of weeks. The last thing Molly's training routine needs is the disruption of ice and snow. She's wearing thermals under her tracksuit today, the beanie hat providing additional protection to her head and ears as her Spotify playlist pumps through her earbuds.

Jamie continues to post on her behalf, and has spoken of a potentially huge opportunity with a leading shampoo brand, but she's not so keen to pose for a video in the shower. Jamie promises it will all be tastefully shot, but it feels like waving a red rag at a charging bull. She only has to get through the next fifty-nine days, and achieve a qualifying time, and her reliance on endorsements will diminish.

At least that's the plan. Of course, she's nowhere near the standard to qualify in two hours twenty-eight yet, but she is focusing on running miles in under six minutes. To qualify she needs to maintain an average of five and a half minutes per mile, which is easy enough at the start, but much more of a challenge when you've been running for twenty miles.

'Right, it's time to up the pace now, Molly,' Finn calls from the centre of the track, his stopwatch aloft. 'I want the next mile as close to five minutes as you can manage. Let's see what you're capable of.'

She glances over her shoulder to acknowledge his words, but almost loses her footing when she sees he is not alone. She recognises the woman as Thea's coach, but it's her flirtatious body language that puts Molly off her stride. Turning back to face the track, she puts her head down, and pumps her legs faster, trying not to think about them. It shouldn't bother her. Finn is free to flirt or date whoever he wants. And yet she can feel her muscles tightening as she grinds her teeth.

She glances back at them again as she takes the next bend. What is that woman's problem? Thea said staff and athletes aren't allowed to pursue relationships, so surely the same rule should apply to coaching staff too?

Molly tries to push the thoughts from her mind, but the more she tries to ignore them, the greater the struggle.

'That's great, Molly,' Finn shouts out as she passes. 'See if you can maintain that pace for the next mile.'

Molly doesn't want to look at them, but dares to take another glance, wanting to confirm that her imagination is blowing the scene out of all proportion, but now the woman is rubbing his upper arm. Why is she doing that? Has he received bad news, and she's comforting him? He didn't mention any sour feelings when he spoke to Molly, so what does this woman know that she doesn't?

Molly yelps as her foot lands, and she instantly pulls up. It's like a knife has been slashed across the back of her left calf, and she sinks to the damp track, raising an arm in the hope of getting Finn's attention. The pain in her leg is excruciating, and she knows instantly she's pulled the muscle. Lying on her back, she tries to compose her rapid breathing, and tries desperately not to catastrophise just how serious this injury could be.

Finn slides over a moment later, asking what's wrong.

'M-my calf,' she manages to stammer between breaths.

'Can you stand? Let's get you off the track so I can assess it properly.'

She allows him to put his arm around her shoulders, and leans in to him as he raises her into a sitting position. He's so strong, and she picks up a waft of his cologne.

Stop it, she warns herself internally.

'On three,' he says, counting, before hoisting her up to her feet.

She winces, as she gently places her foot on the ground, and continues to lean in to him as he supports her weight and leads her to a bench at the edge of the track.

'Was it instant pain, or gradual?' Finn asks, gently running his hands along the injured leg.

'Instant,' she gasps, her breathing still haggard.

There's no sign of Thea's coach any more, though Molly can't be certain where she's disappeared to.

'Can you roll up your trouser leg so I can take a wee look at it?'

Molly obliges, unzipping the cuff, and sliding the material up her leg.

'Do you mind?' Finn asks, as he presses his warm palms against her calf to examine the leg.

'No, it's fine,' she says, straining a smile.

She closes her eyes and grits her teeth, as his hands work the muscle, the massage sore but not painful.

'And you didn't hear any kind of pop or snap?'

She shakes her head.

'Good, well, I don't think you've torn your Achilles tendon, so that's good news. It's probably just a strain of the gastrocnemius muscle. If it's only a mild strain, it should be healed up in a couple of weeks, though you'll have to properly rest and ice it. I can ask your physio to give you a regime of exercises to aid recovery. How is it feeling now?'

His hands are warm on her leg, but his touch is gentle. She snaps her eyes open, suddenly conscious that she's enjoying the smoothness of his touch too much.

'I'll live,' she says, slightly disappointed when he lowers her leg back to the floor, and sits down beside her. 'What were you and Thea's coach discussing?'

She instantly regrets the question, embarrassed by her own envy.

'Oh, you mean Emma? Nothing, really. Just talking work stuff.'

It didn't look very professional, Molly thinks, but doesn't say.

'Can I ask you a personal question?'

'Sure.'

She bites her lip, and then bottles out of asking what's on her mind. 'How much do you think this strain is going to upset my rhythm?'

He looks as though she was going to ask something else, but doesn't question it.

'Well, as I said, it all depends on your recovery time. We've been stepping up your distances, and it's probably that additional pressure that's shown today. It needs to be properly healed before you start running, as otherwise you could strain it again, and worse next time. I think we should take it as a warning that we were pushing it too much.'

'But I need to push, no? I'll never hit the qualifying time otherwise.'

'I have faith that you will, Molly. You shouldn't be so hard on yourself. It's not like you have never run a marathon before. You have muscle memory and that will help massively.'

She can feel his eyes watching her, and when she turns to look at him, his face is so close that she can smell his cologne again.

'Can I ask you something else?' she says quietly, and he nods. 'Well, a little bird told me that you quite like me.' She can feel the heat rising to her cheeks, but continues regardless. 'And I just wanted to let you know that if you want to ask me out, you should.'

He's so close that she's sure he's going to kiss her, so she closes her eyes and leans in, her pulse racing as their lips get closer, but rather than kissing her back, he pushes her away.

'I'm sorry, Molly, we can't.'

She opens her eyes and sees he has slid to the opposite side of the bench.

'I'm sorry,' he repeats. 'The association has strict rules about this kind of thing, and I can't afford to lose my job here.' He stands, and turns his back on her. 'I'll go and get some ice for your leg.'

She watches as he jogs away in the direction of the main building then lowers her face to her hands, unable to understand how she could have misread the signs.

21 April 2024, Tower Bridge, London – Mile 13

My mind can't get past the question: could Jamie have engineered my stalker's return for commercial gain?

I know it's a ridiculous thought, and it bothers me that I could even contemplate betrayal from such a close friend, but then can I really consider Jamie a friend? He was the one who approached me when I narrowly missed out on the bronze, telling me that he had the power to send my career into the stratosphere. I can remember laughing at him, rather than with him, but he continued to pursue me, sharing the financial earnings of other nameless clients, and how it was commonplace for professional athletes to have someone handling that side of affairs for them. I'll admit I was flattered, and though I tried to play hard to get, it wasn't like a hundred other agents were beating down my door, so I signed up. And, on the whole, he's lived up to his word. The endorsement earnings to date haven't been as big as he projected, but then I haven't agreed to do everything he's asked, so I can't hold him wholly responsible. And if he's right about the sports companies being on the hook, then he has lived up to that word, right?

But acting on my behalf in a professional capacity doesn't make us friends. The only lunches we've taken have been business-based, and as he frequently reminds me, 'tax deductible'. So, would his orchestrating something like this – regardless of how horrific it has been – really be a betrayal? Would he even see it in that way if he thought it made commercial sense?

Jamie was the one who suggested I sign up to Instagram, and he was the one who posted those first pictures advertising the sports bra; he was the one who brought this trouble to my door, but he was acting in my best interests, wasn't he?

He volunteered to manage the account for me when the messages from Bistras and his aliases got too much, but could he have been the one sending the messages in the first place? I grind my teeth as I try to picture him playing the opposing parts of antagonist and confidante, but surely there would have been easier ways for him to cash in on me? Just because he had the opportunity and motive to lead this torrent against me, it doesn't necessarily mean he did.

When I gave him full access to manage my account and messages, I then started receiving messages to my number. He is one of only a handful who had that number, and my new one too, but using it would make him an obvious suspect, so why would he run the risk of drawing attention to himself?

He was the one who set me up in that flat, and he was the one who handled all the rental charges, paying it out of what I was earning through the endorsements. I haven't asked to see statements yet, but what if the rent wasn't as high as he claimed, just so he could force me to do more promotions work, flaunting myself online? I dismiss this thought as quickly as it arrives; that would mean he'd been planning this for more than six months, and I just don't believe he's that organised.

But he *was* the only person who knew I was in The Clarendon last night – hell, it was *his* idea I stay there.

I shudder at the thought of him leaving the box of orchids outside my room. I can't be sure he knew they were my mam's favourite plants, but it's possible I've mentioned it at some point over the last three years. And when I phoned to ask if the flowers were from him, he said he wasn't home, which would be true if he was making his escape from the hotel. When I was toying with the idea of not running, wasn't he the one who pushed me to go ahead with it, knowing that he'd already lined up the appearance on *GMB* tomorrow?

I try to chase the conspiracy theory from my mind, because I don't want to consider that someone I know could be so cruel. And whilst I can't escape the uneasy feeling that he is benefiting at my expense, I have no evidence that he's involved in any of this. I know Bistras is behind it in general, but I can't see how Jamie could know him or be connected to all of it. One thing it does show is just how all over the place my mind is right now.

I can feel my vest top sticking to the scar on my back, my increased sweat acting like adhesive. The sun is beating down on us, and without sunglasses, it's making it difficult to see ahead without squinting. What rain was previously on the road has all but evaporated, but it's leaving a muggy, damp smell in its wake.

I feel something brush the top of my shoulder, and start as Kat muscles past, slowing just as she is in front of me. I have no idea how she's made up the time so quickly, and Finn's prophecy that she would tire as we near the halfway point seems to have been in vain. And although I have also been pushing myself too much, whilst I'm struggling with the strain of running too quickly, she actually looks in good shape for this section of the race. Maybe I've underestimated her, and that spells trouble.

I glance over to Thea, whose attention is fixed firmly on the road ahead. She doesn't look nearly as exhausted as I'm feeling. I probably shouldn't be surprised as these two powerhouses have been training nonstop for well over a year for the Paris games, whereas I've had to battle back from the brink. Maybe my belief that I could finish ahead of Kat has been sorely misplaced.

Tower Bridge looms ahead, and this should be a sight that fills me with enthusiasm, knowing we're almost halfway through proceedings, but all I can think is how on earth am I going to be able to keep up with these two for another thirteen miles?

Kat is making no effort to pull away and catch up with the lead group who are already over the bridge and out of sight. I just need to keep close to Kat and then hope I have enough in reserve to race her to the finish line.

The bridge is closed to traffic today, and barriers have been set up on both sides of the road to keep the public from getting in the way, but – my word – there are so many people standing there. I can hear bells ringing, cheering and applause, and am already feeling overwhelmed, but the worst part is that Bistras could be standing amongst them.

There are banners hanging from each barrier, advertising this, that and the other, a rainbow of balloons and too many faces to scan. I can't see Jamie in the crowd, which I guess is a good thing, but the faces are largely passing in a blur, and it's hard to make out specific profiles.

Somewhere ahead there is the flag of St Andrew being waved frantically. I feel dizzy with all the noise and attention, and put my head down, just trying to get through it. But ahead, I spot a waiting motorcycle, and recognise the mirrored Aviators. The bike moves forward as we begin to near. I really wish Zara would phone and rule this cameraman in or out of my investigation.

I hear Jamie's words in my head: I need you to look like you're enjoying yourself.

I force myself to stare down the lens of the camera, and adopt a determined and passionate stare, but without a mirror, I have no clue how it will come across on the broadcast, or whether they're even filming at this moment.

I look down at my watch as it buzzes, telling me I have another picture message. I'm reluctant to check it, but curiosity gets the better of me, and I adjust the strap on my arm so I can see my phone's screen. My heart breaks as I see a topless image of myself. I am in a shower cubicle at the Team GB training centre from what I can tell, and my eyes are closed as I wash shampoo out of my hair. I have no idea when it is or who has taken this shot, nor how without me realising. But it's the second message that makes the hairs on the back of my neck stand:

QUIT THE RACE OR THESE GO PUBLIC.

30

_____

BEFORE

Sunday, 25 February 2024, Streatham, London

The smoke alarm blaring overhead has Molly tumbling out of bed in a heightened panic. At first, she thinks she's dreaming until she runs her hands over her eyes, and blinks several times.

The alarm is deafening, and she's forced to cover her ears with both hands, trying to make sense of why it is sounding now, and what she needs to do next. Unlike a hotel room, there is no list of instructions about where the nearest exits are.

Something must be on fire, she tells herself, immediately hobbling to the kitchen area, and checking the toaster for the whiff of burning, but there's nothing obvious to suggest her flat has triggered the alarm.

So if it's not her flat, it must be one of the others in the block. Probably a false alarm, but she can't bear to stay in the flat with the ear-splitting noise any longer. She slips on a pair of sliders, and a coat, and moves to the door. At the last minute, she thinks about her keys and phone, and grabs them off the nightstand, slipping them into the pocket of her coat.

Pressing one ear into her shoulder, she uses her free hand to depress the handle, but the door doesn't budge. She tries it again, but the door seems to be stuck in place.

This isn't happening!

With both hands, she pushes the handle down as far as it will go, and pulls with all her might, but the door remains closed. She steps away, covering her ears once again. It doesn't make sense. The door can't be opened from outside without a key, and doesn't lock from the inside, so there is no logical reason why it shouldn't open. Removing the keys from her pocket, she searches for somewhere she can insert them into the door handle, but there's no mechanism for a key.

Beyond the door, she can hear other residents grumbling as they make their way along the corridor. She thumps her balled fists against the door and yells for help, but either they don't hear her, or choose to ignore her, as nobody responds.

'Help me,' she yells. 'I'm trapped in here.'

Nobody stops or offers help, and she attempts to open the door again without success. The alarm must have been sounding for at least a minute now, though it feels longer to Molly as panic starts to tighten its grip. The fact that the alarm has yet to be reset suggests it's been caused by more than another resident having a crafty cigarette.

Molly knows she needs to get out of the flat one way or another, and as the door is jammed, she crosses to the window, and stares out at the growing mass of people in dressing gowns, gawking back up at the building. Although they're at eye-level, they're all gathered near the entrance, and nobody appears to be looking in her direction. She bangs on the glass, waving frantically, hoping just one person sees her and realises she's trapped inside. One good thing about being on the ground floor is that if she can get out of the window there's no dangerous fall to worry about.

She needs to get the window open, but when she checks the small pot on the windowsill, the key is not inside where it should be. She lifts the pot to check beneath it, and then runs her fingers over the threadbare carpet in case it has somehow fallen out, but there's no sign of it.

She closes her eyes and counts to ten, trying to calm herself long enough to remember the last time she saw the key or opened the window. It's been months due to the cold wintery temperatures. She opened it the day she moved in to try to clear some of the musty smell, but she can't remember a single time she's opened it since. So where did she leave the key? She would have put it back in the pot where it came from, surely?

Straightening, she tries to turn the handle of the double-glazed pane in case it is still unlocked, but it's as stuck as the door. She thumps her hands against the pane, desperately signalling the group of thirty or so people who are staring back up at the building. Surely, someone will realise not everyone is accounted for? Doesn't the building have some kind of fire marshal who would check?

She's made no effort to engage with any of her neighbours, so there's every chance they won't even realise she's missing. But even if they did, they might just assume she's staying somewhere else for the night.

She pulls out her phone to check the time – not yet 2 a.m. – and then realises the phone is her key to freedom. Checking her recent calls list, she stabs a finger at Jamie's name, and presses the phone to her ear. She can barely hear it ringing over the cacophony of the smoke alarm, and when the ringing stops, she starts shouting into the phone.

'Jamie, you've got to help me. I'm trapped in my flat, and there's a fire—'

She stops when she hears the robotic voice of the answerphone system. She hangs up and tries Thea's number next, but it goes straight to answerphone, suggesting the phone is switched off.

Banging her hands against the glass again in frustration, she searches the dimly lit flat for anything she can use to break the window. It'll mean losing her security deposit, but she has no other choice. But there's nothing big enough or strong enough to break glass. She spies the toaster on the side, and in desperation, unplugs it and throws it with all her might towards the glass; it bounces off without making an impact.

Flashes of blue light up the windows of the building across the road as a fire engine honks and battles around the narrow road. This is when Molly realises that a fire engine would only be called if the block was actually ablaze. Her panic grows.

Grabbing the cord of the toaster, she slams it repeatedly against the glass, but all she achieves is a dented and broken toaster.

Will the firemen see her trapped? Nobody else has noticed her signalling efforts, so what chance do they have?

Abandoning the toaster, she can now see a trail of smoke seeping in beneath her door. Hurrying to the bathroom, she douses a towel in water from the sink, and pushes it up against the gap, coughing as she does so. Pinching herself to check it isn't a nightmare, she hurries back to the window, but the fire engine is still trying to get close enough to the building to be able to tackle the blaze.

She limps back to the door, and pulls down on the door handle one more time, and this time it opens a crack. She's so surprised that she lets go of the handle, before quickly scooping the sodden towel from the floor, and putting it over her head and shoulders. The door opens easily, no longer stuck, and she ventures out into the smoke-filled corridor, a robe pulled tightly around her pyjamas. Keeping herself bent over, she hurries along the hallway, out past the mail lockers, where a fireman spots her and drapes an arm around her shoulder. He hurries her away from the building to where the crowd is gathered.

'Are you all right?' he asks over the din of voices and alarm.

She tells him she was trapped, but is okay, and he tells her to wait for an ambulance to arrive to be checked over. She agrees and he hurries away, but she doesn't see where he goes. Daring to turn back and look at the building, she sees bright orange flames dancing in the window of a flat on the top floor.

The fire engine pulls to a halt behind the crowd, and one of the firemen dismounts and hurries to the front of the group, telling them to move away from the building. She follows the flow, but can't help wondering why the fireman who led her out of the building didn't do the same. And then she wonders how he got into the building ahead of his colleagues.

The hairs on the back of her neck stand, as she senses someone watching her, but as she scans the panicked faces around her, she can't see the figure who led her to safety. Shivering in the early-morning breeze, she can't help wondering whether the fire was deliberately started, and if he was there in the corridor the whole time, preventing her door from opening.

31

_____

NOW

21 April 2024, Shadwell, London – Mile 14

My stomach turns as I stare at the topless image on my phone's screen, and the message beneath it.

QUIT THE RACE OR THESE GO PUBLIC.

My skin crawls at the thought of somebody maliciously taking the picture and then deciding to threaten me with it. I'm not doing anything wrong in the image, but I don't want the world to see me exposed in this way. And the message suggests this is just the tip of the iceberg; what other pictures have they taken that they also intend to share if I don't quit? And more importantly, who in the hell is doing this to me?

The camera angle is acute, indicating the picture was taken from above, which suggests whoever took it was in the cubicle beside mine, rather than poking a camera through the curtain. My eyes are closed, my face pointing towards the stream of water. This isn't the shower in my flat. This was definitely captured at the Team GB facility, but there's no date stamp, so I can't tell how recent it is.

My eyes mist over, and I just want to scream out. This isn't fair! I have trained hard, and battled to be here today, and this person – or these people – are doing everything within their power to throw me off course. But why me? What did I do wrong to warrant this level of attention?

I can't see how Bistras could have got past the security desk at the Team GB training centre, unless he posed as a cleaner and snuck his way in. But I'm sure they must do due diligence on any staff, so surely he couldn't have slipped through the net? I know he has form for misdirection – he posed as a fireman, after all – but it would have taken months of planning to get into the building undetected. And even if he had got past security, I'm not sure how he would have managed to get into the female changing rooms to take the picture.

So, if not Bistras, then who?

Someone with access to the building and changing rooms.

An image of Jamie's face forms in my head, and I picture him in the building, telling me to make a pass at Finn. He had signed in and been given a visitor's pass that day, but did I ever see him leave the building? What if he'd hung around, snuck into the changing rooms, and taken the picture? But to what end? It isn't in his best interests for me to quit the race, is it? I mean, me not finishing the race because of my stalker would increase the drama for tomorrow's interview, but surely it makes more commercial sense for me to finish the race *despite* the presence of the stalker? Nike and Adidas aren't going to be offering money to an athlete who failed to qualify for the Paris games.

It can't be him. But who else would have access to the facility and motive for wanting me to withdraw?

My eyes fall on the back of Kat's hot-pink vest ahead of me, and my heart skips a beat. It has to be her!

Unable to control my rage, I reach out and pull on her shoulder. She yelps, but I persevere, accelerating so that I fall in line beside her.

'Is this you?' I demand, waving my arm towards her.

'What the hell is wrong with you?' she grizzles back.

I stab a finger towards the screen. 'You sent me this picture to try and get me to quit the race.'

She tilts her head slightly to look at the screen, before bunching her nose in disgust. 'You're out of your fucking mind,' she says, pulling free of my grip, and powering forwards.

'You're the only one who could have taken it,' I yell out, forcing my legs to increase my own pace to try to keep up. 'I'm going to report you to the committee for what you're doing to me.'

She doesn't respond, pushing on again, and waving her hand dismissively. I try to chase after her, but every time I get close, it's as if she has been given a fresh shot of adrenaline and manages to evade my reach.

I take a screenshot and forward it to Zara so she can see what's happening, but I'm frustrated that she still hasn't got back in touch.

I can't understand how or why Kat would be working with Bistras, but I can't see how it could be anyone else. The messages have all come through from the same withheld number; the same withheld number that has been phoning with that stupid robotic laugh, so they are connected even if I can't yet see how.

What I do know is that they've overplayed their hand by sending me this picture. Showering at the Team GB facility was a necessary requirement after training, and I nearly always showered at the end of the day, so all I'll need to do is let the committee know all the times I was there and they'll be able to prove that Kat was also there at those times. It's not exactly a smoking gun, but maybe they'll be able to check CCTV to see who went in and out of the changing rooms when I was in there showering. There can only be a small number of potential suspects, and Kat is going to be top of that list. Gloria Hutchinson won't be happy to learn that she's acted this way.

I glance back over my shoulder to fall in line with Thea, but suddenly my foot catches on something, and then I'm rapidly flying forwards, my pulse racing as my mind instantly prepares for impact. My arms shoot out to protect my face, and as I see the concrete racing up to meet me, it's my right knee that connects with it first, and I yelp as I feel a burning sensation tear through my flesh. I scream out in agony as the runners behind do their best to hop, jump and skip around me, so they don't join me in a heap. I don't attempt to stand until they've passed, and wince as I bend my right arm to examine the bloody gash on my elbow. I blow at the grit, and use the bottom of my vest to dab it clean.

I see race stewards approaching and Thea appears at my side, offering to help me to my feet, but I tell her to keep running. She looks pained to leave me, so I force a smile and tell her I'll be fine.

I wait until she's moved on before turning over to examine my knee. The sweat on my legs has already made the blood run down to my sock, and the air blowing against the open wound makes it sting.

The two race stewards ask me if I'm okay, and whether or not I bumped my head. I assure them that I didn't, but one of them is keen to call a paramedic to my aid. I tell him I don't need attention, but as they try to lift me to my feet, I can't help but cry out. I'm grateful there are no spectators in this part of the race, so they won't have witnessed the embarrassment of my fall. I look down to try to see what caught me, but there are no obvious obstacles in the road that my foot could have connected with. I guess maybe one foot struck the other because I wasn't paying attention, but I really don't know.

The stewards escort me to the side of the road where there are security barriers despite the lack of crowd.

I can still just about make out Thea and the others further up the road. The longer I stay here, the less chance I'll have of getting back to their pace. This fall and injury really is the last straw. I have spent the day battling against fate, but maybe it would just be easier to give in and admit defeat.

I'm about to relay this message to the race stewards when I hear someone calling my name.

32

Monday, 26 February 2024, Brixton, London

Molly stifles a yawn as the tube train reaches the station and the doors beep open. She scans the faces of the passengers in her carriage, checking for the final time that none of them look familiar or are paying her undue attention, before turning and exiting the train. The air is warm and humid on the platform, but she takes a seat on a bench, and waits until the rest of the alighting passengers have headed for the exit sign before she tightens the pack on her back and limps towards the escalators up to street level.

It's been four days since her tight calf muscle forced her to stop training, and although she's supposed to be laid up in bed resting it, the fire at the flats this morning has given her a new mission. It took the fire brigade until 8 a.m. to extinguish the flames and another hour until the building was declared structurally sound, and the residents allowed to return. Those on the top floor, closest to where the fire began, have been told to collect valuables and relocated to temporary accommodation until a cleaning crew can put in necessary fixes.

The whole place smelled like burnt toast, and any desire to return to sleep was quickly dispelled by the sound of everyone else having to get ready for work. Having been on edge for six hours, certain her stalker was the one who led her from the building, Molly opened her laptop and began searching for the doorbell camera's footage of the night's events. It was what she found that had her begging Detective Zara Freeman for an urgent meeting.

Freeman said she would be at court first thing, but told Molly to come to the station just after lunch. So, with her laptop in her backpack, she took the two trains to get to Brixton, but the strapping around her leg is doing little to limit the pain, and so her trajectory up to street level is slow and laboured.

She messaged Finn to explain she wouldn't be able to make it to her physio appointment until later this afternoon due to a personal issue, and without delving into the detail, he promised to pass on the message. He probably thinks she's trying to avoid bumping into him after her attempt to kiss him last week, and maybe on some subconscious level he's right. He hasn't attempted to discuss the incident with her, and maybe that's because rebuffing the advances of his athletes is commonplace for him. Making the first move certainly isn't routine for Molly, and she's still not over the pain of his rejection. She understands that there are rules in place, but surely if they were discreet, they could get away with it? Unless, of course, he just isn't interested in a relationship with her, and blaming the rules was his way of trying to let her down gently. She hadn't thought of it like that before, but is now convinced that's probably the more likely reason.

Either that, or he's already embarked on something clandestine with one of the other athletes, or Thea's coach even. She was certainly being a bit too friendly, even flirtatious, with him. And yet Thea and Jamie both suggested that Finn was into her, so either they're both off, or he really is just keeping her at a professional arm's length. Ultimately, he didn't say he didn't want to kiss her back, so maybe there's hope for something more once the Paris games are complete; assuming she makes it that far.

Reaching Brixton Police Station, Molly has a knot in her stomach that she can't ignore. She reported fake-Oppenheimer to the police weeks ago, and despite her obvious fears – it's clear he knows where she lives – they've done nothing to stop him. And last night he was close enough to her that he could have done anything and nobody would be any the wiser as to his identity.

She needs to share the camera footage with them. This isn't a movie, and she doesn't have the resources to catch this guy on her own.

As she heads in through the door, she recognises the young officer behind the windowed desk from when she was here over a month ago. If he recognises her, he doesn't show it. She explains she has an appointment with DC Freeman, and he asks her to take a seat while he lets Freeman know she's arrived. Ten minutes pass, and then Freeman appears at the secured door, beckoning Molly to follow her through.

The corridor is much darker and cooler than the front desk, and as they move further into the belly of the station, Molly can't escape the feeling that she's done something wrong.

Freeman leads her to an interview suite, where she invites her to sit and explain the purpose of the meeting. Molly tells her about the fire last night, and how she'd tried and been unable to escape her flat at first, and how, fearing she'd be suffocated, she managed to get out.

'And that's when I saw him. Only... I didn't realise who he was at first. I thought he was a fireman because of how he was dressed, but he was there before the fire engine had parked up, and rather than joining the others, he disappeared into the darkness.'

'Slow down, Molly,' Freeman says, scribbling notes on a pad. 'Who did you see?'

'The person who's been terrorising me.'

Freeman's eyebrows knot with confusion. 'You saw your stalker?'

'Yes.'

'At your flat?'

'Outside, but yes.'

'Can you describe him to me?'

'I didn't see his face... at least, I didn't look at his face because I thought he was a fireman, and I was just so relieved that someone had come to help me.'

'Where was he when you saw him?'

'In the corridor, but I now know he was outside my flat, and he's the reason I couldn't get the door open.'

Freeman looks flummoxed again. 'You think this man – this fireman – was blocking your door in some way?'

Molly nods, but doesn't speak. Instead, she slides the pack from her shoulders. Unzipping the bag, she extracts her laptop, and opens the lid, turning it to face Freeman.

'What's this?'

Molly presses play, and the black and white footage from the doorbell fills the screen: floods of half-dressed people pouring past the field of view, before a figure in a helmet and dark coat approaches the door.

'Is there any sound?' Freeman asks.

'It's muted because all you can hear is the fire alarm sounding. Watch what he does.'

Freeman leans closer to the screen. The man's face is obscured by the helmet, but what looks like a grainy hand grabs hold of the door handle for what appears to be at least two minutes, and the figure's head leans closer to the door as if he's listening in. He eventually releases the handle and disappears from view, and a moment later the door opens, and Molly emerges, hurrying out of shot.

'I tried to open my door several times and it wouldn't budge,' she explains. 'I tried breaking my window as well, and then finally the door opened and he approached me as I made it to the end of the corridor.' She takes a deep breath. 'I believe this is the man who has been messaging me online, the same man who had the trainers delivered to my dressing room at Broadcasting House, and the same person who started the fire in the upstairs flat.'

'You believe?'

'How else do you explain this guy's behaviour?'

Freeman lowers her pen, her brow furrowing as she tries to work out the best way to answer the question. 'Honestly, what you've shown me looks like a fireman trying to get into your flat to offer help while all hell breaks loose around him. I'm not dismissing what you're saying, but there's nothing conclusive in this.'

'He doesn't come from outside, though,' Molly continues, prepared for the challenge. 'Watch again, and you'll see he comes from the opposite direction of the other people. He isn't coming from outside; he must have emerged from upstairs somewhere.'

Freeman replays the footage, and scribbles the note down. 'That doesn't mean he started the fire. For all I know, he came past your flat to go and knock on all the other doors first.'

'I checked the footage, and found this.'

Molly opens a second file. A large man in a similar dark coat, carrying a holdall, but without a helmet, moves past the camera, pausing momentarily to stare at the door, before moving on.

'This was half an hour before the alarm went off. I think he came past, went upstairs, started the fire and came back down.'

'Not as far as I'm aware. I want you to find him, because I'm telling you that he was determined to keep me trapped in my flat for as long as possible.'

Molly can't contain her relief, finally feeling as though she's getting back some control of her life.

33

NOW

21 April 2024, Shadwell, London – Mile 15

There is a figure standing beyond the barrier, but I can't see who it is at first as my view is blocked by one of the stewards. It takes all my effort to strain my neck so I can see.

'Finn? What are you doing here?'

'Are you okay? I saw you trip.'

The stewards are eyeing him suspiciously until I inform them he's my coach. They prop me against the railings while they go in search of a First Aid kit.

'I'm done,' I tell him, and there's a sense of relief in admitting defeat.

Finn leaps over the barrier and then lowers himself to his knees to examine my leg. Wrapping his warm hands around my calf, he starts to manoeuvre my leg backwards and forwards.

'Does this hurt?'

I wince, biting down, and nod.

'The good news is it isn't broken,' he says, offering a smile and a wink. 'You'll live.'

The shock-induced adrenaline is starting to dissipate, and my heart rate is returning to a more regular rhythm. I look up to the road and can just about see the group I was leading, and it's like watching sand slipping between my fingers.

One of the race stewards returns, and Finn snatches the First Aid kit from him and cleans my wounds, before strapping plasters over them. He moves with such speed that I can still make out the last runner in the pack.

'On your way then,' he tells me, hopping back over the barrier as if it isn't even there.

'I told you: I'm done.'

'No, you're not.'

My brow creases. 'I am. What is the point in trying to fight the inevitable? Between Bistras and fate, I just can't take any more.'

'The Molly Fitzhume I know isn't a quitter.'

'Yes, she is.'

'No, you're not. Five months ago, you up and left your home to move to an unfamiliar city to train for an event despite an injury that others would have retired after. You've shown me more determination than anyone I've ever met, and the one thing I know to be true is that you *will* start running again today. But the longer you leave it, the harder it will be to catch back up with the others.'

'They're already way too far ahead—'

'Rubbish! You can still catch them, Molly. You have eleven miles to make up the time, and you're more than capable.'

'But my knee—'

'Is just cut and bruised. You've run through worse injuries.'

I look back up the road as the last runner disappears from view. To my right, the first of the straggler pack has just appeared, and they will catch up to us within ninety seconds.

'But my stalker—'

'Listen, I will be at the sidelines keeping you safe. Okay? I won't let anything bad happen to you, which is why I am not going to allow you to throw in the towel. We all fall sometimes, Molly, but we do it so we can learn to stand up and carry on.'

I try bending my plastered knee, and it stings, but it bears my weight.

'You will never forgive yourself if you give up now. Your split times are good, and despite this little rest stop, you can still bring it home inside the qualifying time. I really care about you, Molly, and I can't let you give up on your dream.'

His face is so close to mine that I'm not certain he isn't about to kiss me, but he must realise this because he takes a step backwards.

'What about Kat, though? If she finishes ahead of me, the qualifying time won't matter.'

'You don't need to worry about Kat. Just focus on finishing the race. Trust me!'

Deep down, I know he's right: I won't forgive myself if I quit now.

'You can't afford any more stoppages.' He hands me a glucose gel pack and two painkillers. 'Take these and focus on your breathing. Remember how much you used to love running, and get back to that. I know you can catch them.'

I squeeze the glucose gel into my mouth and down the painkillers, and hand both packs back to him.

'I'll meet you at the next water bottle stand in just over five minutes. Get going.'

I take a deep breath and push myself away from the barrier. My right knee throbs with every step forwards, but I force the pain from my mind, breaking into an uneasy jog, until I'm comfortable with the level of pain. It will be a while until the painkillers kick in, but the ache serves as a reminder that nothing good comes without hard work.

The enforced rest stop has done more good than bad, and my body doesn't feel as tired as it did before. I slowly increase my pace, conscious of the stragglers gaining on me. I must be at least two minutes behind the others in front, but Finn is right that they are catchable if I can run fast enough. The sun is now hidden behind a wave of fresh cloud, and the relief from the heat is welcome. In fact, as I look up at the horizon, I can see darker clouds approaching too, so there's a real chance we'll see more rain before the race ends.

I call Zara again on my watch, but there's still no answer. I can't tell whether she's seen the last picture message I sent, of me in the shower, and I can only hope that she has and has already contacted the security team at the Team GB training facility to work out who could have taken it. I think about all the times when I thought I was being watched in the building and how dismissive Zara was after Bistras's arrest. I don't think she thought I was lying, but just getting carried away. Well, that picture proves it wasn't all in my head.

Her answerphone kicks in again.

'Zara, did you see my message? He's threatening to release compromising photos of me if I don't quit the race. I need you to come and protect me. Please? Phone me back.'

Ahead of me is a motorcycle and cameraman, but from this distance I can't see whether he's wearing mirrored Aviators. I am all alone on this stretch of road, and although there are occasional race stewards in their high-visibility coats, it would be so easy for Bistras or whoever to make their move on me now. Finn said he'd meet me at the next water station, but that's not until after the next mile marker.

I don't like how isolating this section of the course is. Where are all the spectators? Maybe I'd be safer allowing the stragglers to catch up with me; there's safety in numbers, after all. But to do so would mean not hitting the qualifying time.

The noise in my head is just so loud that it's impossible to concentrate on any one string of thought. Oh, what I would give to be back in Dumbarton, running through the tall grass, the cool wind on my face; knowing where all the rises and dips are, and able to leap over or round each one.

The road ahead looks flat and clear, so I allow my eyes to close and focus on my breathing. In through my nose, deep into my lungs, and then exhaling through my mouth. In and down, and then out. Right foot, left foot, right foot, left foot. It's just about finding the right rhythm. I can picture the Dumbarton hills, and for a moment I'm transported back there; back to a time when running was just about the joy of escaping my monotonous life. Somewhere along the way, I've forgotten how much fun running can be. Although competition can add welcome pressure, it becomes more goal-orientated, and less enjoyable.

I cautiously open one eye to check for obstacles, before snapping it shut, almost able to feel the tall grasses tickling my knees as I run through them. I can feel the smile breaking across my face. The wind blows through my hair, and I finally feel at peace. My mind empties of all my fears, and I am one with the world.

My concentration is broken when my headband erupts in a cacophony of noise. If it's Bistras's withheld number, I won't answer it, but when I glance at my watch, I see Zara's name and relief washes over me. However, the respite is short-lived, when I hear the fear in Zara's voice.

'Your tip-off was correct: Bistras *has* escaped.'

34

BEFORE

Molly keeps her head down, pumping her arms, her breathing fast but steady. Music is blaring through her ear buds, blocking out all background noise, allowing her to focus on maintaining her rhythm. In the two weeks since she pulled up with a tight calf muscle, she has followed the strict exercise regime set by her physio, worked out in the swimming pool every day, applied heat and ice interchangeably and today is her first time back on the track. Finn had said they would take it easy with a five-mile stretch, with six-minute miles, but she's been gradually increasing her pace, determined to test the calf muscle fully.

It just feels good to be back outside, though the thick band of grey cloud overhead suggests rain could be due imminently. The predicted forecast for the race itself – only forty days away now – is for mild and dry conditions, but that is subject to change, and she hopes it will at least be dry. She's run marathons in the rain before, and whilst not as bad as overbearing heat, the calmer the conditions, the better.

She glances over at Finn, who is waving to say she's completed her fifth mile, but she ignores the gesture and continues running. Her leg feels good, and she's already several weeks behind schedule, so stopping now just seems counter-productive. At least he's on his own out here. Every time she's seen him since he rejected her advances, he's made sure to have someone else in the room with him; usually the physio. There is logic to the physio being included in discussions relating to Molly's training – especially while recovering from injury – but Molly can't help thinking Finn doesn't want to be alone with her in case she tries to come on to him again. She wouldn't, not after he made his feelings abundantly clear, and she misses the easy-going banter they used to share. Everything is just too formal now, and she's wondered about requesting Finn be replaced, but to do so would mean to have to request a replacement from the Head of the Olympic Committee herself: Gloria Hutchinson. And then Molly would have to explain why she is struggling to work with Finn, and that could threaten her potential place on the team.

'Come on, Molly, let's not aggravate the injury,' Finn calls to her, as she passes him again.

She doesn't acknowledge his request, pretending she didn't hear it.

Up ahead, she sees Kat warming up, and suddenly the idea of staying out on the track isn't as appealing. When Molly passes, Kat glares back at her. They haven't spoken since the night when Molly's drink was spiked, but she's remained true to her word and hasn't named any of the other athletes who were also at the club, and so far no drug tests have been requested. Not that Molly would be in any danger if she had to do a test now. Thea has suggested Molly just keep out of Kat's way, but that's also meant Molly hasn't seen much of Thea either.

As Molly comes around the final bend, Finn steps out onto the track and waves her down, forcing her to slow. There's no way to pretend she hasn't seen him, and so she stops beside him.

'Couldn't you hear me shouting?' he says as she removes her ear buds, and she just shrugs. 'How is the leg feeling?'

'Yeah, fine,' she says, trying to get her breath back. 'I could keep going.'

'Let's not push it, okay? The plan is to increase your mileage every day until you get back to twenty, and then we'll see where we go from there.'

She follows him from the track, back into the NAS building, and to his office where the physio is already waiting by the massage table.

'Any twinges?' she asks, when Molly has lain down and lowered her tracksuit bottoms.

'No, it feels good.'

The physio slowly moves her hands along the muscle, checking for tenderness and inflammation. Molly can see Finn over by his desk, his eyes averted, but is that intentional? He could leave the room, but has chosen to stay. Molly can't get to grips with his mixed signals.

His phone rings, and when he's answered it, he stares directly at her, forcing Molly's cheeks to blaze and her to look away.

'There's an officer from the Met Police here to see you,' Finn says.

'Me?' Molly asks, uncertain which of them he is speaking to.

'Yeah. Tell me I shouldn't be worried. If Gloria gets any hint of impropriety—'

'What do you take me for? I haven't done anything wrong.'

A knock at the door is followed by one of the reception team escorting Detective Freeman into the room. She shows her identification to Finn and the physio and asks them to leave. Finn gives Molly a troubled look, but she mouths for him not to worry.

'I tried calling you,' Freeman says, when they're alone, 'but you didn't answer, so then I tried calling at your flat, but you weren't home, so I figured you'd probably be here.'

Molly pulls up her tracksuit bottoms, and swings her legs over the side of the massage table. 'What's so important?'

'Well, there's two things actually. First, I should give you the good news: I've found your mystery fireman.'

Molly leaps from the table and hurries to her, not willing to trust what she heard. 'You found him?'

Freeman nods. 'Yep.'

'And? Who is he?'

'I can't give you his name, for reasons that I will come on to, but we were able to use facial recognition to make an identification. The man in question isn't from the UK, and doesn't have a criminal record here, but he does have something of a chequered history in his native Lithuania. Interpol have an outstanding warrant for him, in fact.'

Molly's mouth drops open. 'For what?'

'I can't divulge that either.'

'You've arrested him for the fire and sending the messages?'

Freeman shakes her head. 'I cannot say for certain that the man in question is responsible for the messages you've received, as that isn't something I'm able to investigate directly.' Molly opens her mouth to interrupt, but Freeman speaks over her. 'I have referred your case to our cyber-crime team, and they will be taking that side of the investigation forwards. You'll need to provide your phone to them so they can do what they need to do. It's only temporary, but once they've downloaded all the necessary data, you'll get the phone back.'

'So where is he now? In custody?'

Freeman shakes her head again. 'Unfortunately, whilst the video clips you sent me can be tied to the person in question, because they were obtained illegally, we're not able to prosecute him with what happened at your flat.'

'Obtained illegally? They were taken from the camera in my doorbell.'

'Exactly. A camera that is recording people's movements without their knowledge. I'm afraid to say, because the filming is outside the boundary of your property, and there are no signs warning passers-by that they're being recorded, the footage captured is in breach of data privacy law. Did you fit the doorbell yourself?'

'No, a friend did. Well, a friend's brother.'

'They usually put stickers in with these doorbell cameras and it would have said to put one up, but I've checked your flat and there's no such sticker or notice. That's the bad news. I have to formally tell you that you either need to take down the camera, or put up a notice to warn others. You also need to destroy any footage captured to date, or risk being sued by anyone you've recorded.'

Molly stares back at her blankly, waiting for a punchline that isn't going to arrive. 'I don't understand. So, have you arrested him or not?'

'I have spoken to the man in question. He was arrested due to the outstanding Interpol warrant, and is being deported in the coming days. However, we are not able to charge him with anything here.'

'Then what was the point? You think this will stop him? He managed to get into the country before without being stopped, so what's to stop him coming back?'

Freeman sighs. 'I understand your frustration, Molly, and I

appreciate that this isn't the news you wanted to hear, but it's out of my hands.'

'Tell me his name. I want to know who's been stalking me for the last four months.'

'I'm sorry, I'm not allowed to give you his name.'

'But what about the fire he started?'

'It is believed that the fire started as a result of a cigarette left unattended, probably by someone squatting. Fire investigators have been over the scene and there is no physical evidence tying the man in question to the flat.'

'But on the video he comes from the direction of the stairs.'

'Even if the video hadn't been obtained illegally, it doesn't place him in that room or even upstairs. I'm sorry, Molly, I know how much you want it to be him—'

'I just want this to be over.'

'Then, my advice to you is to move out of the flat. Find somewhere else to live that's low-key, and keep your head down.'

Despite Freeman's reassurances that fake-Oppenheimer is leaving the country, Molly is certain it won't be the last she hears from him.

35

NOW

21 April 2024, Canary Wharf, London – Mile 16

I want to tell Zara that I already know Bistras has escaped, having seen the headline in the German newspaper, but I allow her to speak first, so I can continue running. I scour the faces of the few gathered spectators, searching for him.

'I just heard back from my counterpart in Berlin,' she continues, breathlessly. 'She said he was being transported to a new prison, and there was some kind of mix-up – she was vague on the detail – but the transport vehicle never reached its destination. Whilst there is no reason to panic—'

'No reason to panic? *He is here!* I've been telling you all day that he's back.'

'His passport was confiscated when he was charged, so travel out of Germany is going to be all but impossible. There's no reason to leap to the conclusion that he's returned to the UK.'

'Other than to kill me, you mean?'

The phone line crackles as Zara sighs loudly. 'I understand your fear, but logic tells me that he is far more likely to be hiding out in Germany, or trying to return to Lithuania. He knows the authorities at every port are looking for him, and he is unlikely to attempt to flee the country.'

She isn't listening to me, and I'm struggling to contain my growing anger and frustration. 'And what if you're wrong? What if he's already out of the country, and in London to finish me off?'

'I don't think that is the case—'

'He's been messaging me, and left the plant outside my room.'

'He wasn't outside your room at The Clarendon. I had a friend view the hotel's CCTV footage, and the person who left the blue orchid didn't match Bistras's description.'

I'm thrown by this statement, and I can't tell if she's just saying it in an attempt to make me feel better.

'But it must have been him. He left me a message on a card just like he left in my dressing room at the television studio.'

'Well, unless he's lost a shedload of weight, it wasn't him. From what I've been told, the figure who left the plant was tall and thin.'

'But you have his face? You can run a trace, right?'

'He was wearing a motorbike helmet, so no, but either way, it wasn't Bistras outside your door.'

'A motorbike helmet? So it was a delivery man? That doesn't mean Bistras didn't set it up. He probably hired the guy to leave it there, *exactly* like he did at the television studio. Don't you see the pattern here?'

'Molly, nobody is taking your feelings for granted, especially not me. That is why I wanted to phone you straight away. Whilst I firmly don't believe your life is in danger, I think it would be safer for you to withdraw from the race and wait with one of the stewards until I can get an officer to your location. There are police on site, and if you let me know which marker you're near, I'll have an officer meet you there.'

I feel my head shaking as I continue to run, still looking at the segments of spectators. 'No, you have to come here and find him. I've trained too hard and for too long to let him stop me. I'm not giving up on my dream because of him.'

'I am on my way, Molly, but I don't want you taking unnecessary risks.'

'If I don't finish this race, I can kiss goodbye to the Olympics.'

'I'm sure the selection committee would understand if we explained why you need to withdraw.'

I can picture Gloria Hutchinson's face, trying to cover her sheer delight that I won't be competing.

'Not an option,' I say firmly. 'They can't make exceptions, and excuses won't help. I need to prove I've recovered from my back injury and that I won't let the team down in Paris. I *have* to finish this race. I need you to find Bistras and arrest him.'

'I will do my best, but do you know the expression looking for a needle in a haystack?' She sighs again. 'Okay, here's what we'll do: I will get Bistras's face sent to every officer already on site, so they know who to look out for; that should help narrow the search. What mile are you up to?'

'Approaching the Mile 16 marker soon.'

'Good, okay, well, if you haven't seen him already, we know to focus our attention on the miles between you and the finish line. What area are you in?'

I look around me for any obvious landmarks, but can only see a pharmacy and estate agents.

'Somewhere between Canary Wharf and the Thames? Hold on.' I scan the road ahead of me. 'Wait, there's a school coming up.' I squint as I try to read the name and have to accelerate to bring the words into focus. 'The Arnhem Wharf Primary School.'

'Okay, give me a second, I'll try and see where you are on a map... It's coming through now. You're on Westferry Road. Oh, Jesus, you're about as far from the finish line as you could be. It really doesn't narrow the search as much as I was hoping.'

'He's definitely here. He sent me a picture message of me being sick at the side of the road, which he took, so he can't be too far away. He's sent threatening messages as well, telling me to withdraw from the race or he'll publish topless pictures of me. If I quit the race, he wins.'

'I've seen the messages you forwarded. Can you give me the number he's sent them from, so we can try and trace his location?'

'The number is withheld every time.'

'Shit! Okay, what about when he phones? You said something about a laughing voice?'

'The number is still withheld, and I think it must be a recording as it sounds exactly like when he phoned me that night after training. He wants me to know it's him doing this to me.'

'Are you running in a group?'

'No, I'm on my own at the moment. I fell over – it's a long story.'

'Is there anyone nearby you *can* run with? I'm just thinking he's less likely to act if there's a witness or witnesses around.'

Despite my increased speed, the road is twisty, and the pack ahead are nowhere in sight.

'I'll do my best to catch up with someone.'

'Good. Listen, Molly, I'm sorry I didn't take your concern seriously earlier. It's been one hell of a night here, and I thought you were... it doesn't matter what I thought. What's important now is that we keep you safe. I've asked my counterpart in Berlin to keep me posted on any updates as to whether they catch up with him, and will keep you posted. Without a passport, he won't be able to leave the country, but that doesn't mean he doesn't have the ability to get hold of false travel documentation, so we can't rule anything out.'

It's a relief to know she's on my side, and that I'm not just losing my mind. With everyone insisting that he couldn't be behind this, I was starting to believe I was crazy, or that he had an accomplice, but now I know he's just a twisted sociopath, and for some reason that brings a level of calm to my mind.

'If you see anything suspicious, you need to get to safety and phone me straight back. I am on my way, but it's going to take a while to get to your location with all the diversions in place.'

I thank her and end the call.

There should be a water stand after the next marker, and knowing that Finn will be there to make sure Bistras can't interfere with my bottle again is good news.

I continue to puff out my cheeks, and pump my arms as I focus back on just getting along the road. I need to push all thoughts of Bistras from my mind. Zara is on the case, and she will stop him. There are blocks of flats and local businesses lining both sides of the pavement, and small groups of spectators gathered at various points – no large crowds. My knee isn't even aching as much as it was before. In truth, I'd forgotten all about it while speaking to Zara, so hopefully the painkillers Finn gave me are doing their job.

A smattering of applause breaks my concentration, and when I open my eyes to check for obstacles, I see there is a crowd of five or six spectators ahead, near a traffic camera.

And then my gaze falls on Otto Bistras standing behind them.

36

BEFORE

*Sunday, 24 March 2024, National Sports Centre, Crystal Palace,
London*

With only four weeks to go until the marathon, Molly is
determined to reach her target of twenty-six miles. Finn is still
discouraging her from pushing herself too much, but his priority
isn't her making the qualifying time for Paris. So, although he'd
capped her running time to ten miles this morning, as soon as he
left for the day, she went back out onto the track and managed to
put in another ten. So she's quietly pleased with herself for getting
a twenty-mile stint under her belt, even if it did have to be
completed in two sessions with a warm down in between.

Finn is still insisting that she take whole-day breaks between
practice runs, out of fear that she may trigger either injury, but in
truth her back has never felt better, and although there is still
some tenderness in her calf, her physio's post-run massages are
helping with that. She is so close to her goal now that she can

practically taste it. With so little time left to achieve her dream, she has to push herself.

She would speak to Finn about the reasons for his reticence, but he still refuses to be alone with her, and their professional relationship has become stilted as a result. She should be free to discuss anything relating to her running with him, but she no longer has confidence that he has her best interests at heart. When they started working together, it was agreed that he would help her reach a point where she could achieve the necessary qualifying time, but now it's as if he doubts she'll succeed, and therefore doesn't want to waste his time. Either that, or he's being too cautious with the calf strain.

The sky is darkening by the time she makes it back to the NAS building, and when she checks her watch, she isn't surprised it's after six. Sunday operating hours means the building will be closed up by seven, so she has less than an hour to get showered and changed before security comes asking questions. There are no other athletes or staff about as far as she can tell and she heads towards the changing rooms, though with her ear buds still in, she can't hear any other sound anyway.

The changing room is empty and there's no obvious sign anyone else is about as all the lockers are closed and no clothing or towels have been left out. Removing her ear buds, she strips down and ties a fresh towel around her chest. Another benefit of showering in the NAS building is that they launder all the towels.

After shutting her clothes and valuables in locker seven – her favourite number – Molly heads into the shower area. All are vacant, so she chooses the one furthest away, with the protection of three solid walls. She pulls the curtain across and switches on the tap. A burst of hot water erupts from the shower head and she steps into the spray, slowly allowing her shoulders to unwind.

She lathers shampoo on her head, but freezes when she hears

a door slamming nearby. She'd swear that was the door to the changing room. She quickly washes the shampoo out of her eyes and hair, and switches off the shower, straining to hear anything else, any sound of movement, or any indication about who came or left the changing room. She was certain she was the only one here, but didn't check the toilets. It's possible that someone could have been sitting quietly in one of the cubicles, but given the fact that Molly thought she was alone, she now feels uneasy about who may still be around.

She didn't hear the door go twice, which means either someone was in here and left, or they're still here now. Reaching for her towel, she heads out of the shower area, now checking all of the toilet cubicles, but finding all the doors open, and none in use. Back in the changing area, everything looks as it was before. Molly can't prevent her paranoia piquing, and returns to the shower area and toilets to double-check. There are no obvious hiding places, but she inspects every nook and cranny just in case.

'Hello?' she calls out, surprised by the apparent fear in her own voice.

She stands still and listens, but nobody responds.

'Hello?' she tries again. 'Is there somebody else in here?'

Still no answer. She performs her check of the showers and toilets again, this time in reverse, and finds herself back in the changing area, without finding anyone.

Too freaked out to hang around, she decides it's time to get dressed and get back home.

Opening the door to the locker, she starts when she sees the A5 white envelope with her name scrawled on the front. She steps backwards, as if the envelope itself could be contaminated in some way. She's certain it wasn't in her locker when she put her phone and wallet away minutes earlier. She would have noticed it, surely? So how has it now appeared? She had to use her key to open the locker, and that hasn't left her possession, so how could anyone else have left the envelope?

She checks behind her, suddenly feeling as though she's being watched.

This can't be happening again.

And yet the envelope is there. In her locker. With her name on it.

Snatching the envelope, she turns it over in her hands, before ripping into it and sliding out a small card. The breath catches in her throat as she reads the printed message.

BEST OF LUCK AT THE RACE.
I'M RIGHT BEHIND YOU.
XXX

He's here. Somewhere. He left this for her.

With the tears now beginning to fall, she reaches for her phone, locates Freeman's private number and dials. Freeman answers on the third ring, and Molly quickly explains what's happened, how her stalker is back, as she'd feared he would be.

'That's impossible, Molly. The man we saw outside your flat is in Germany as we speak. He was found guilty of multiple stalking offences on Friday. He's been sentenced to years behind bars.'

'But he was here. He left this message.'

'He couldn't have, Molly. If it helps put your mind at ease, I will tell you his name – off the record, you understand, but so you can Google him yourself and see that I'm telling the truth. The man you recorded outside your flat was identified as Otto Bistras. A Lithuanian incel that the German police have been chasing for years after a number of models, athletes, singers and actors accused him of sending lewd messages to them. Sound familiar? He's under investigation for similar offences in separate cases in

Sweden and Italy as well. I have no doubt that the man who was stalking you is Bistras, and that he won't be bothering you any more.'

'But if he didn't leave this message, then who did?'

Molly blurts out the question before she's even had time to consider the options. Does he have an accomplice; someone to do his bidding now that he's been caught? But who? And why? What sick enjoyment does he get out of terrorising someone in this way?

'The National Academy of Sport has CCTV, right?' Freeman counters.

'Only at reception. There are no cameras in the changing rooms for privacy reasons.'

'But the security team is still there now, right?'

'Um, yes, well I suppose they must be.'

'Then I suggest you go and report this incident to them. Maybe they know who else is still inside the building.'

Molly agrees and dresses quickly, but keeps both eyes on the door into the changing rooms throughout. When she's locked her locker and put her backpack straps over her shoulders she goes to leave, but is stopped by a troubling thought: what if the security guard left the message? If it's just the two of them left in the building, the last thing she should do is rely on him, or spend any more time than is necessary in his presence. So, as soon as she makes it to the reception desk, she scans her way through the barriers, wishes him good night and runs through the doors, not stopping to look back over her shoulder in case he's right behind her.

37

NOW

21 April 2024, Mudchute, London – Mile 17

My heart is in my throat and I can't breathe. I can see the monster who has haunted my dreams and he is staring in my direction. I want to run away – in any direction that will take me away from him – but my fight or flight instinct won't kick in. I blink several times, thinking my mind is playing tricks on me, but I am almost certain it's him.

He's standing behind a group of six who are dressed in navy overalls, and who I'm assuming have just emerged from the gated factory behind them. Is he with them? No, as I stare longer at the group, I see he is a couple of metres behind, using them as some kind of shield.

I don't think he's noticed me yet, so I slow, and dart behind a wall that is jutting out. I take several breaths, and attempt to dial Zara, but the line goes to voicemail.

'He's here,' I whisper, though I'm not entirely sure why as he shouldn't be able to hear me from here. 'I'm still on Westferry Road, near some kind of furniture manufacturer. I need you here.'

I end the call, but my whole body is shaking, and I don't think it's the exhaustion from running. I can't believe he's here. This is the one thing I've been dreading since opening the door to my hotel room this morning, though deep down I've been secretly hoping Zara was right and I *have* been overreacting.

Wiping the sweat from my temple, I brush stray hairs out of the way, and slowly poke my head back around the edge of the wall. The group is still there and one or two are pointing towards the wall, presumably discussing where I've disappeared to. I can't see Bistras from here, but I dare not move any further forwards. If I can't see him, then he can't see me, and that feels like the safest conclusion for now.

But I can't stay in hiding forever. Finn said I could still catch Kat so long as there are no more unnecessary stops, but I can see the seconds slipping away before my eyes. If I stay here much longer, I will blow my remaining chance of qualification, and he will win. But if I rejoin the race and he sees me, there's no knowing what he will do, and if he is intending to harm me, he will still win.

I look back along the road from where I've just come, but I can't see any race stewards. I did pass one when I was speaking to Zara, but I can't remember how far back that was. I've no doubt there will be more further ahead, but I'll need to get past Bistras to reach them.

I try Zara again, without success, so I dial Finn's number.

'Hey, I've just made it to the water station. Where are you?' he says excitedly.

'I'm between the sixteenth- and seventeenth-mile markers.'

There's a pause. 'Okay, you're going to want to up your pace a little more if you can manage.'

'I can't,' I whisper.

'Okay, well, maybe you just need some more liquid hydration. Is it your knee slowing you down?'

I glance back at the group, but I still can't see Bistras behind them, so I duck back behind the wall.

'He's here, Finn.'

'Who's where?'

'Bistras,' I grizzle. 'My stalker. He's at the side of the road.'

'Jesus! You're sure it's him?'

'Certain.'

'Oh, God, can you alert one of the race stewards?'

'There are none nearby.'

'What's he doing? Has he threatened you?'

I bury my face in my hands. 'I don't think he's seen me yet. I'm hiding behind a wall near a shuttered sandwich shop. I'm scared, Finn. I don't know what to do.'

He doesn't reply at first, and I hate being this vulnerable in front of him, but I can't contain the tremors in my hands.

'Listen, I'm probably about three minutes away from you. I'll come to you now, but I'll have to try and navigate around obstacles. Can you stay where you are?'

If I lose another three minutes, I will never recover the time, and so if I wait for Finn I might as well just withdraw from the race.

I blink away the tears as my vision blurs. I'm not prepared to let him beat me.

I tell Finn to stay where he is and end the call. I take a long, deep breath to compose myself, and then sprint out from behind the wall. My eyes immediately dart to the group of workers in their overalls, and I can see the hulking figure of Bistras moving away from them, his back to me. It's possible I can run past without him noticing, but how long will it be until he comes for me again? I can't spend the rest of the race jumping at every shadow, fearing the inevitable.

I have to take a stand!

Clamping my jaw tight, I veer to the left, and pump my arms as fast as I can, balling my fists, and focusing my gaze on one thing: the retreating Bistras.

I scream out in a guttural roar when I am only metres from him, and then I leap into the air, just as he starts to turn, but he's too late, and I land on his back, driving him into the metal struts of the heavy-duty fence enclosing the factory beyond it. We crumple to the floor, but I manage to maintain my advantage, sitting astride his right arm, while he blindly flaps and panics beneath me. His body mass is significantly larger than my own, and I have to battle to keep him on the floor. With my hands still balled, I pummel his chest and back, catching his chin in the process. He yelps in fear, but I don't relent.

A moment later there are pairs of hands on me, trying to drag me off him, but I shake myself free and continue to hit him wherever I can. Again, the hands come, and this time they do manage to drag me clear and I now see that the two men holding on to me are from the group of factory workers. They're holding my arms firm as if *I'm* the villain in this scenario.

I glare at Bistras, as he plants his hands on the pavement, and tries to push himself up.

'Grab him, not me!' I tell my captors. 'He's a criminal.'

They exchange glances, uncertain what to do, and in their defence, I can see why they would have doubts about him being the aggressor in this situation.

'Phone the police,' I yell at one of them, a woman who appears to be recording the whole episode on her phone. 'His name is Otto Bistras, and he's the son of a bitch who's been stalking me for the last five months. Don't let him escape!'

Bistras is now back on his feet and is brushing dirt and dust from his trousers. He straightens and looks at me, and that's the moment I realise what a horrendous mistake I've made. The man staring back at me looks terrified, and although his hair is parted in the same way as Bistras's, this man's hair is white, rather than platinum, and his glasses are bifocals, rather than the square rims I was sure I saw.

How could I have got it so wrong?

Now that I can see the man up close, it's obvious he isn't Otto Bistras, but I was so certain that's who I saw, that I now scan the immediate vicinity in case they somehow switched places, and he's still lurking nearby, but there's nobody else around.

'Do you know this woman?' the man holding my left arm asks the bewildered man, but he shakes his head earnestly, his bottom lip trembling.

'I am so sorry,' I say to him. 'I thought you were... I made a mistake. I'm sorry.'

He doesn't acknowledge the apology, instead turning to the two race stewards who have now joined us.

The guy holding my left arm releases it, and he tells the stewards what happened. His shaved head bears a colourful tattoo of a serpent. He must be at least six foot five, and towers a good six inches over Bistras. His chest is broad, but I reckon it's more muscle than fat.

The stewards eye me cautiously.

'I'm sorry,' I say, pulling my remaining arm free of the restraint. 'I made a mistake. I thought this man was escaped convict Otto Bistras, and I tried to apprehend him, but I see now he isn't.'

They look at me like I've just tried to argue that the earth is flat.

'I'm so sorry,' I say again to the man, but my offer of a hand is quickly rebuffed as he cowers behind the race stewards.

I know I should wait until the police arrive so I can make a formal statement, but this stoppage has already cost me too much time, so I tell the race stewards to find me at the end. I need to get on.

I'm mortified that I could have made such a shocking mistake. That poor man. He didn't deserve the pent-up frustration I unburdened on him, but what it shows me is just how much of an effect Bistras's escape is having on me.

I hurry along the road where the Thames bends around the Isle of Dogs, past Canary Wharf College, and past Mudchute DLR station. I keep my eyes on the pavement, looking for Bistras, but also conscious that my mind could still be playing tricks on me. I'm still shaking when I make it to the water station where Finn is pacing frantically.

'What happened?' he yells, as I stop to accept my bottle from him.

'I thought I saw my stalker,' I say, 'but turns out it wasn't him. How far behind Thea and Kat am I?'

He checks his watch. 'I started a timer after they went by. You're three minutes behind, but I know you can do this. You need splits twenty seconds quicker than theirs for the remaining nine miles, and you'll be fine. Give it everything you've got.'

I take a long drink of water and toss the bottle to him, before starting up again.

As I make my way along East Ferry Road, through the heart of London's docklands, I can barely feel the ache in my knee and elbow. There are more applauding crowds ahead, and I spot another St Andrew's flag which has me pumping the air with my fist in solidarity. I also spot one of the motorbikes and a cameraman waiting for me to approach, and I put on a determined and psyched expression for Jamie's benefit. And speaking of the devil, I'm not too surprised when I see his name appear on

my watch as my phone rings. I tap the side of the headband to
answer the call, but my blood runs cold when I hear the sound of
the robotic laughing monkey.

38

BEFORE

Saturday, 30 March 2024, Brixton, London

Molly takes a deep breath before raising her hand and knocking at the door. The air around her is sweet from the smell of freshly baked cookies in the box she's carrying, but she still can't be certain this is the right step. She hears movement beyond the door, and realises it's too late to back out now.

The door opens a crack, and a half-dressed Kat stares back at her in amazement.

'What the hell do you want?'

Molly takes another breath, trying to recall the words she practised in the mirror this morning.

'I know we haven't seen eye to eye,' she says, 'and I wanted to clear the air.' She extends her arms, offering the box, but the gap in the door doesn't widen. 'I bought you some cookies from the Danish patisserie near the track – Thea said they're you're favourite. I was hoping maybe you could invite me in and we could have a cookie and a cup of tea?'

Molly hadn't meant for her tone to sound so needy, but she can't help feeling intimidated by Kat. They've barely exchanged more than two words since Molly began training at the National Academy of Sport, but if looks could kill, Molly would already be dead by now.

Kat looks down at the box. 'So, they're for me?'

Molly nods eagerly, and pushes them closer to the door, the gap finally widening enough for Kat to pull the box through. Offering an olive branch was Thea's idea, and Molly feels sorry for her, being caught in the middle of this pointless feud.

Kat opens the lid of the box and looks inside, the sweet smell getting stronger. Molly is salivating and her stomach gently grumbles.

'Listen, I've got company at the moment,' Kat begins, glancing back over her shoulder. 'Can you give me five minutes to get dressed and we can go grab a coffee downstairs?'

Molly nods, her cheeks flushing for not even considering that Kat might have hooked up with someone the night before – or be in some kind of relationship. Molly has become so accustomed to being alone that it never crossed her mind that Kat wouldn't be.

'Sure,' she says, 'I'll see you down—'

But the door has already closed.

Exhaling a sigh, Molly turns and heads back along the corridor, stopping to knock at Thea's door to provide an update. But if Thea is inside, she doesn't come to the door, probably already at the track, so Molly continues on and back into the warm, muggy air. A blanket of light grey cloud hangs over the area; it's surprisingly humid for the time of year, though the predicted thunderstorm this evening should ease the atmospheric pressure.

Outside the front door, Molly stops. There are a couple of cafés that she walked past on the way to the building, and she can't be certain which one Kat meant.

She pulls out her phone so she'll look like less of an oddball standing there waiting. She rereads the message from Detective Freeman, once again assuring her that fake-Oppenheimer – or Otto Bistras to use his actual name – is sitting inside a German prison, but Molly can't escape the feeling that she's still being watched. And despite Freeman's assurances to the contrary, they haven't actually proved he was the one who sent all those abusive messages, or that he was the one who paid for someone to deliver the trainers to her dressing room. And they probably never will.

What if they're wrong and the real culprit is still at large?

The stress is causing her to lose sleep and she needs as much rest as possible between track days. The marathon is three weeks tomorrow, and while the rest of the team is getting closer to the qualifying time, Molly is only just completing twenty-six-mile stints, and isn't anywhere near the time. Finn assures her she is on course, but she sees the uncertainty in his eyes whenever he says this.

She's spiralling again, and the stress of trying to clear the air with Kat isn't helping. She'll be glad when it's all over.

Ten minutes pass, and Molly is just starting to think Kat has stood her up, when she appears at the door, dressed in her Olympic team tracksuit, almost as if she's trying to make a statement. Molly notices she hasn't brought the box of cookies with her, but hopes that isn't a bad sign.

They walk in silence, Molly unable to think of anything to say – she's never been comfortable with small talk – until they arrive at one of the cafés. Kat suggests they sit at one of the outside tables, and as soon as she's sitting, she tells Molly she'll have an Americano. Midway through sitting down, Molly straightens again and heads inside to place the order, a little put out, but she tries not to let it bother her. The important thing is she's managed to get Kat to the table to speak; now is the time to strive for peace.

Collecting their order, she carries the two paper cups outside, and places Kat's before her, before sitting, and removing the lid of her tea so it can cool.

'Thanks,' Kat says. 'So what is it you want to talk to me about?'

Molly can't be sure if the slightly aggressive tone is because of her, or if it's just Kat's natural manner.

'As I said upstairs, I don't want there to be any animosity between us. We're both professional athletes, right? We both have the same dream: standing on the podium in Paris. But competitors on the track don't need to be competitors off the track as well. You know?'

When rehearsing last night, she'd decided to play up to Kat's ego a little, and now she hopes it pays off. She can't see the two of them becoming best friends, but she just wants to put an end to all the bitterness in the air.

'Go on,' Kat says, taking a sip from the steaming cup.

Molly hadn't really prepared much more, hoping to break down the barrier with that one line.

'Um, well, I know that you feel threatened by my presence, and I understand—'

'I don't feel threatened by no one,' Kat snaps back.

Molly can't remember the exact conversation she had with Thea, but she's sure that's how she had described the cause of the hostility.

'Sorry, I... um, I didn't mean it like that. I meant I understand why you might worry that your place on the team is at stake, but I just—'

'You think I'm worried about your privileged arse keeping me out of the team?' she scoffs. 'You really do have a high opinion of yourself, don't you, princess? I've seen the times you're putting in right now, and you're so far off the pace all you'll see in the race is me miles ahead of you.'

Molly can feel the conversation slipping away; this isn't how it went in her imagination.

'Please, Kat, all I'm trying to say is—'

Kat stands suddenly, the table shaking in her wake. 'You think you can buy my friendship with some cookies and a coffee? How out of touch are you?'

Molly's own patience is wearing thin. 'I'm not trying to buy you. I am trying to patch things up with you, but clearly the massive chip on your shoulder is holding you back from accepting this peace offering for what it is.'

Kat clicks her tongue, grabs her coffee cup and stalks away.

Molly knows she should go after her and do whatever she can to fix things, but she doubts there's anything she can say now to heal the rift.

Frustrated, she remains where she is, and slowly drinks her tea, trying to calm her own rising anger.

When she's feeling calmer, she unlocks her phone again and sees a new email. It's from the marathon committee, confirming her place and number for the race. At this, any remaining anger dissipates instantly.

Although she's been trying to picture the race and manifest success, seeing her actual competitor number makes it hit home: she will be there come hell or high water.

She tried to take the moral high ground with Kat, but she isn't going to waste any more time worrying about what others think of her. This is her chance and she is more determined than ever to do whatever it takes to win her place in the Olympic squad, even if it does come at Kat's expense.

39

NOW

21 April 2024, Canary Wharf, London – Mile 18

The robotic monkey's laughter echoes through my head, even after I've ended the call from Jamie. There must be some kind of mistake. I scroll through my list of recent contacts, and it definitely says Jamie's phone made the call. I dial back, but as soon as the line connects, all I hear is the monkey laughing at me again.

What the hell?

I stare at my watch to make sure it's definitely Jamie's number I'm connected to, but as I stare at his name, the reality slowly dawns on me.

If we do this in the right way, you'll have the biggest brands falling over themselves to make you their summer poster girl ahead of the Olympics.

My suspicions about Jamie were right after all. It makes sense now. He was behind everything: the flat with extortionate rent; the adverts on Instagram; the anonymous online messages; the messages to my mobile number even after I changed it; and the orchids outside my hotel room. These thoughts and suspicions felt like paranoia before, but now I have the evidence.

What I don't know is how he connects to my Lithuanian tormentor Otto Bistras. Or whether he even does.

I scroll to Zara's number, press the call button, and am relieved when she answers.

'It's Jamie,' I shout breathlessly as I cross the road in front of a towering skyscraper.

'Molly? Can you hear me? The signal here is dreadful.'

'Jamie is the one who's been working with Otto Bistras,' I practically shout.

'Molly? Can you... me?'

I look at my phone's screen but my signal is on less than a bar, and I can only assume it's because of all the towers surrounding me.

The line disconnects.

My mind is all over the place as I round the next bend. I replay the conversation I had with Jamie first thing, each sentence taking on a more sinister edge now that I know his secret.

Everything that's been building in the last five months has led to this.

This race could set you up for life.

I figured you'd have enough on your mind without having to worry about all that.

But what troubles me most is why he would now let me know that he's been behind today's torment. He could have continued phoning and messaging from the withheld number and I'd have been none the wiser. It doesn't make sense why he'd give up his anonymity, unless there's some reason he no longer needs to hide his identity. I shudder as my mind starts to jump to further conclusions.

The headband blares out a ringtone as Zara calls me back.

'Molly, can you hear me now? Is that better?'

Her words are stilted, but I can just about make out what she's saying.

'I have... news for you... Bistras is back in...'

'Zara? Say that again, you broke up.'

'Molly... you... me?'

Damn these buildings!

I try to increase my pace, keen to get out into the open again. There are so many people cheering from behind railings, but it's all so overwhelming that I don't even acknowledge any of the chants of my name.

My whole body aches as the additional exertions start to take a toll. Making up three minutes to catch up with Kat and Thea feels just too much.

I hear Mam's voice in my head, and a lump forms in my throat: Every passing second is another chance to turn it all around.

I've fought for too long to give in, and grinding my teeth, I force my legs to move faster, in spite of the pain now pounding through my calf and thigh muscles.

Zara's name appears on my watch again, and this time when I answer I can hear her perfectly.

'Can you hear me now, Molly?'

'Yes. Can you hear *me*?'

'I can now. Did you hear what I said about Otto Bistras?'

'Only that he's back. I thought I saw him on the side of the road.'

'Impossible; he is in custody in Germany as we speak.'

I splutter. 'What?'

'That's the great news. Turns out there was an accident during the prison transfer and the van rolled down some kind of embankment, which is why it didn't show up at its destination. Bistras and the two prison officers were found at the site half an hour ago and are being taken to hospital for treatment. Bistras has a broken collarbone, which seems like some kind of poetic justice if you ask me. Off the record, of course.'

She chuckles, but I don't share the joke.

'You mean he's been in Germany all this time?'

'Yep, in a locked cell in the back of an armoured van. That's the good news: he isn't in London and isn't back to get you.' She pauses. 'I thought you'd be pleased?'

So, Jamie wasn't working with Bistras? At least that reconciles *that* question.

'And you're sure he's been there all night? With no access to a phone?'

'They had to cut him out of the van, so there's no way he could have escaped, and he wouldn't have had access to a phone either. Whoever has been messaging you today, it isn't Bistras.'

'Then it must be someone else. I've suspected it before; you remember after he was originally arrested, I told you somebody was still watching me and tormenting me? Do you believe me now?'

'I'm sorry that I doubted you before.'

'I don't need your apology, I need you to find my agent Jamie and arrest him: he's the one who's been behind all of this.'

'Your agent?'

'He phoned me a few minutes ago and I heard the laughing monkey. It's him, Zara. It's been him all along.'

'But why?'

As I say it out loud, it all becomes clear. It's obvious, and I now realise I should have taken the thought more seriously before now.

'To make me some kind of poster girl for fighting back against cyber bullies, so he can use me to make money. I'll explain more when I see you, but right now, you need to find him and stop him.'

'That makes no sense. He's your agent, right? He wouldn't need to go to all this effort just to make money off you. I don't buy it.'

'I phoned him back and the monkey was laughing. I don't know why he would be so cruel as to make me think Bistras was behind all of this, but I have no other answer.'

'Enough is enough, Molly,' Zara says sternly. 'I really do think you need to stop running, and get to safety. Where are you now? I'll come to you, and then you'll be safe.'

'I'm just leaving Canary Wharf, heading towards Poplar and then on to Shadwell. But if I quit the race, I will regret it for the rest of my life.' I pause. 'Just find Jamie, and put a stop to his games.'

'Can you send me his mobile number, and I'll have a trace run on it.'

'I can't while I'm running. His number should be on his website.'

'Okay. I'll speak to my team, and call you back as soon as we know where he is.'

40

NOW

21 April 2024, Poplar, London – Mile 19

I can't stop staring at the crowd, unable to escape the feeling that I'm being watched, and that someone – maybe more than one person – means me harm.

I don't want to believe that Jamie could have been behind the messages and threats, and the more I think about it, the less it makes sense. The bit that bugs me most is that he's no longer hiding the fact he's behind it all. It's possible that he's just forgotten to hide his number now, but that seems less likely. Ultimately, he knows I've reported my stalker to the police and that Zara has been supporting me. He would know that I'd tell her about today's messages and calls, and that I would show her my phone so the police will have the evidence that he's behind it all. There's no way he'll get away with it. Even if he planned to kill me before the end of the race, I've already reported his actions to Zara, so they'll come for him. Why would he throw away his job, prospects and freedom just to terrify me?

Unless he has another motive I've not even thought of yet.

My knee is stinging, and when I look down at the strapping Finn applied, I can see a bloody patch and a thin trail of blood running down my shin. The skin above the strapping is pink and swollen, and will turn to a yellow or purple bruise over the coming days. One thing's for sure, I'm going to need a rest after I finish this race.

If I ever finish this race.

The thought jars.

I was ready to believe that Bistras was planning to kill me in front of a live audience, but if Jamie's been behind it all, then should I assume he has the same intention? And how does Bistras fit into all of this? I know he was outside my flat, because I saw him on the doorbell camera footage, but was he the one sending the messages? Or was it Jamie? I can no longer separate the two, or determine whether they were working together or independently.

I feel as though my pace has dropped right off. I can't remember how long it's been since I passed the Mile 18 marker, but I can see the next marker in the distance.

I search for Finn's number on my watch and hit the dial button. It cuts straight to answerphone, so I hang up and try again. He'll know my splits and he'll be able to tell me how far off the pace I am. He said he'd be monitoring me from the sidelines to keep me safe, but I haven't seen him since the last water station.

I try re-dialling him for a third time, but either his phone is switched off or, wherever he is, he has no signal.

Where is he?

There should be a glucose gel station coming up just before the next marker, so maybe he's waiting there for me.

Despite the ache in my right knee, I push myself onwards.

They say it's the mind hitting the wall that prevents most runners from completing marathons. The body can ache, but it's how the brain processes those signals that determines whether an entrant completes or withdraws from an event. The human body can be put through all manner of challenges and torture, but it's the brain that tells the runner whether to keep going. And my cynical mind is screaming at me to stop. My motivation for continuing today was qualification for the summer games, but if that's no longer possible, then there really is no point in persisting with this charade.

The road narrows ahead, and I spot the familiar barriers draped in advertising, which means there are more crowds coming up. Maybe Jamie and Finn are amongst them.

But then I spot a motorbike and cameraman at the side of the road, and when I see the mirrored Aviators, my heart skips a beat. The bike starts up, the camera raised so I can barely see the cameraman's face. I realise now that in all this time I haven't actually seen his face, just those damned sunglasses. He was the reason I fell the first time, and he always appears when I'm least expecting it.

Always watching. Always focused on me and not the other runners.

I know now he isn't Bistras, because Zara says he's back in custody and never left Germany, but that doesn't mean this guy isn't involved somehow. Could he be working with Jamie? Or could he be...?

With renewed energy, I surge forwards, but rather than focusing on the course, my target is the man on the back of that motorbike. There is a cheer as the spectators see me take the next bend, but they have no idea what's going on. I focus my glare on the Aviators and push through the pain barrier.

'Show me your face!' I yell out, as I try to ignore the agony of my knee. 'I know it's you, Jamie. Show me your goddamned face!'

The motorbike has accelerated to stay clear of me, but that only drives me to push myself harder and faster. I start waving frantically at the camera, hoping the rider notices and slows.

'Stop,' I yell next, because there's no way I can maintain this pace if the bike continues to accelerate.

The cameraman turns and appears to say something to the rider who slows and indicates, pulling to a stop at the side of the road. I hurry over and demand he lowers the camera, but when he does, I see it isn't Jamie, but someone much younger; someone I've never met before. He can't be much older than twenty, judging by his stubble and acne-covered chin. There is a strong smell of body spray emanating from his leather jacket as well.

He removes the sunglasses, asking if I'm okay, and whether they want me to call one of the race stewards.

Before I can answer, my watch vibrates and when I look, I see there is a message from Finn. I can't see him in the crowd, but he did say he would be there to keep me safe. It means so much to have him championing me.

I gasp as my eyes fall on the content of the message.

IF YOU PERSIST, I WILL KILL YOU BEFORE THE FINISH.
I'M RIGHT BEHIND YOU, BUT NOT FOR MUCH LONGER.
xxx

It doesn't make sense. First Jamie, now Finn?

The young cameraman still looks concerned, but he is nothing to me now, as I know he didn't send the message. I wave away his concern, and break into a sprint, trying to shake away the sense that none of this is real, and that I'm trapped in a nightmare from which I cannot wake.

I try to phone Finn, but his phone is still switched off. My brain whirs as I try to take it all in. If his phone is turned off, can he have sent the message?

I try Jamie's number, but again his answerphone cuts straight in without ringing.

Could they be working together?

But if so, to what end?

I am so confused right now.

41

NOW

21 April 2024, Poplar, London – Mile 20

I'm not even looking where I'm going, my mind unable to process the realisation that Jamie and Finn have been working together against me. I thought we were a team, all striving to achieve the same goal, and now I feel utterly betrayed. I was so convinced that Finn was fighting against feelings for me, but was that all just part of his act? It makes sense: I'd be less likely to suspect him of anything if I was attracted to him romantically. And it was Jamie who planted the seed of the idea in my head.

I have been a prize fool.

If you persist, I will kill you.

Finn is the one who's been pushing me not to give up today, so why has he suddenly changed his tune? He made out like his own career was on the line because of me; it just doesn't make any sense. I don't want to believe he's involved too.

I reach the stand with the glucose gel packs and there's no sign of him. I shouldn't be surprised, now that he's revealed his true intentions.

I grab two of the packs, and stop long enough to yank off the lid of the first and press the small plastic tube between my lips. I squeeze the packet and the thick liquid crystals squirt into my mouth. I discard the used packet in one of the kerb-side rubbish bags, and repeat the process with the second. All I know is I'm going to need all the energy I can get if I'm to finish this race.

It's no longer about qualifying for the Olympics, now I just want to reach the end, and see Finn and Jamie brought to justice.

Running again, I take the next bend quicker than I'm expecting, and have to catch myself before I crash into one of the security barriers. The ground here is slicker than it has been, which must mean there's been a recent downpour. I'm going to have to be careful as I can't afford to slip and injure myself further. The road ahead of me is long and straight, but my eyes widen when I see the pack of runners about two thirds along it. The group can't be more than forty seconds ahead of me. I must have been running far quicker than I gave myself credit for.

I can't see Kat or Thea from here, but they can't be too much farther ahead than that group, so I still have a chance.

This is all the encouragement I need, and I lower my gaze, focusing on my breathing and willing my body to give an extra yard of pace.

I don't even look at my watch when my headband starts ringing, and when I answer, it is more of a relief than I'm expecting to hear Zara's voice.

'How are you getting on? Any more sightings of your agent?'

'Not yet.'

'Where are you now?'

I briefly look up. 'Some kind of high street as far as I can tell.

I've just passed several blocks of flats, and now there are shuttered shops and restaurants.'

There's a pause on the line. 'I've got you. You're on Poplar High Street, nearing the West India Dock.'

'How do you know where I am?'

'I'm tracking you on the official race app. You're doing pretty well, all things considered.'

I'd forgotten all about the app providing location information for each runner. And if Zara can track me through it then so can anyone.

'That's how Jamie knows exactly where I am too.'

'It's possible, yes, but do you really think he means to do you harm? I don't see what's in it for him.'

I don't understand the incredulity of her tone.

'It doesn't matter what his motive is, it was his phone that had the laughing monkey. And what's more, I think Finn is working with him.'

'Wait, your coach too? What makes you think that?'

'He sent me a message – telling me to withdraw or he'll kill me before the finish line.'

'When was this?'

'About four minutes ago.'

'Can you send me a screenshot?'

I wrestle my phone from the pack on my arm and do as instructed, keeping one eye on the runners ahead of me.

'Good, thank you. My team have just been to your agent's office and there's no sign of him there. We've checked traffic cameras and his vehicle hasn't been seen since arriving back at his apartment last night, but he isn't there now either. I have got permission to trace his phone, but it is currently switched off. We need him to put it back on so we can try to triangulate his signal. Is it usual for him to have his phone switched off?'

'He's an agent: it's practically glued to his ear. It's switched on all day and night.'

'It's definitely suspicious that it's switched off then. In my experience there are only two reasons people switch off their phones: they've run out of battery, or they don't want to be traced. We will try and locate both Finn's and Jamie's locations somehow.'

'Why are they doing this to me?' I ask, hearing the strain in my voice.

I hear her take a deep breath.

'Can I be honest with you?'

'Please.'

'It's possible neither your agent nor your coach are involved in what's happening.'

Does she think I'm making this up?

'I'm not going crazy. The messages came from their phones, and I heard the monkey when Jamie phoned me.'

'I don't doubt you did, Molly. I don't think you're crazy, but let me ask you a question: why would your agent or coach want to harm you? It goes against their own interests.'

'I don't know. I've been asking myself the same question. But I know what I heard and saw. And why else would they have their phones switched off when they know I might phone? How else do you explain it?'

'I'm no expert, but it's possible someone has cloned their numbers and is using those to throw you off the scent.'

'Is that even possible?'

'As I said, I'm no expert, but something just feels off about this. In all the meetings the two of us had, there was no reason to suspect either of them of wrongdoing, and if they *are* involved, I don't understand why they would make it so obvious it's them. I'll pass their numbers to our cyber team and see what they can find out. In the meantime, you could help me out. If either Jamie or

Finn phone you again, and you hear that laughing voice, don't
hang up. The longer the number stays active, the easier it will be
to trace where the call is originating from. Oh, and Molly, be care-
ful. Whoever is behind this is smart and isn't finished with you
yet.'

42

NOW

21 April 2024, Limehouse, London – Mile 21

Almost another mile down but my legs and arms feel so heavy that the thought of five more fills me with dread. I've been running for over two hours, but it feels twice as long.

Could Zara be right and Jamie and Finn are being used as pawns in someone else's sick game?

I've never wanted something to be more true. It was the thought of them betraying me that hurt the most – either one of them or both together.

I'm still no closer to figuring out who is behind this. It feels like most of the jigsaw pieces are there, but without the key piece or an idea of what they're supposed to create, it's virtually impossible to put them together.

Pulling my phone from the sleeve tightly secured around my forearm, I open my messages and review what the stalker has sent today.

First there was the card with the orchids. I sent a picture of it to Zara.

I'M RIGHT BEHIND YOU.
SEE YOU AT THE RACE.
xxx

The block capitals, the statement about being behind me and the three kisses at the end of the message are all consistent with the card Otto left with the running spikes in my dressing room, which is why I assumed the flowers were from him.

The next message came through on the withheld number just before the ten-mile marker. It threw me so much that I didn't really study the words.

YOU SHOULD HAVE TAKEN THE HINT AND LEFT THE RACE.
I'M RIGHT BEHIND YOU, BUT YOU WON'T SEE ME COMING.
xxx

Although the block capitals are there and the kisses, the 'I'm right behind you' appears in the second line this time. Is that significant? Does that mean it was sent by someone else? Or am I reading too much into it? And what hint should I have taken? The flowers? The phone calls?

And why is this person so determined that I leave the race?

Zara challenged why Jamie or Finn would want me to with-draw, as it's not in their best interests, so I'm becoming more convinced it can't be them.

The question is: who has most to gain from me abandoning the race?

My gaze focuses on the hot-pink vest top only fifteen or so yards ahead of me, now at the back of the second pack of runners.

I don't think Kat realises just how close I am to her, and for now that's how I want to keep it. I need to hold back until the finish line is in sight. Of course, I have to hope she doesn't have a burst of energy in reserve as well. But it is clear to me that she has the greatest motivation for me not crossing that finish line as I'm the biggest threat to her position on Team GB.

But how would she be able to orchestrate all of this while competing in the race? Like most of us, she has a phone strapped to her arm, but I know how much of a distraction using it is. Would she be able to maintain her pace and be making prank phone calls? I'm also not sure how tech savvy she is to be able to hide her number and clone those of Jamie and Finn. Though I suppose it's possible she could have someone on the outside helping her with the messages and phone calls.

And then there's the last message, received two miles ago:

IF YOU PERSIST, I WILL KILL YOU BEFORE THE FINISH.
I'M RIGHT BEHIND YOU, BUT NOT FOR MUCH LONGER.
XXX

It's the first time they've physically threatened me, but that tells me they're worried that their plan isn't working. The intimidating phone calls and creepy messages haven't impeded my efforts, and even when they twice messed about with my drinks bottle, I'm still going. And with just over five miles remaining, they're getting desperate.

That said, if they're serious about the threat to kill me, I'm going to have to watch my step.

I need to focus on what I can figure out myself. I can't just sit back and wait for my future to be decided for me.

I slide my phone back into the pouch on my arm, and slowly increase my speed until I'm beside Kat. She looks horrified to see me there and tries to up her own pace, but I can see how much of a struggle it is for her.

'I need to talk to you,' I say. 'I'm thinking about withdrawing.'

The lie doesn't sit comfortably, and as tempting as it is to make it a truth, I only say it because I want her to believe I'm no longer a threat.

'Why?'

I gesture in the direction of the blood-stained strapping of my right leg.

'It's agony,' I tell her, though my aching muscles are causing me greater discomfort.

'Looks sore. You should get it looked at by one of the St John Ambulance people.'

'I will,' I reply, accepting it's a good idea.

We continue onwards, because I don't know how to phrase what I want to say. She's already denied taking the topless photograph, so I can't just accuse her again and hope she cracks. What I need is to trick her into revealing the truth.

'How come you're not running with Thea?' I ask next.

'She's further ahead; I couldn't keep up.'

Good for her, I don't say.

'I'm surprised she's putting in such an effort,' I say instead, 'given she's already qualified for the games.'

Kat shrugs at this, maybe already sensing that something is off. 'It's good for conditioning, I suppose.'

'Is that why you're doing this? Conditioning?'

'We both know I wouldn't need to be running today if it wasn't for you competing, so stop with all the fake tenderness and tell me what you really want.'

So much for the softly-softly approach.

'I know you've been trying to get me booted out of the team, but what have I ever done to you?'

'You've got some nerve, do you know that?'

'So, my drink getting spiked the night after the team meal was just bad luck? Messing about with my stuff in the locker rooms when nobody else is about? Sounds exactly like what someone would do when they feel threatened.'

'You ought to rein your neck in, love, and stop judging others by your own standards.'

How dare she judge me?

'That's where you and I are different: I would never do anything to bring harm to a fellow athlete.'

'If it wasn't for you, I'd be at the track training for my Paris events right now, instead of being forced to run a marathon just to prove I'm better than you.'

It's not quite the confession I was hoping for, but at least she's not hiding her disdain.

'So if I throw in the towel, you'll stop your little games?'

'What are you banging on about?'

'Oh, please. The messages? The phone calls? The threats?'

'Not this shit again! I already told you I didn't take that poxy picture. Wait, is this just some ploy to try and mess up my race? Spin on.' She shakes her head dismissively. 'Why have you always got to play the victim? Do you get some kick out of people feeling sorry for you, is that it? You're sick in the head.'

I shouldn't be surprised that she's denying it.

There's only one way I can beat Kat, and that's to finish this marathon ahead of her.

With all my might, I bite down hard and force my feet to move quicker, though it feels like I'm running through tar. They say the final five miles of a marathon are the toughest, and I have a feeling this is going to be the longest twenty-five minutes of my life.

In my periphery, I can see Kat is trying to match me, but she's struggling and a small gap opens between us. I know I can't maintain this pace, but I just need to keep her behind me until I cross that finish line.

I physically jump when my headband bursts into life, and see Finn's name on my watch.

'I know who's behind it,' I say, but stop when I hear the robotic monkey laughing back at me.

I remember what Zara suggested, that this must be someone else using Finn's number, and I resist the immediate urge to hang up. I glance over my shoulder, but Kat's phone is still in the pouch on her arm, so I don't think she can be making the call. I look into the crowd of spectators gathered behind the barrier up ahead, looking for Jamie. I can't see him, but I do spot Finn waving frantically at me. I can't hear what he's trying to yell over the din of the crowd but given he has his phone in his hand, he's either completely innocent or no longer worried about hiding his intentions. I need to put as much distance between us as possible, just in case, so I push myself into the middle of the road.

I hear Zara's words in my head: *If either Jamie or Finn phone you again, and you hear that laughing voice, don't hang up. The longer the number stays active, the easier it will be to trace where the call is originating from.*

I grind my teeth harder, the robotic laughter grating at every nerve-ending, but knowing Zara will be doing all she can to trace the number. I don't want to believe that Finn has betrayed me but if he is then I want Zara to nail him.

The laughter continues unabated as I pass the twenty-one-mile marker, and I'm praying it will end soon when I hear a voice calling out a name down the line; a name I'm very familiar with, and suddenly the world splinters before my eyes.

43

BEFORE

Saturday, 20 April 2024, National Sports Centre, Crystal Palace, London

Dr Stanway crosses her legs as she reads the notes on the pad before her. Molly has made it clear that she doesn't need therapy, but Finn has insisted that ahead of the games all of the Olympic team are required to speak with a counsellor.

'But I haven't qualified yet,' she argued when he raised it again last week.

'*Yet* being the operative word,' he responded with a kind smile. 'And you never know, it could do you the world of good.'

He didn't elaborate on what he meant, and she didn't push, uncertain that she wanted to know the answer. If Finn thinks she'd benefit from therapy, does that mean the mask she's been carefully holding up all this time has finally slipped? How many of the other athletes can see she isn't coping with the pressure?

Freeman hasn't been any help either. There have been so

many odd things happening that can't just be coincidence. Phone calls from withheld numbers at stupid times. When she answers the phone, it's always the same: a robotic voice laughing at her.

It started in the early hours of each morning, but since Molly has started switching off her phone every night, the calls have been coming through when she's in training. It's almost like whomever is behind this campaign knows when the most awkward time to call is. And it's like they have a sixth sense to know exactly when her phone will be on.

All Freeman suggested was blocking all withheld and private numbers, but Molly is fed up with having to make so many changes to her own life. Someone is doing this to her, and they need to be stopped.

And then, two days ago, she started receiving WhatsApp messages from an unrecognised number. The first made out like they were a friend who'd lost touch, but the moment Molly acknowledged the message, she was sent an image of a piece of paper with the handwritten words:

DIE BITCH

'The number is unregistered,' is all Zara was able to tell her.

'But can't you trace the number? Triangulate the signal or whatever they say in the movies?'

'The phone needs to be switched on for that to happen. Whoever is sending the message is turning off the phone as soon as the message is sent. We're trying.'

What Zara hasn't confirmed is whether Otto could be sending the messages from prison. Whilst he shouldn't have access to a phone while behind bars, Molly has watched enough crime shows to know there are always ways and means. She desperately hopes it is Otto because at least he can't physically harm her. But if it's some unknown assailant, then she isn't safe.

'Molly?' Dr Stanway says in her sing-song manner. 'Are you still with me?'

Molly's mind snaps back to the interior of the therapist's office, unable to remember what question Dr Stanway just asked.

'Listen, Doc, I'm fine. Okay? Can you just scribble that in your report so we can both get on with our days? I should be out running, not stuck in here.'

She doesn't want to come across as aggressive – a bad report from the doctor and there'll be no way she's considered for the team regardless of what time she manages to achieve next Sunday.

'Can I be honest with you, Molly?' Dr Stanway says, removing her spectacles.

Molly meets her stare, the doctor's blue eyes so bright they resemble the cloudless sky beyond the window. Her short bob perfectly frames her cheeks, and her designer dress suit screams of a life of privilege. Molly doubts this woman has ever had to work as hard as she has.

'Sure,' Molly says, raising her eyebrows dismissively.

'I have spoken to a lot of athletes in the last decade – sports is kind of a special interest for me – and I have yet to meet a single individual who is relaxed before an event. That's why I'm asked to meet with them in the first place. And you, with what I understand is your last chance at making the Olympic grade, expect me to accept that you're not feeling any level of pressure ahead of Sunday's marathon?'

'Of course there's pressure, but I've been training for this all my life. It's not like it's the first marathon I've ever run. I'm a long-distance runner, and I know what's required of me.'

'But it can't have been easy for you, though, right? I mean, your dream was on the brink of collapse when you injured your back last year. And now here you are, fighting back, striving to achieve your dream. If I was in your shoes, I wouldn't be sleeping properly.'

Molly's eye twitches, but she hopes the doctor doesn't notice. Molly can't remember the last time she had a decent night's sleep. Certainly not since she moved to London. She would give anything to just be back in Scotland, where the air is cleaner and the streets kinder.

'How are you sleeping, Molly?' Dr Stanway asks next.

Molly inwardly screams, realising the doctor is paying far more attention than she gave credit for, before taking a deep breath, ready to roll out the rehearsed lie.

'I go to bed at ten most nights and don't get up until six. Eight hours a night is pretty good, I think.'

Stanway chews on the end of her glasses. 'Again, forgive my bluntness, but you don't look like a woman getting eight hours' sleep a night.'

Molly bolts up, ready to storm out, but something holds her back. She only agreed to meet with Dr Stanway today because Finn said the Olympic Committee would be less than impressed if she didn't. If she doesn't see the session through, they'll be equally unimpressed.

'I don't have to stay here and take this abuse,' she says instead, hoping to play the victim card.

'It was merely an observation, Molly. I didn't mean any offence.' She sighs and slides her glasses back onto her nose. 'Listen, you don't need to be afraid to speak to me. I'm not your enemy, and everything we discuss will be treated with confidentiality. I won't share the output of this session with anyone. Please sit down.'

Molly hesitates, before retaking her seat, puffing out her cheeks.

'Thank you,' Dr Stanway says. 'Your coach, Finn, mentioned you'd been suffering at the hands of a stalker. Can you tell me about that?'

So Finn does have concerns about her. What else has he told the doctor?

'No judgement,' Dr Stanway adds, when Molly doesn't answer.

The doctor continues to stare, Molly becoming more uncomfortable with each passing second of silence.

'I'm going to share something from my own life, in an effort to put you more at ease. Okay?'

Molly doesn't answer, doubting anything can make her any less uncomfortable.

'When I was at medical school, I had to deal with a fellow student who became obsessed with me. We went on a blind date – we were set up by friends – but I knew pretty early that we weren't suited.'

She pauses, as if expecting Molly to blurt out all the gory details of her own trauma, but continues again when Molly remains silent.

'He kept showing up randomly whenever I'd be out. I thought it odd, but all my friends said I was just being paranoid and there were perfectly rational reasons he would also be at the Student Union bar and campus library at the same time as me. Then, I went home to visit my parents in the Cotswolds, and I ran into him at the only pub in my parents' tiny village. I reported him to my tutor, who said they would speak to him about it.'

Molly stares over at the door, desperately hoping Stanway picks up on the hint.

'Of course he denied the allegation, and that seemed to tip him over the edge. He started sending me threatening messages, really abusive stuff, accusing me of being a slut and trying to get him kicked out of medical school.'

Molly sits forwards. 'Jesus! What did you do?'

'I shared the messages with my tutor, and he was given a written warning and when that didn't stop him, he was kicked out of the school.'

'Good riddance,' Molly says, wishing her own issues could be so easily resolved.

'The point of the story is so you understand that you're not alone. I understand the stress and anxiety a stalker can cause. You wouldn't be human if it wasn't affecting you in some way.'

'That's part of the problem, though,' Molly admits. 'I don't know who is responsible for what is happening to me. It could literally be anyone.'

44

NOW

21 April 2024, Shadwell, London – Mile 22

'Hurry up, Seb, we're going to be late for your sister's event.'

I know I didn't imagine the woman's voice, speaking over the sound of the robotic monkey's laughter. The call ended immediately after, but I have replayed the line in my head over and over, and I know what I heard.

Seb is a common enough name, I suppose, but I desperately want to believe it's purely coincidence that the person behind the laughing monkey shares the name with Thea's brother.

When she first spoke about him, Thea said, 'He talks like a robot, but he managed to rebuild the toaster when he was like two.' She said his autism makes him view the world in a different way and one of his special interests is technology and gadgets. She called him 'a tech genius', and isn't that exactly the sort of person who would be capable of cloning Jamie's and Finn's numbers and using them against me?

It can't be him.

I try to call Finn back but his phone is once again switched off. I don't leave a message.

I briefly met Seb when he came to my flat to install the video doorbell. I didn't get any sense that he was dangerous. Being autistic doesn't make him a bad person, and if anything, the guy I met showed huge empathy for what I was going through, and was falling over himself to try to help me better protect myself. So it can't be the same person who's been sending threatening messages and creeping around the locker room taking inappropriate pictures of me in the showers. He wouldn't have been able to get past security without Thea signing him in, and she wouldn't have left him unsupervised in the female changing rooms.

Zara challenged me on Jamie and Finn's motives for trying to get me to withdraw from the race, and I can't think of any reason Seb would want me not to finish either. I'm no threat to his sister, and he must know we're friends, so it has to be coincidence.

Right?

I am back on The Highway, a long stretch of road leading from Limehouse towards the north end of Tower Bridge. I've already run along this stretch of road once today, albeit in the opposite direction. Some of the men's elite runners pass by on the other side of the road, and I am envious of the energy and determination on their faces. They're yet to circle the Isle of Dogs so are about nine or so miles behind me. What I would give to have another nine miles' worth of energy, but I'm running on adrenaline fumes right now. It's a struggle just to keep one foot moving in front of the other. I almost stumble when I look down, and immediately look up, praying muscle memory will keep me upright until the finish line.

Hurry up, Seb, we're going to be late for your sister's event.

The woman's shrill voice echoes around my mind. If not Thea's brother, then who else could this Seb character be? I'm certain I've never met another Seb before, but that doesn't mean he isn't someone who's been following my career from a distance. Jamie made sure all and sundry knew I was on social media, so there's every chance he's just another creep whose interest was sparked. And this Seb also happens to have a sister, although that doesn't necessarily narrow the search much.

I keep returning to Thea's brother. He would know my number if he'd checked his sister's phone. Apart from Jamie, Thea is the only other person who knew I would be at The Clarendon Hotel, because she'd asked if I wanted to meet for a smoothie last night and I said I was going to bed early at my agent's insistence. I don't know if I ever told her about Mam's love of orchids, but I suppose there's a chance it may have come up over the last few months.

Has he been spying on us both?

No, that doesn't make sense in my head either. There just isn't any reason for Thea's brother to want me out of the race.

Is it possible her brother could be behind all of this, maybe out of some misplaced sense of loyalty to his older sister? Maybe he thinks he's helping her by chasing away her competition. But how do I ask without alienating her? I have to remember it's possible the voice I heard calling for Seb could be yet another trick to drive my suspicions from where they should be.

I look ahead to try to spot Thea, but I can only just see the pack ahead of me. I need to catch up with her somehow and ask whether I'm going crazy or whether there's a chance her brother could be behind this. She knows him better than me, and hopefully she can say enough to put my mind at ease.

I start as my phone pings, and my watch reveals another message from 'Finn'. I don't want to read it, but I'm hoping it will tell me more about my antagonist.

**LEAVE THE RACE NOW OR YOU'LL NEVER RUN AGAIN.
THIS IS YOUR LAST CHANCE.**

45

NOW

21 April 2024, Tower of London, London – Mile 23

Another threat, only this time, the sender has dispensed with the three kisses. Is that significant? Do they now know that I know they're not Otto Bistras?

I think back to that image of the German newspaper they sent when I was near Rotherhithe. The translation revealed Otto had escaped prison, and yet that doesn't marry up with what Zara told me. A traffic accident while he was being transported from one prison facility to another could be viewed as an escape attempt, but I'm not sure it would be so newsworthy, especially not front-page fodder.

I need to look at it again, so I slide my phone out of the plastic pouch and flick back to the images, pinching the screen to zoom in to the English translation. No matter how closely I stare at the screen, the writing is blurred, so it's impossible to read what the rest of the article says.

I hear Zara's voice in my head: *Whoever is behind this is smart and isn't finished with you yet.*

And then Thea's voice: *He is a tech genius.*

Could the image of the newspaper be faked to make me believe that Otto was behind today's terror? And then, when they heard that he'd been found, they decided to apportion the blame to Jamie and Finn? It feels like a light bulb moment.

And yet how would this person know that Otto was missing, and then that he'd been recovered?

Unless they can hear everything I'm saying on my phone?

This thought is a sucker punch to the gut, and it takes all my effort not to double over. The phone in my hand suddenly feels like a contaminated brick. If they've managed to clone Jamie's and Finn's numbers, who's to say they haven't installed some kind of surveillance software on my phone?

I can see the end of Tower Bridge, and more of the elite men's team on the opposite side of the road. The road bends down and around the Tower of London, the brick walls dominating the skyline. The site is so steeped in bloody history that it almost feels fitting that my own journey is nearing its end here.

I catch sight of the message again on my watch, but I feel less scared about the threat than I probably should. It stinks of desperation, and maybe I'm being naïve, but it feels like I'm somehow gaining the upper hand; my perseverance and continually ignoring their threats means they're resorting to desperate measures.

LEAVE THE RACE NOW OR YOU'LL NEVER RUN AGAIN.
THIS IS YOUR LAST CHANCE.

I forward the message as a screenshot to Zara, so she's aware that my stalker is still at large despite her assurances that Bistras is back in custody. Their last threat was to expose nude pictures of me online, but I've not had any alerts that such an act has been carried out, but that doesn't necessarily mean this is an empty threat. Despite my confidence, I shouldn't underestimate how far they're willing to go.

Thea is up ahead, having seemingly dropped back from the pack of runners she was with. I call out to her. She must not hear me at first, because she doesn't turn, but I continue to bellow her name until she looks back, and slows long enough to allow me to catch up.

'Hey,' she says, something like shock in her voice.

'Hey,' I reply, unsure where to begin. 'Are you as exhausted as me?'

'Tired, but only three to go.'

I don't know how to phrase my question. Essentially, I need her to tell me if Seb could be capable of all of this.

'Are you expecting to see your mum and brother at the finish line?' I ask instead.

Her brow furrows as she glances over, and in fairness it is a bit of a left-field question for this stage of the race.

'No, Mum hates coming into central London.'

I have a vague memory of her telling me this before, but I note that she hasn't mentioned her brother. If I ask her about him directly, she might twig that something is off, and I'm not yet ready to outright accuse him of something he has no involvement with. I must tread carefully.

'Are you planning to celebrate tonight?' I try.

'Celebrate?'

'The culmination of months of hard work. I just wondered whether you and Kat had made plans with any of the other athletes.'

I use a sad tone when I ask this, hoping she'll take pity rather than automatically jump to conclusions. She'll know that I will have been kept out of the loop if there are plans to paint the town red.

'I think Kat may have plans, but I'm not sure,' she says unconvincingly.

'If not, maybe you and I could do something?'

She briefly looks over and meets my stare. I'm convinced she'll be able to see through my charade, so I try to adopt a sorrowful frown.

'Maybe.'

'We could ask your brother along,' I push. 'I feel like I haven't properly thanked him yet for sorting out that doorbell camera for me.'

She fires a second glance, but I can't read her expression properly.

'Seb doesn't do well in social situations.'

This isn't working. I'm running out of time. If he's going to be waiting for me at the finish line, then I need to know what to expect. The time for subtlety is over.

'I need to ask you about your brother,' I say, struggling to get the words past my heavy breaths. 'I think he's been messaging me.'

I pause, trying to judge her reaction, but she keeps her face focused on the road ahead so it's impossible to see if there's surprise or disbelief in her eyes.

'Impossible,' she says uncertainly. 'He doesn't have your number.'

It's an interesting response. I was expecting her to ask what he's been messaging.

'I think he's been threatening to hurt me,' I pant.

She glances back at me for the briefest of moments, but not long enough for me to read her expression.

'Seb wouldn't do that,' she says with something close to incredulity. 'You must be thinking of someone else.'

I chance my hand. 'He's been prank calling me, but I think I heard your mum calling him at the end of the message.'

This time she definitely looks over, her glare a mixture of fear and anger.

'Must be some other Seb. My brother barely knows who you are. He wouldn't be messaging or calling you.'

Something feels very off. She's so adamant, which I guess she would be as a loyal sister, but as a friend I would have expected some kind of empathy towards me as well. There's something in the back of my mind that is so close, but I can't quite see.

'I know what I heard, Thea. All I'm asking is whether it's possible he's trying to frighten me in order to help you in some way? You said he's autistic and takes things literally, so maybe he's somehow misunderstood something he's heard or—'

'My brother wouldn't do something like that. You're being paranoid.'

There's that defensiveness again.

'Why would Seb be trying to get you to withdraw from the race?'

The breath catches in my throat. How does she know that's what he'd said? I didn't tell her that part yet.

'Um, I mean, assuming that's what the messages have said. You said the person who's been messaging you wants you to quit, right?'

She's trying to backtrack now, and suddenly that voice in the back of my head is getting louder. I haven't told her what the messages said. Did Thea put Seb up to this?

I don't want to listen to the voice. Thea is my friend and has been nothing but supportive of me. Maybe they're all right when they say my paranoia is getting the better of me. And yet...

What do I know about the person behind all of this? Assuming they're not working with Otto Bistras – and I hope I'm not making a mistake with that assumption – that means I have two stalkers acting independently of one another. The shoes in my dressing room were definitely Otto, I think, and that's because of the Oppenheimer book that was included in the box. And if that's true, then Otto was also behind the earliest messages on my Insta, and the negativity that was spread about me. But can I say for certain that he was responsible for all the messages?

I know that Otto was the one who trapped me in my flat when the smoke alarm sounded, because he escorted me out, and I had the footage of him on my doorbell camera. Zara told me he'd been arrested and put on remand back in late February – almost two months ago – so does that mean Thea and Seb have been behind everything that's happened since?

That would mean the flowers this morning, the messages and the phone calls are all them.

They have my telephone number, and Thea was the only person apart from Jamie who knew I was at The Clarendon last night.

She's looking back at me now, trying to work out if I noticed her slip. I try to smile back, but I'm not certain the expression is convincing. I can't let her know that I know.

The thought is so crazy that I want to laugh out loud, but now that it's bouncing around inside my head, I can no longer ignore it. I thought she was my friend. Why would she do this to me?

46

NOW

21 April 2024, City of London, London – Mile 24

I'm being ridiculous. I have suspected so many different people today, and surely Thea is the last person whose name should make the list. There is nothing for her to gain in seeing me fail. And if she was responsible, then how does that marry up with all the care and support she's shown me throughout Otto's campaign of terror?

When he first started messaging, she was the one who showed me how to block him. When he broke into my dressing room, she was the one who encouraged me to go to the police and held my hand throughout. She was the one who rescued me when Kat or one of the others spiked my drink, and she has been nothing but supportive of my training and competing today. And she has already qualified for Paris, so whether I qualify or not has no impact on her future. Her place on the plane is guaranteed, and although I know she's friends with Kat, I don't think she'd sacrifice one friend for the sake of another.

I've lost my mind. Finally the paranoia and terror have taken a toll and I can no longer trust my own thoughts. I should have listened when Dr Stanway warned me about the impact of all the stress. Maybe I should have heeded her warnings and tried yoga or meditation to calm my out-of-control imagination.

I continue to run beside her, feeling as though I should apologise for daring to question Seb. It was wrong of me to put two and two together and jump to the wrong conclusion.

And yet...

My suspecting Seb wasn't without reason. Zara has been telling me that the person behind today's messages and calls is someone with a better than average understanding of technology. And he definitely fits that mould. But based on our one meeting, I wouldn't have said he was someone capable of elaborate plans and a desire to hurt others. If anything, I'd say he was much more of an empath, and as such I can't really understand why he would have any involvement in something so clandestine; unless it was to please someone he cares greatly for.

I don't want to be thinking such unkind thoughts about Thea, but something just adds up in my head.

Thea knew the syntax of Otto's messages to me because she was the first person I showed them to. She saw the types of messages he was anonymously sending via Instagram, so it probably wasn't too difficult for her to take on his persona. And I wouldn't have seen the frayed edges because I was so convinced that Otto was the only one behind it. I feel like such a fool.

She's been the closest thing to a best friend I've had in almost a year, and I don't know what I've done to cause her to act out like this. I am no threat to her chances in the team, and maybe I've just been naïve to think she was being a good friend; maybe it was all fake from the very beginning and I was just so lonely that I over-looked the deceit.

But where does that leave me? Hypothetically, if she is somehow involved then she doesn't want me to reach the finish line, which is only two and a half miles away now, so if she is planning something, then that moment is rapidly approaching.

As is the Blackwall Tunnel, in very close proximity.

A shadow crosses my soul. Although closed to traffic today, it is the only place along the route where spectators are prohibited from watching the race. And with no obvious motorbike and cameraman nearby, that stretch of tunnel would provide perfect cover if Thea wanted to do me harm.

As if reading my mind, she glances back over her shoulder at me, and, maybe I'm just imagining it, but I'm sure I spot a momentary grin.

I try look behind me, hoping to spot another pair of legs gaining on us; at this point, I wouldn't even care if Kat has found a second wind, as there's no way Thea would lash out at me with a witness around. But there's no sign of Kat, nor any other runners for that matter.

The tunnel is coming up so quickly, and my instinct tells me that I'm not safe to be alone inside with Thea. What if she's carrying some kind of weapon? What if this has been her plan all along? To get me somewhere alone where she can carry out her plan? Surely that's the only logical reason for why she allowed me to catch up to her in the last mile.

I look down at my watch, and stab at the screen, desperate to get hold of Zara and tell her everything, but the number fails to connect and a message flashes up on the screen to tell me I have no signal. Is that just because I'm in a patchy area for the network, or is this all part of Thea and Seb's plan?

I'm running out of options as the roof of the tunnel looms ever closer. I can stop running, and hope that Thea continues on through without slowing, but how will I know that she's exited and isn't just waiting for me inside? I could wait until someone else catches up to me and then head through beside them, but how long will I have to wait? I'm already in danger of not hitting the qualifying time, so I really don't have any time to waste. That only leaves me with one other option: I need to outpace Thea and hope I have enough energy reserves left to get me through to the other side and the next race marshal.

I'm so exhausted already and I know I have barely enough energy to complete the course, let alone accelerate, but I have no other choice. I'm going to have to time it carefully. The only thing currently in my favour is that Thea doesn't know that I know what she's planning. Maybe the element of surprise will be enough to see me past her and out the other side. The only thing I can't be certain of is how much energy she has in reserve. I know for a fact that she hasn't been running to her ability today, and if I try to accelerate and she manages to keep pace with me, there will be nothing preventing her achieving her aim.

'I'm sorry,' I offer as the underpass looms.

'Sorry for what?' she pants back without looking at me.

'What I said about your brother. It was just me getting my wires crossed, I guess.'

She doesn't answer, and I'm not really expecting her to. Deep down, I now have real belief that she's involved, even though every bone in my body is desperately hoping I've got it wrong. My apology is as false as her; just trying to buy myself some time before I make my move. The longer I leave it, the better chance I have of making it back to daylight.

The tunnel is approximately 1,350 metres long and should take about four and a half minutes to run, but given the sheer exhaustion I'm currently feeling, I'll be lucky if I can complete it in that time.

'He's lucky to have a big sister so willing to back him,' I puff, desperately trying to keep my legs from bursting into a sprint too soon. 'I certainly know how lucky I feel to have a friend like you supporting me. I know it sounds lame, but you've become like a sister to me.'

I cringe at the cheesiness of the statement, but my desperate mind is hoping I can trick her into thinking I don't suspect her or Seb, and so she decides not to carry out her plan. If I can play on her empathy, then maybe I can keep her from lashing out.

My phone vibrates, and I dare to look at the message on my watch, but the words blur and I have to blink several times. Even when my eyes focus, I still don't believe the words that stare back at me.

DROP OUT OR THE BOMB TRIGGERS.
REPORT IT AND MORE WILL DIE.

My mind immediately pictures the devastating scene in Boston in 2013 when two brothers set off pressure cooker bombs. Three people were killed and many others maimed. The message has come from a withheld number again, so she's clearly ditched the plan to hold Jamie and Finn accountable. But is this threat real or just a last, desperate bluff?

Surely, my friend wouldn't sink to such depths. But then has she ever really been my friend? How long has she been planning my downfall, and more alarmingly, why? What have I ever done to warrant such vitriol and anger?

I look at her, but she isn't holding her phone, so the message must have come from Seb. We enter the tunnel, but I slow, no longer sure of my own mind. The absence of people here is alarmingly apparent. My heart races. What if it's planted...

'Is this you?' I yell at her, pointing at my watch.

She slows before stopping.

'Finally! The penny drops.'

I'm not expecting her to outright admit she's been behind the messages, and I'm temporarily speechless.

'Drop out of the race, Molly. There's no shame in it. Drop out now or there will be consequences.'

'A bomb. You expect me to believe you're a terrorist of some kind and have planted a bomb along the route?'

She doesn't answer, but there's a twinkle in her eyes.

'I'll tell the police. I'll tell Zara what you've done.'

'Good luck with that. The fact that there's no evidence won't exactly help you.'

'I have the messages on my phone. That's all I need to show her.'

'Oh, please, do you really think Seb will allow those to stay on there? The software he installed the day he fitted the doorbell will take care of any breadcrumbs.'

'Why are you doing this to me? I thought we were friends.'

She scoffs at this, but no explanation is forthcoming.

I'm wasting valuable seconds not running. I'm about to start again, when she steps in front of me.

'Drop out or you'll regret it, Molly. We're not messing about here.'

I look beyond her shoulder at the long length of tunnel ahead of me. If they were going to set off a bomb, this would be a prime location, but why would they want to set off a bomb in London and throw the whole city into chaos? Even without evidence, if I told Zara what she's admitted to then they'd definitely investigate the two of them, and would Seb really be able to keep quiet under cross-examination?

Kat can't be much further behind us, and I can't afford to let her get ahead of me. And I can't allow Thea to bully me into giving up my dream. I push past her, and start to run again, my leg muscles straining under the need for me to rest.

With a deep breath, I stretch my legs longer, pumping my arms with all my might, willing the lights in the ceiling to pass by quicker.

'Where do you think you're running off to?' she calls out from behind me, and I quickly realise she has started running again.

I want to get away from her, but having her behind me and out of sight makes me much more vulnerable to an attack. I don't believe she has planted a bomb in the tunnel, but that doesn't mean she hasn't planned something else. A coming together that can be innocently explained away afterwards.

'Run, rabbit, run,' I hear her voice echo around the chamber, and the shock in it gives me the impetus to keep swallowing up road.

But I have no choice now. If I slow, she'll catch up to me and I'll be at her mercy, powerless to stop her doing whatever she intends.

'I'm coming for you, Molly. I will catch you.'

I've lost count of the passing seconds, as I focus on just staying ahead of her at all costs. My legs will give in at some point; my lungs are already burning under the strain. But if I can just get back out into the sunlight, I'll have survived.

Have I overestimated her ability to catch me in a head-to-head race? I dare not look back in case she's just attempting to lull me into a false sense of security. I just have to focus on the road ahead. That's all I have left.

47

NOW

21 April 2024, Victoria Embankment, London – Mile 25

Every step I take feels like I am running through tar. My head is screaming out for my body to move at pace, but it's like someone has hit the slow-motion button and I can no longer continue. My body shifts awkwardly as my arms continue to pump by my sides, but I can't raise my knees as quickly. I am slowing and there is nothing I can do about it.

Thea is still chasing after me, and I now have no doubt that she means me harm. The only thing I don't know is why. Why is she so desperate for me not to finish this race? So desperate that she'd claim to have planted a bomb, knowing I will report her.

But if I can't prove she's involved then there's no reason for her to try to silence me before the end of the race, right? Or is that just wishful thinking? What if she's now panicking about the repercussions of her actions and isn't thinking straight? What if she now thinks the game is up and decides to attack me regardless?

Emerging from the Blackwall Tunnel, it is a relief to see the sky above me, and I almost want to break down in tears to celebrate the fact that I have survived. For now.

But I can still hear Thea's feet slapping at the road, and there's no way she can't be gaining on me now. We are back out in the open, but there are no supporters lining the road here, and my belief that I'd be safe if I just made it through the tunnel now feels misplaced. I don't want to look back, but curiosity gets the better of me and I dare to sneak a glance. For a moment, I don't see Thea back there, and it's like my prayers have been answered, but then I realise she's switched sides and is coming up to my right. Where are all the motorbikes that have been dogging my journey all day?

I can't go on. My energy is spent, and I have done everything in my power to stay out of her clutches, but I have nothing left. I'd like to think she wouldn't be stupid enough to attack me in broad daylight, but desperate people are capable of desperate measures. There was no bomb in the tunnel but that doesn't mean she hasn't had Seb plant one somewhere else. But where?

A flash of yellow appears up ahead, and for the first time in over a mile I see a glimmer of hope. Thea is so close now, but I'm certain she won't attack me with a race marshal watching on. In fact, I hear her drop back as I focus my course on getting closer to him. It's the first time I actually allow my pace to slow, as I am not sure I'll be able to stop before I get to him otherwise.

I am breathless as I reach him. 'There... bomb...' I try but my brain is working faster than my respiration and the words are inaudible.

Thea flashes past, firing me a warning glare, but not slowing as she reclaims her lead.

'Are you all right, love?' the kindly marshal asks, the bristles of his moustache hiding his lips. 'You need medical assistance?'

I still can't breathe, struggling to find the composure I need to report the message.

'Bomb... police,' I try again, but he isn't understanding me.

I need to know why Thea is so keen for me not to finish this race. She's had so many chances to harm me in the run-up to today, and has shown nothing but care and empathy, albeit acted, so what is it about today that has triggered this? And is it just today or was she the one messing with me before now?

'Shall I call for the medics?' the marshal asks again, but I shake my head.

'Tell the police there is...' My words trail off as I think back to the message.

Report the bomb and more will die.

It makes no sense. If she wants to kill me then why use it as a threat? Why not just wait until I cross the line and then detonate?

With innocent people's lives at stake, of course I would report it. Surely she knows I'd do that. I'd have to be a narcissist to keep quiet. The police will probably evacuate the area and possibly end the race early.

My eyes widen as the connection fires inside my head. That's exactly what she wants to happen. A bomb threat at this point would cause pandemonium. It would mean I'm unable to finish the race and will miss out on the qualification time. It won't impact her as she's already booked her spot on the plane, as has Kat – unless I manage to finish ahead of her today.

'You want me to call the police?' the marshal asks, trying to interpret my breathless words.

I quickly shake my head, and I'm about to tell him not to bother when I see Kat cruise past me, her head down, her running almost rhythmic as she concentrates on swallowing the final miles.

Thea knows better than anyone how long I've been dreaming about qualifying for Paris; how my heart is set on it. Revenge is a dish best served cold and what better way to extract revenge than by seeing me humiliated and broken by failing to achieve my dream?

I don't know why she is doing this to me, but I know she will do anything to stop me finishing the race. Me reporting a bomb threat will end the race prematurely and guarantee I don't qualify, and I will be the cause of my own downfall. I can practically see Thea cackling at that, and it's all the more reason why I don't believe the bomb is anything more than a bluff. Of course, if I'm wrong, then it isn't just my life I'm putting in danger.

48

NOW

21 April 2024, Victoria Embankment, London – Mile 26

I try phoning Zara because I want her at the finish line to arrest Thea for what she's done. Even though I can't prove it, if Zara knows who she's looking for, that should help narrow her search for evidence. I hate the thought of Thea getting away with this.

Zara doesn't answer her phone, so I once again leave her a message, hoping she hears it in time.

I refuse to look at my watch as my broken body pounds the road. I've passed the entrances to Southwark Bridge, the Millennium Bridge, Blackfriars Bridge and Waterloo Bridge. The spectators have been cheering me on, waving their flags and singing my name as I pass, but I haven't paused once to look at any of them or acknowledge their support. My focus is on qualifying ahead of Kat, and keeping a very close eye on Thea. If I see any sign of Seb near the finish line, then I'll have no choice but to cave to their demands.

My trainers are rubbing against blisters on my heels and beneath my toes, and my right knee throbs with every step, but the pain is driving me on. And more importantly I *am* gaining on Kat. Unfortunately, the rain has returned once more, and the course is slicker than I'd like. There are so many tall buildings either side of the road, but they are offering little shelter as the wind is blowing the rain into my face; an invisible yet powerful force.

Across the water, the London Eye spins and that means I am nearing Westminster Bridge, which is where the course will bend and head towards St James's Park. I have watched this part of the race so many times, and have always thought how flat it looks. Yet now that I'm running it, this straight section of Victoria Embankment is much steeper and more uneven and seems to stretch forever.

I groan each time my right foot connects with the road, and I really don't want to think about the damage my obstinacy is causing. The one question I will ask myself once I cross the finish line will be: was it worth it? I guess time will tell on that one.

I look up to Kat, trying to gauge the distance between us, and either she's somehow sped up, or Thea has slowed, because the two of them are running shoulder to shoulder, as thick as thieves. Kat made no secret of her disdain for me, but could that mean she's been in cahoots with Seb and Thea this whole time? Is that why Thea is doing this: to help her true friend, Kat?

There is a bike and cameraman ahead of the two of them, and when he spots me, he turns his camera in my direction. I dread to think how I must look. If Jamie is watching he'll probably be cringing, all the major sports brands deciding not to return his calls.

I can see Big Ben ahead and the time on the giant clock says it is close to 11.48, which means it's almost two hours and twenty-five minutes since we set off. I need to hit the finish line by 11.51 or I won't have qualified in time. Success is driven by moments like this. It is what separates the winners from the gallant runners-up. I have been through too much to have it all snatched away from me.

There isn't a bomb at the finish line, I tell myself, pushing the memories of the Boston atrocity to the back of my mind.

I turn right at Westminster Bridge, past the Houses of Parliament, the crowd's cheering growing, along with their number. This is the first moment Thea turns and looks over her shoulder. Seeing me, she whispers something to Kat, who then also turns and looks at me. I glare at them both, and push through the pain barrier. I just need to get ahead of them.

They just want to see me fail. There is no bomb.

I am so exhausted as I make it onto Birdcage Walk, but the crowd is so loud here, especially when they see three British runners together. They are waving their flags, and ringing bells, and it's all quite overwhelming. If I had any strength left, I would try to take in the whole scene, but all I can see is Kat's pink top. They are barely ten yards ahead of me, but I have no energy in reserve. I will lose in a flat-out race, so I need to time my over-taking manoeuvre if I'm to stand any chance of getting ahead of them.

My eyes dart right and left, looking for any sign of Seb, or anything resembling an unattended package.

The wind is now blowing the rain from the left of me, and I have to keep wiping at my face, as it's blurring my vision. There are police officers standing beside the barriers watching the crowd. I want to call out to one of them – any of them – to tell them to stop Thea, but my mouth is so dry and I have no energy to speak.

There's no sign of either of them tiring, but they're definitely running slower. I have no choice but to pull beside them as the penultimate bend of the course comes into view ahead. Kat glances at me, and I can see the panic in her eyes. Her face is drawn, her energy levels clearly as low as mine, but both of us push ourselves through the wall, forcing our faces forwards in case this ends in a photo finish, the difference between winning and losing a matter of centimetres.

I still can't see Seb, so I was right to ignore the message about the bomb, right? They wouldn't kill all of these innocent people just to get at me. Would they?

My elbow catches Thea, and I'm suddenly aware of how close we are, and I try to deviate slightly as I don't trust her, but she follows my course, and continues to bash into me.

'Hey,' I try to shout, but only soundless air escapes.

Still she brushes into me, and we are now a clear metre away from Kat, who is able to focus on just running in a straight line. I don't have the stamina to be running extra steps away from the running line.

I cannot believe Thea is still so determined to stop me finishing that she's even prepared to do it in front of the cameras.

The crowd continues to cheer, and I can barely concentrate on putting one foot in front of the other. I am so tired.

A steward in the middle of the road points out the final bend. It is now or never. I need to find the last drops of adrenaline to give me an edge.

I flick out my elbow, catching Thea's arm, and then I attempt to accelerate.

Thea has also accelerated, and catches up to me easily, suggesting she has the beating of me in a head-to-head.

The finish line is in sight, but as I try to see beyond Thea, my foot lands awkwardly, and then with alarm, I'm once again tumbling forwards, and no amount of sway will correct my descent. I crash to the floor, and scream out in agony as my elbows scratch at the hard surface. There is an audible gasp from the crowd behind the barriers, and as I dare to look up, all I see is Thea and Kat crossing the finish line.

And in that moment, my dream dies.

49

NOW

21 April 2024, Westminster, London – Finish Line

It's like someone has slowed time. From the floor, I see Kat and Thea raise their hands in celebration, and briefly embrace, before accepting fresh pink towels from their coaches, posing for photographs and then Thea catches my eye with a triumphant look. She waves at me and then vanishes from sight, and I can't see where she's gone and my mind races with the possibility that my ordeal is far from over.

The droplets are falling heavily, but I don't feel them as they make contact and run down my skin. Pressing my hands into the ground, I try to push myself up, but the grazes to both palms sting, and I tuck them back in to my body. With my knee swelling and the sting of fresh wounds, I hadn't even registered that I am injured anywhere else.

I am suddenly surrounded by bodies, arms reaching beneath

mine and hauling me up, and like a puppet without strings, I allow them to. The fight has abandoned my body. They fire questions at me, but I don't really hear them, instead gripping onto the fore-arms, and trying to straighten myself. The yellow plastic of their waterproof coats creaks beneath my fingers, but I push them away from me and hobble forwards. The finish line is so close, and yet might as well be lightyears away. It's like wading through tar as the rain continues to fall, my vest already soaked through and hanging from my frame. In my periphery, I can see hands applauding and flags being waved, but there is no sound other than that of my heart breaking.

Once again, I have come so far, only to fall at the final hurdle.

I have no idea how close my nearest competitor is, so I have to keep moving despite the lethargy and stabbing sensations at every muscle and sinew.

I will finish this race, even if I have to crawl over the line.

My knee buckles, and I'm momentarily falling forwards again, until I adjust my leg and just about manage to keep upright. I see Finn appear between the struts of the overhang. He is holding out a pink towel ready to catch me, and that becomes my only focus. I have nothing else to give.

Crossing the finish line should be cause for celebration, but I crumple into Finn's arms instead, him wrapping the pink towel over my shoulders. It smells fresh as a field on a warm summer's day, and I can't help the tears flowing as the emotion breaks free. I want to tell him about Thea and Kat, but it's like my brain and vocal cords are at an impasse. I bury my face in his shoulder instead, and allow him to lift me into his arms, and carry me away from the flashing cameras and the hum of questions from the media.

How could I have let her beat me?

And then I think back to the last message. There's been no

explosion, but is that because I didn't cross the line in time? What if it was more than a threat? I need to make certain that there isn't a device near the finish line. I push myself away from Finn and stumble uneasily back towards the stanchion.

'Molly, where are you going? The paramedics are this way.'

I feel Finn pulling me back, but he doesn't understand.

'There's a bomb,' I say, breathless, but his face balls in confusion.

'Don't be ridiculous. Come on, you're delirious.'

I search for a uniformed officer, but the only official I can find is one of the race marshals.

'You need to tell the police there might be a bomb,' I try to tell him, but he's wearing a headset and can't hear me properly.

Finn is still pulling at my arms, and apologises to the marshal, making excuses.

'No, you don't understand,' I plead again. 'There's a bomb. Thea... and her brother...'

But then my eyelids close and I collapse into Finn's arms.

* * *

I wake, stretched out on a gurney in the back of an ambulance, a paramedic shining a torch into my eyes, Finn speaking on my behalf, showing them my injured knees. I try to speak, but I am so dizzy, and I can barely string more than two thoughts together.

It's like I am in a nightmare from which I cannot wake. I don't want to be here. I want to be back on that course two minutes ago when Thea and I were neck and neck and my dream was within touching distance.

Did Thea trip me? Is that what happened?

It all happened so fast, and all I can remember is something catching at my foot. A loose stone? A carefully placed foot? Who knows?

The paramedic's gloved hands are smooth as they run the length of both my legs, and she offers apologies as she begins to unfasten the bloody and sodden dressing from my right knee. It sticks and pulls where some of the blood has dried, but although my brain registers pain, the signal is at the back of the queue, and I don't make a sound.

Finn appears at my side, brushing straggled hairs out of my face, and pressing a cold compress against my forehead. I hadn't realised how hot my face was until the ice-cold packet hits my temple. It eases some of the pain instantly, and my hearing clears.

'I've been trying to call,' he tells me, though I'm barely listening, 'but I lost network access after I saw you at the rehydration station near Canary Wharf.' He lifts his phone into my field of vision and I see the words 'NO NETWORK' in the top corner of the screen. 'It's the darnedest thing. Can't make calls, can't send messages. I kept trying to get in touch to tell you where I'd meet you, but it was impossible. I saw you briefly near Limehouse, but I don't think you saw me. I was waving because I wanted to tell you that my phone was screwed and that I'd try and meet you further down the road. You were running with Kat, so I figured you were safe from your stalker.'

At least I was right about the bomb threat being a bluff, but it doesn't make defeat sit any easier in my gut.

'Thea and her brother are the ones who've been messaging me,' I say, the words sticking to the roof of my mouth, as I finally verbalise her betrayal.

'Thea? As in Team GB's Thea?'

I nod slowly, but his face creases with confusion.

'But why would she—'

'I don't know why, but it was her all the time.'

He lifts the icepack from my forehead and presses the back of his hand against my temple instead.

'Listen, Molly, you're exhausted and probably dehydrated. You don't know what you're saying right now, but hang tight, and I'm going to go and get you some water.'

'No, wait,' I say reaching out for him, but he isn't listening and trundles out of the ambulance.

How am I going to convince anyone of Thea's actions? It's my word against hers, and I'm going to be perceived as just bitter and envious of the fact that she qualified and I didn't. There's a chance that Zara might believe me, but without evidence, her hands are tied. And how can I even be sure I'm safe now? The race is over and I didn't qualify, so they won, but will they really stop there? What if they are planning to silence me for good?

The paramedic cleans and dresses my knee, before strapping it into a splint that fixes my leg in a straight position. She tells me it's just a precaution, but due to the swelling I should have it X-rayed just in case. The floor of the ambulance bounces as she heads out through the door, but I still don't feel safe.

How could I have been so stupid?

And that's when I spot Thea staring at me from across the street. Dressed in a bright yellow cagoule, she looks like a mirage through the heavy rainfall. She's pacing backwards and forwards, not staring at me, maybe talking on a phone. I sit up and try to focus my gaze. No, she isn't on a phone, she's trying to find a way through the nest of barriers setting this area apart from the park. And before I can register the fact that she's trying to escape, she forces herself between the barriers and disappears into the park.

There are so many people milling about that nobody will notice if I escape.

There's no way I'm going to let her get away with this. I need her to be here when Zara turns up, and so I push the blanket from my legs, and slide my legs over the side of the gurney, and attempt to put weight on my right leg. It twinges but holds, and I don't hesitate, clambering out of the ambulance and stalking across the road, slipping through the barriers, and then through the gates and further into St James's Park.

50

NOW

21 April 2024, St James's Park, London

I hobble through the wrought-iron gates. The drizzle continues to soak everything in its path, including the towel still draped around my shoulders. I'm so tired I can't control my body's shivers. But I don't relent. I need answers and the only person who can provide them is walking – not running – away from me.

She is moving slowly, but doesn't once turn back to check if I am following. My gut tells me she knows I'm tailing her, and there's also a voice in the back of my head warning me that I'm taking a huge risk to be following her into the unknown. For all I know, she wants me to give chase so she can get me alone and attack me. But we're in a public park, and although there aren't many people around as the rain continues to fall, it's not like we're alone.

We continue along the straight stretch of path, passing a wooden coffee hut, from where the tempting smell of hot chocolate emanates. Thea doesn't stop, and so neither do I. The hood of the yellow cagoule is pulled up and around her head so I can't see where she's looking or what she might be thinking about.

We're moving in a south-easterly direction, the path lined with knee-high wired fences, signs warning visitors to stay off the bright green grass beyond. I'm tempted to call out, but I don't want to trigger her to break into a run. If she takes off now, there's no way I'll catch up. It's all I can do to drag my strapped knee and maintain this slow pace.

Checking my phone, I see that my last message to Zara still hasn't gone through, so she has no idea that Thea is behind it all. And she doesn't know that I have left the marathon course. I should have told Finn where I was going, but he might have tried to talk me out of it, and I can't let Thea go without hearing the truth from her. She has stolen my dream from me and I need to know why.

As we near the footbridge crossing the lake, she takes a sharp turn to the left and walks beneath the shroud of low-hanging branches, still making no effort to turn and see if she's being followed. There's no reason for her to be walking through the park after the marathon. She should be properly warming down with her coach; but then again, I've made a mess of assessing her character up till now, so how can I be certain of anything?

I look at my phone again, but I have a 'NO NETWORK' message in the corner. I can feel the hand of Seb at work here. They don't want me phoning the police.

Now my gut is telling me just to cut my losses and return to where Finn is probably searching for me.

And that's when Thea suddenly breaks into a run, darting to the right as the pathway splinters in two. I try to increase my pace, but my right knee is in too much pain, and I'm barely jogging.

We're right beside the lake's edge, and there is nothing but an ankle-high barrier preventing us from entering. I'm struggling to keep sight of her yellow jacket as we pass a terraced bar where a handful of people are sheltering from the rain, but Thea disappears behind a long bend in the path. What triggered her sprint? Did Seb send her a message warning I was behind her?

I follow the path around, no longer sure what direction I'm heading in. I look in all directions, but apart from a couple beneath an umbrella and a guy walking a Westie, there's no sign of Thea. Her yellow coat was so distinctive, but it is nowhere. I continue along the path, assuming I will eventually reach the footbridge, when I spot what looks like a neat garden, and just beyond it a small, ramshackle cottage. It looks so out of place, like something out of a horror movie, with the dark sky overhead giving it a menacing vibe.

Duck Island Cottage is fenced off and warns of no admittance, but I can't help feeling it would be the perfect place to hide, and then I spot a flash of yellow in the window, and realise this was her plan all along. I lift my legs over the fence and move closer to the cottage, hoping a passerby will see me and call the police, but there is nobody on the path in either direction.

The door is ajar, and creaks as I push it open. I don't want to enter in case Thea has managed to arm herself, so I call out her name, and ask her to step outside. I strain to hear any sound, but there is nothing over the thunder of my heart in my ears.

'Thea, I know what you and Seb have been doing,' I call out, setting my phone to record a voice note, 'I just want to know why.'

I take a further tentative step, but there's still no sound. Did I imagine the flash of yellow? I'm about to turn and leave, when the light-headedness returns, and realise Finn may have been right about the dehydration. I crash to the cold, hard stone floor and my eyes start to close when I see a figure in yellow standing over me.

51

NOW

21 April 2024, St James's Park, London

I don't know how long I'm passed out for, but when my eyes open again, I can see Thea has closed the door to the cottage, and is sitting at a wooden table, staring daggers at me. Her hair is wet and scraggly, glued to her cheeks, and although it's dim, I can see the mania in her eyes.

'How does it feel to lose everything?' she asks, unzipping the cagoule and pulling the hood down.

'I want to know why, Thea. You're supposed to be my friend.'

She cackles, witch-like.

'I tried to be your friend, Molly, but then I realised what a narcissist you are. I remember when you turned up at my flat after your interview on the television. All you were worried about was someone being in your dressing room. Did you once stop to ask how I was, or whether you were disrupting my plans? No. Like usual, you had to make everything about you! That was the moment I realised who you really were, but no matter how much distance I attempted to put between us, you kept coming back, like a lost puppy.'

This is the second verbal assault she's levied at me today, and this one is as painful as the last, but it still doesn't justify what she's done.

'Why didn't you just tell me to back off if you didn't want to be my friend? Why did you let me crash at your place if I was becoming overbearing?'

'Because they say you should keep your friends close, but your enemies closer.'

I try to straighten, the hard floor uncomfortable on my lower back, but my elbows are too sore to prop myself up. And my head feels even dizzier than before.

'I'm not your enemy, Thea.'

'You took everything from me, Molly, and now you get to experience how excruciating that is.'

'What did I ever take from you?'

She plants a foot either side of my waist and leans over, her eyes venomous.

'You're the reason Otto will probably spend the rest of his life behind bars.'

'Otto? Why the hell would you care what happened to him?'

'Because I love him.'

Something isn't right: my mind is spinning, and I'm beginning to question whether Finn was right, and I've entered delirium. Why do I feel so light-headed?

'Wait, you know Otto Bistras?'

She grins maniacally at the realisation that I hadn't figured out their connection.

'Of course I do. Otto has been like a guardian angel to me; always there to help keep my career on track, so to speak.'

My mouth drops. Is this just another of her lies to try and trip me up?

'You're lying,' I challenge, keen to eke out as much detail as I can for the recording.

She shakes her head, and there's something about the look of sincerity in her eyes.

'But how? When?'

'I was at my wits' end five years ago. I'd just taken silver in the 10,000 m at the national championships when I was selected at random for a drug test. I knew I would be kicked out and never race again, and that's when Otto saved me. He managed to switch my test and someone else took the fall.'

I remember her mentioning Caroline Hoebeck's disgrace, but I hadn't realised Thea was the cause. I need her to admit what she's done.

'You're the reason Caroline was banned from competing again.'

There's something pathologically wrong with the way her lips curl into a smile.

'Otto told me he didn't want to see me waste my opportunity; he was like an angel sent by God. Whenever an obstacle appeared in the road, he stepped in to clear it. Short of money? He gave us some. Mum too busy dealing with Seb's meltdowns? Gave me the love and encouragement I craved. Another competitor threatening my place? He ensured they had second thoughts.' She pauses and glares at me. 'I owe him everything, and now you've taken him away from me.'

I was aware that Thea didn't have an easy upbringing, and with no father in the picture, I suppose I can understand her latching on to someone like Bistras if he came to her rescue when her dreams were so close to failure. The longer I can keep her talking, the better the chance that Zara will find us.

She spots the phone in my hand and snatches it from me before I can hide it.

'Ha! Thought you could record my confession, did you? I wouldn't bother. Seb stopped the recording within seconds of you starting it. He's been watching your activity all day long, but you being you didn't give up. Even when we told you there was a bomb at the finishing line.'

She shakes her head in admonishment.

'Tut, tut, tut – what would people say if they knew how selfish you were, not reporting it? Better destroy the evidence in case it gets out.'

She throws my phone to the floor, and I see the screen crack on impact.

'Don't worry, you won't need that where you're going.'

What does she mean by that? I need to get up. I'm too vulnerable down here, but when I try to adjust my arms, I crash back to the floor, banging my head against the stone, but barely feeling the impact.

'Be careful, you're in a bad way, Molly. You never should have ingested ketamine so soon after the race.'

'What are you saying? I didn't...'

But I can't finish the sentence as light scratches at the edge of my vision. I remember this feeling, and I'm terrified about what's to come again.

My head lolls from one side to the other as I try to focus my mind on survival, but I'm losing control and it won't be long until I'm no longer able to fight back. Thea takes a step forward, leaning over me and holding something out but my vision blurs in and out so much I can't quite see what it is. A vial of some kind, maybe.

'I didn't want it to come to this, Molly, but you had to keep running, didn't you? If you'd just quit the race, none of this would be happening right now. But oh, no, you couldn't do that, could you? Instead you had to go and put it all together, and made me admit my part in it. And with Otto not here to help, you've forced me to take matters into my own hands.'

I continue to stare at the vial between her fingers. 'Did you drug me while I was passed out?'

I think she nods, but can't actually see as I'm seeing double.

'And it was you who spiked my drink in the club that night.'

I'm not sure if I actually say the words or if they're in my head.

'Otto is where he deserves to be,' I say, hoping to make her see sense. 'He's a twisted pervert, Thea. Can't you see that? First he preyed on you when you were vulnerable, and then he came after me.'

Her mouth curls into a snarl as if she's sucking on a wasp.

'He didn't come for you. You had some creep messaging you online and you jumped to the wrong conclusion and had my Otto locked up.'

I close my eyes, unable to focus on speech and sight. 'You can't be serious. It was your Otto who was stalking me. You saw the messages.'

'No. No. They were from some guy called Oppenheimer. You lied to the police when you told them they were from Otto.'

'It was the police who identified him, Thea. There was a recording of him outside my flat the night he tried to burn the building down.'

'There you go again with your lies.'

'I'm not lying, Thea. I have footage of him dressed as a fireman and leading me from the building.'

'No, you don't. He wasn't there.'

I hear the doubt in her voice.

'I swear to you, Thea, that he was there. I have the video on my phone, which I could show you if you hadn't broken it. But Seb would be able to see it if he has control of the phone like you claim. Ask your brother to watch the video and then you'll see how close he got to me.'

She's silent and I hope I am finally getting through to her.

'No. You're lying. You're just trying to fib your way out of trouble.'

Before I know what's happening, she's grabbed one of my hands and is trying to haul me up and onto her shoulders. I suddenly realise just how precarious a location we're in. If she gets me outside and pushes me into the water, I'll be helpless to prevent her, and my broken and drugged body will drown.

'Please, Thea. You're a victim as much as me. If we go to the police we can—'

But I'm winded as my midriff collides with her shoulder, and now I'm facing downwards and can feel the blood rushing towards my head.

Where the hell is Zara?

'Please, Thea,' I try earnestly, as we move closer to the cottage door. 'I'm not lying, and from what the police told me, I wasn't the only person he's been stalking online. He wasn't imprisoned because of what he did to me, but for what he had done to others.'

Light falls onto us as the door opens, and I feel a rush of air against my cheeks, but suddenly I'm weightless, and we're both flying backwards into the darkness. We collapse onto the floor, but I barely feel the impact as the drug addles my mind. There is a commotion beside me, but I can't see a thing as the world above and around me spins.

Is this death? Has she thrown me into the water and I don't even realise?

There is yelling somewhere distant, and then I feel an urgent slapping against my cheeks, and it shakes me long enough to open my eyes.

'Can you hear me? I need you to drink this.'

Something sharp is pressed to my lips and I'm unable to prevent the cool liquid pouring into my mouth and down my throat. I try to open my eyes and see Kat staring down at me, cradling my head in her lap.

'I think Thea might have drugged you, Molly. I've called for help, but I need you to stay with me. Hopefully the sugar will keep you conscious long enough until they get here.'

52

NOW

My head is all over the place as I am chauffeured from one room to another. First it's a trip to wardrobe, and a discussion occurs as if I'm not even there, and three outfits are bagged up and carried by the poor girl whose voluntary work has earned her the title 'runner'. She takes me to have my hair fixed (her words, not mine), then it's to another room where someone moisturises my face, and then paints on layers of makeup to hide my blemishes. The irony that they're covering up my marathon battle scars for an interview where they plan to discuss the race isn't lost on me.

Kerry – the runner – rifles through the bag and removes the three outfits, systematically holding them up to me one by one before picking a pale-blue satin blouse and navy pencil skirt.

'The audience will only see you from the top up,' she reassures me when I try to adjust the large strapping over my knee.

'I'd be much more comfortable in my trackie bottoms and T-shirt,' I say, but she thinks I'm joking and laughs away my concern.

It's been four days since Thea drugged me again and tried to make it look like an accidental drowning. Had Kat not followed us into the park on Sunday, I wouldn't be here now. It's been four days of police interviews, with the press camped outside my tiny flat, while my body slowly tries to recover from the ordeal.

'Are you ready to go?' Jamie asks a few minutes later when I'm changed. I can hardly recognise the reflection staring back at me in the full-length mirror.

'I guess so,' I say as nerves knot in my stomach.

If Jamie's nervous, he isn't showing it. In fact, I'm not sure I've ever seen him so happy. He's beaming from cheek to cheek, and although he's not due to appear on camera, I'm certain he's had his crow's feet touched up. He collected me from my flat at 6 a.m., and when I told him I really didn't want to appear on television, he dismissed my reluctance as nerves and told me I had made a commitment and couldn't back out. Since we arrived, he's been networking like crazy, and you'd think I was royalty by the way he's been introducing me to people.

'You're due on at half past seven, which is prime time for the morning shows. Viewers at home will be eating breakfast and getting dressed to the sound of your voice, so this really is your chance to sell yourself.'

I open my mouth to interject, but he continues before I can.

'You're here to tell them what you went through at the weekend. Okay? I know you're not comfortable blowing your own trumpet, but the nation wants to hear your story, Molly. They need to know the horrific nightmare you've been through and how you overcame all that adversity.'

I picture Thea's tearful face as Zara arrested her and put her in the back of the waiting patrol car. Kat told me she'd seen me bolt from the ambulance and, fearing I was seeking some kind of reprisal against Thea, she followed behind, but lost sight of me when I entered the cottage. It was only when retracing her steps that she heard our voices coming from within. She later admitted that she genuinely thought she would be saving Thea rather than me when she burst through the door. I didn't ask whether she would have acted in the same manner if she'd known what was really going on. And had the vial of ketamine not rolled out of Thea's hand, she may not have figured out what Thea was planning.

Jamie is about to speak again when Kerry appears and tells me I need to head onto the set now, so that I'm in place for when they return from the news. He wishes me good luck, and then watches as I'm led like a lamb to the slaughter. I know I'm being overly dramatic, but it's so warm, and there are so many bright lights, I've never felt more out of my comfort zone. Give me a soggy London street over this any day of the week.

I'm introduced to the two hosts: one whose shirt and tie and receding hairline make him resemble an accountant on the verge of a nervous breakdown; the other so gaunt the bright red cardigan hangs from her frame like a cloak of blood. They both tell me how brave I am and how I've made Britain proud, but I don't think they realise their flattery is making me feel more uncomfortable rather than less.

There are a variety of newspapers spread out on the desk in front of me and them, and as I flip over one of the tabloids, I'm shocked to see my haggard face staring back at me. In the image, I'm on all fours, one leg caked in blood, and an expression of agony stretched across my face. I can just see the corner of Buckingham Palace in the background of the shot. I had no idea there were photographers that close to the finish line. I flip over the next paper and see the same picture but from a different angle. It appears I am the focus of all the sports pages. Jamie didn't warn me that my performance was so prevalent in the news. What have I let myself in for?

The floor manager gives a thumbs up and the presenters welcome back the audience. They then talk about all the courageous participants in the marathon who raised a record sum for charitable causes. And then they tell the story of a woman who succeeded despite huge adversity, and it's only when I see a red light appear above the camera that I realise they're talking about me. I nervously say hello, but they immediately launch into their questions.

'Tell us about the campaign of terror your stalker has put you through over the last five months,' the female presenter asks, her face a picture of faux concern and empathy.

Zara has been very clear that I'm not to discuss the ongoing investigation into Thea's actions before, during and after the marathon, so I attempt to navigate any specifics of race day. Instead I talk about the messages Bistras sent, the phone calls, the fire alarm at my flat, and his shadowy presence. It galls me that I can't tell them how systematic Thea was in coordinating the calls and messages and how she was even prepared to resort to murder to cover her tracks. I still don't know how I could have missed the signs about her.

The presenters share alarming facts about the threat of cyber stalking, how 25 per cent of women aged between eighteen and twenty-nine have reported some form of online stalking; 65 per cent of all online users have experienced some form of harassment; and 38 per cent said their harasser's identity was hidden. We take phone calls from viewers concerned that their children are being targeted by online bullies, and from one woman who says her cyber stalker found out where she lived and came to her house and threatened her. Before I know it, the interview is over and I have no idea what I've said in the last twenty minutes. It can't have been too bad as Jamie is waiting in the wings with a proud smile on his face.

'That was perfect, Molly,' he tells me. 'You were natural and sincere. It couldn't have gone better, even if we spent all night rehearsing it. My phone has been ringing hot all morning with other outlets that want to interview you, and both Nike and Reebok have increased their offers. I reckon we can hold out and start a bidding war for your signature. If we handle this right, you'll never have to do an honest day's work for the rest of your life.'

I picture Thea again.

Zara has said she is suffering with something akin to Stockholm Syndrome; she blamed me for Otto being locked up and went to extreme lengths to continue his stalking, hoping I would tell the police I'd made a mistake and he'd be released. And when that failed, she wanted to make me suffer by snatching my dream at the final step. It doesn't feel right that I should profit from so much misery caused by one man.

'There's someone here who wants to speak to you,' Jamie tells me when we arrive at the dressing room they've assigned to me.

I'm not sure who I'm expecting when he opens the door, but Gloria Hutchinson is sitting on the small armchair in the corner of the room.

'I'll leave you to it,' Jamie says, closing the door behind him, more than just a twinkle in his eyes.

'How is your knee?' she asks, standing and offering me the chair.

'Sore,' I admit, hobbling in, but choosing to prop myself up against the wall.

'Finn tells me there shouldn't be any lasting damage, and you should be fit enough to resume training in a week or so.'

My brow furrows. 'Training for what?'

She sits back down, and fixes me with a firm stare. 'For the Olympics, of course.'

'But I didn't meet the qualifying time.'

'True, but given the circumstances you faced, and the fact that a spot in the team has suddenly opened up, we're willing to take a chance, so long as you're prepared to work your socks off in the weeks leading up to the competition.'

She's offering me a place on the plane; I should be jumping for joy, but it's what she's not saying that troubles me most.

'You want me to take Thea's place?'

'Obviously, given the current police investigation, and what Thea has admitted, it would be wildly inappropriate to have her flying the flag in Paris. The place is yours if you want it.' She pauses a moment, and offers what I think is an attempt at a smile. 'I'm not one who enjoys admitting when they're wrong, but you've surprised me, Molly. I hadn't realised what you've been facing in the last few months, and you suit the image of underdog over- coming adversity that the press have painted you as.'

'The papers have blown it all out of proportion.'

'That's as may be, but like it or not, you are now the face the press will associate with our team at this summer's games. You're a role model to so many facing abuse and harassment, both online and in person. We want you in our team, Molly.' She takes a breath. '*I* want you in our team.'

EPILOGUE
NOW

10 August 2024, Stade de France, Paris

When you've been dreaming about something for four years straight, nothing can prepare you for when the moment arrives. The track is dry, and the sun is bright. There is a gentle thrum of noise as the filled stadium anticipates the athletes stepping out, ready to take their places on the track. My bowels have led me on a merry dance this morning as nerves threaten to get the better of me. But I know what I'm capable of. I sailed through the heats and semi-finals of the 1,500 m event.

It's been a crazy four months. When I'm not training with Finn, Jamie has been ferrying me from one photoshoot to another, or from one television studio to the next. He said I'd never have to do an honest day's work again, but I took that to mean life would be easier, not harder. Every day is a haze, but it's all been building to this second, and now it's time for me to step up. I'm more nervous than I was in Tokyo three years ago, and maybe that's because I know this really is my last chance to do what I was born to do.

The steward listens in to his headset before ushering the twelve of us to head out onto the track. The crowd cheers wildly as local favourite Beatrice Longchamp walks out and waves at them. I am the fourth athlete to reach the track and can't help smiling when I see the array of Union Jacks and St Andrew's flags waving back. I wave at the crowd, and offer a prayer of thanks for their support.

The remaining competitors join us, and we are moved towards the start line. Standing side by side, there are no starting blocks to concern ourselves with, just a painted, curved line that we will all stand on.

'Are you ready for this?'

I turn, and smile at Kat, who is stretching her calf muscles, and smiling back at me.

'As ready as I'll ever be, I guess,' I say.

Kat and I will never be best friends, but there is now a mutual respect between us. I can see how much athletics means to her, and I hate myself for ever thinking her competitive nature could spiral into something so sinister. And it was only when we started to unpick our respective relationships with Thea that it became clear she'd been manipulating us both. Secretly telling Kat that I was trying to steal her place on the team, she created a pantomime for which she was the puppeteer, alienating us both in the process. Maybe if we'd compared notes sooner, we'd have realised what she was up to.

We've had to overcome our differences in order to help Thea's defence team. As much as she should be punished for her actions, I still maintain that she needs victim support as well. Kat agrees that what occurred earlier this year was pretty messed up, and neither of us want to see Thea suffer more than is necessary. Her brother Seb is also a victim, but more from his sister's manipulation. The Crown Prosecution Service has yet to make a decision as to whether to prosecute him as well.

'Best of luck,' she tells me, with a wink. 'May the best runner win.'

A camera passes along the track, pausing momentarily for each of us to smile or wave at the viewing crowd back home. I've never enjoyed being the centre of attention, and if I've learned anything this last year, the peace comes from being able to close the door at night and shut out the intrusive world. I don't use social media, and Jamie is the only one with the ability to post on my behalf. It's a necessary evil that he protects me from.

The race marshal invites us all up to the line, and checks that our feet are where they should be. We all put our strongest foot forwards, and then we set our arms in position, ready to pump as soon as the starter pistol fires. I can no longer see Kat in my periphery as my eyes are focused only on the track ahead. I've been preparing for this moment for four years, but in truth everything I've done in my life has been leading to this moment. I prayed for one more chance to compete on the highest stage and now it is here.

I take a breath and then the pistol fires.

ACKNOWLEDGEMENTS

Now that you've got your breath back, let me say a big thank you for reading *Every Step You Take*. I hope you enjoyed it (and will now tell all your friends to read a copy). Please do get in touch via the usual social channels and let me know what you thought about it.

Weirdly, this is the second book I've written this year inspired by something I read on social media. Where my last book, *The Trail*, was motivated by a tweet from my agent, the idea for this book was stimulated by a reply posted by the super talented writer Ola Tundun.

In April 2023 I invited my fellow writers to sum up their currents works in progress in three emojis, and I would then proceed to guess what their book was about (procrastination really is a writer's best friend). Ola responded with an image of a woman running, an anxious face, and a face with a tongue sticking out. Knowing that Ola is a writer of romantic comedies, I jokingly replied: "During the London Marathon, a runner realises her stalker is also competing and must figure out who he is before her own finish line emerges." But the idea stuck and sometimes you just have to step back and marvel at the magic of creativity.

And I will hold my hands up and confess that I have never run the London Marathon, so any glaringly obvious inaccuracies are as a result of my misunderstanding, rather than any of the runners who've helped during my countless hours of research and discussion.

I'd like to thank my wonderful agent Emily Glenister, who is always only a phone call or email away when Imposter Syndrome sets in. It means so much having someone to champion my books and I'm indebted to her honesty and support.

I'd also like to thank the other Emily in my writing life, my brilliant editor Emily Yau at Boldwood Books. She is so good at challenging me to write better endings and explore character backstories, two skills I struggle with. The whole team at Boldwood Books deserve huge credit for the work they do in producing my books in the array of formats available. From line and copy editing, proof-reading, cover design, audiobook creation, and marketing. The fact that you're reading this acknowledgement is testament to the brilliant job they do.

My children are an inspiration to me every day, and as they continue to grow so quickly, I am eternally grateful that I get to play such an important role in their development. They continue to show one another affection, patience and kindness, and make being their dad that bit easier. I'd like to thank my own parents and my parents-in-law for continuing to offer words of encouragement when I'm struggling to engage with my muse.

It goes without saying that I wouldn't be the writer I am today without the loving support of my beautiful wife and soulmate Hannah. She keeps everything else in my life ticking over so that I can give what's left to my writing. She never questions my method or the endless hours daydreaming while I'm working through plot holes, and for that I am eternally grateful.

And thanks must also go to YOU for buying and reading *Every Step You Take*. Please do post a review to wherever you purchased the book from so that other readers can be enticed to give it a try. It takes less than two minutes to share your opinion, and I ask you do me this small kindness.

I am active on Facebook, Twitter, and Instagram, so please do stop by with any messages, observations, or questions. Hearing from readers of my books truly brightens my days and encourages me to keep writing, so don't be a stranger. I promise I *will* respond to every message and comment.

Stephen (a.k.a. M.A. Hunter)

ABOUT THE AUTHOR

M.A. Hunter is the pen name of Stephen Edger, the bestselling author of psychological and crime thrillers, including the Kate Matthews series. Born in the north-east of England, he now lives in Southampton where many of his stories are set.

Sign up to M. A. Hunter's mailing list here for news, competitions and updates on future books.

Visit M. A. Hunter's website: stephenedger.com/m-a-hunter
Follow M. A. Hunter on social media

X x.com/stephenedger
f facebook.com/AuthorMAHunter
O instagram.com/stef.edger
BB bookbub.com/authors/stephen-edger
g goodreads.com/stephenedger

ALSO BY M. A. HUNTER

Adrift

The Trail

Every Step You Take

THE

Murder

LIST

THE MURDER LIST IS A NEWSLETTER DEDICATED TO SPINE-CHILLING FICTION AND GRIPPING PAGE-TURNERS!

SIGN UP TO MAKE SURE YOU'RE ON OUR HIT LIST FOR EXCLUSIVE DEALS, AUTHOR CONTENT, AND COMPETITIONS.

SIGN UP TO OUR
NEWSLETTER

BIT.LY/THEMURDERLISTNEWS

Boldwood

Boldwood Books is an award-winning fiction publishing company seeking out the best stories from around the world.

Find out more at www.boldwoodbooks.com

Join our reader community for brilliant books, competitions and offers!

Follow us
@BoldwoodBooks
@TheBoldBookClub

Sign up to our weekly deals newsletter

https://bit.ly/BoldwoodBNewsletter

Milton Keynes UK
Ingram Content Group UK Ltd.
UKHW041926010424
440450UK00004B/98

9 781805 495727